Quiet POWER

J.L. DRAKE

QUIET POWER

QUIET MAFIA SERIES

Cover Design by Spellbinding Design
Editing by Lori Whitwam
Formatting by RedDoor Author Services

Dedication

To my dear friends Liz Clark and Jamie Johnson for not only being dedicated readers of mine from the start of my career, but for spending countless hours with me spinning and relishing our love of all things dark, twisted, and evil.

Thank you!

List of Main Cast

Capri Family
Piero – Don & Elio's father
Andrea – Elio's mother
Elio – Underboss
Francesco – Consigliere
Niccola – Caporegime
Vinni – Caporegime
Donatello – Soldier
Gain – Soldier
Ernesto – Soldier
Harris – Soldier
Bosco – Uncle (brother to Piero)
Noemi – Aunt (married to Bosco)

DeSimone Family
Roberto – Don & Mariano's father
Bria – Mariano's mother
Mariano – Underboss

Sides
Wyatt Burn – Sienna's best friend
Gail Burn – Wyatt's sister
Aldo – Elio's trainer
Anna – Capri family friend
Aurora – Capri family friend
Tieri – Capri friend/Santoro Brother
The Finder – Capri friend/Santoro employee
Sienna Giovanna – Also known as Alessia Coppola
Stefano Coppola – Don

You'll be introduced to these characters as you read:
Coppola Family/Friends
Rosa – Nonna
Pippo, Betto, and Lotto – The uncles
Salvo – Stefano's best friend

Crossover Characters
Devil's Reach Trilogy

Recap

To my readers:

It's important to remember who fits where, so let's break it down, starting with *Quiet Wealth*.

Ready?

Elio and Sienna meet when they are very young, and over the next ten years, they develop a deep and tender relationship. Elio and his family suddenly disappear, leaving zero trace of where they went. Sienna is left heartbroken and alone.

Present Day
Sienna, now a journalist for a newspaper in Tuscany, lands an exclusive job with a man named Mariano

DeSimone. *FYI, we don't like him.* Meanwhile, Elio is running his syndicate with his father, Piero.

Sienna Giovanna agrees to go to a work party with Mariano as his date and spots his partner, who just so happens to be Elio.

They meet, and it's hot. Emotions surge to the surface, and it burns in them both. He tries to get back into her life.

Moving ahead.

Dating a member of the mafia brings the wolves out to play, and the best way to take down the Capri underboss is by hurting the one person he loves.

Now, for the Coppola family.

They are the second biggest mafia family and rule the mid-section of the country. They play dirty, and the boss is a young hothead named Stefano who would like nothing more than to have Sienna all to himself. *Yeah, I know, I know. When you know the truth, it gets icky.*

More stuff happens. They end up in New York where a gangster gets killed, Sienna is involved, and Elio realizes there's way more to the story about who is trying to hurt his family than he thought.

A family meeting is held, and they decide not to go public that Elio and Sienna are dating and keep Mariano in the dark on their plans.

The book ends with Sienna running into her long-lost mother, and guns are drawn. *It's all very dramatic and leaves the door open to more questions.*

Okay, on to *Quiet Secrets.*

Elio isn't feeling good about Sienna's mother showing up with two other men, Oscar and Ugo. Or the fact that his father's *consigliere*, Francesco, seems to know Elenora, which only confuses everyone further.

Elenora isn't overly warm or forthcoming with the information her daughter deserves, and right off the bat, that doesn't go over well. However, she does discover Ugo is her cousin.

Elio and Sienna keep their relationship quiet while Sienna digs into Mariano's life, trying to connect the dots on what he's up to.

Anna comes on the scene. She is the daughter of a family friend who doesn't like that Sienna is catching Elio's eye—not that she has any problem finding other men to play with.

Stefano Coppola starts to encroach further into Capri territory. Elio calls on an old friend from his past to help take down some people in New York. Trigger is more than happy to offer his help.

A bomb goes off in the city and knocks Sienna out cold. *Yes, the bomb was meant for her.* She wakes to find herself in a house with an old lady who tells someone that Sienna's there and to come and get her.

She escapes, Elio finds her, and more secrets are revealed, but more questions come to light.

Elio's Nonna Greta seems to know who Sienna really is and wants her gone from the family, like, yesterday. *So, yeah, Nonna knows something you don't.* Nonna doesn't like Elio having a mind of his own now and tries to manipulate him into seeing Sienna as someone bad.

Not to mention Elio's Aunt Noemi *(who is married to his Uncle Bosco, and they are also Niccola and Vinni's parents)* seems lost and is living with Nonna Greta. *So, you know that can't be fun.*

Elio, who is being led down a very dark path by Nonna Greta, starts to doubt who Sienna is. *You must remember, she is his grandma, after all, and grandmothers are supposed to help mold their grandkids and hand off wisdom. After a lifetime of loving and learning from her, he would never suspect her of lying...not right away. I know you're mad at him, but try to see it from his angle too.*

Elenora leaks some secrets here and there *(A beyond frustrating woman. I sometimes want to throat punch her, too.)* but leaves the biggest one to the very end.

Sienna hands over proof to Elio that something big happened with Nonna Greta. He goes to his father and Francesco and explains what's going on. Things turn bad quickly.

More stuff happens...I'm flipping the pages and scanning...

Oh, yes, here we are. Now for the ending. Ready?

Sienna comes face to face with Mariano, who now knows she was lying about being with Elio.

Mariano stuffs her into a car with the help of Greta's *consigliere*, Abramo.

Greta tells Sienna she knows who she really is, gives her a train ticket to leave, then dumps her on the side of the road.

Elio tries to find Sienna but gets tricked and ends up being jumped by Stefano's men. He arrives home and finds out something huge.

Sienna gets picked up by Ugo and her mother. Elenora reveals that Sienna is actually the daughter of Theo Coppola *Oh, yeah, by the way, he's dead, from long ago.*

Plot twist!

Sienna tries to go back to tell Elio her huge news and finds his entire family at his house.

Somehow, they already know who she is, and Andrea confronts her with it.

Sienna, devastated, leaves a note, calls Ugo, and goes to a hotel. She needs time to figure out what she wants to do with this new information.

And breathe!

Now you are caught up. You are about to get one hell of ride in this next story.

So, hang on, go somewhere quiet, take notes if it helps, and enjoy!

Chapter ONE

We called it the boomerang effect, the kind of love that couldn't be broken. It could stretch and bend but always returned to its rightful shape.

Elio

Two Weeks Ago

Sweat dripped down my face, and my body begged me to quit. Aldo, my trainer, even threatened to leave if I didn't slow down. But I wanted this, needed this. After the shock of finding out that Sienna was a Coppola, and that I had been manipulated by my own beloved nonna, my world had flipped upside down. All through my childhood, my nonna had taught me what I needed to know about my world. As she helped my father groom me to take over the family business one day, she shared her knowledge and gave me the confidence I needed to be the man they needed me to be. It was all those things that made the level of betrayal that coursed through me so untamable. If I stopped, I knew I'd snap. I was not going to leave this ring until I could no longer feel.

"Boss," Niccola called, but all I could see was dust as I kicked, punched, and jammed at the eighty-pound bag that swung from the ceiling. "Elio!"

"He's not listening," Aldo panted. "He wore me out, and now he's determined to fight his way through the bag."

I blocked their chatter and used my arm to swipe at the sweat that dripped from my brow.

"Great," Niccola groaned. "Well, I've got a reason for you to stop." He paused. "Mariano was sighted near the dockyard."

Good.

"I have Gain and Donatello tailing him."

I've been planning my kill.

I saw him glance at Aldo out of the corner of my eye. "All right." He stepped closer. "Sienna left."

My punch wavered and the bag swung out to the side in a twist.

"She left a note, too."

That stopped me mid-punch, and I ripped the tape from my swollen hands. I tossed the sticky ball on the floor of the ring as I ducked under the ropes and dropped to the floor. Aldo tossed a towel at me as I grabbed my water, downing nearly all of it.

"When?" I grunted.

"The camera showed five-fifty, sixteen minutes after Nonna left."

"Note?"

"It's in the kitchen at the Hill House." Niccola nodded. "She also wrote something in flour, and I'm not sure what it means."

I nodded once, grabbing my keys, and headed out the door to the Hill House.

Once behind the wheel, I steadied my breathing and allowed my mind to slip back to memories of the night before.

When the house finally settled after the shock of Sienna's news, I was left with my head still spinning as I relived the night's events one by one. I'd left Nonna in the kitchen with Abramo making calls to ensure we had extra protection. We were unsure of just what the repercussions would be once the news of who Sienna really was got out. Nonna firmly believed the Coppolas might be heading this way and that they'd planted Sienna in our lives to spy all those years ago.

"I thought you could use this." Mama handed me a glass of rum and sat down beside me, nursing her own drink. It wasn't often that Mama dipped into the hard liquor, but tonight was a different story.

"Elio, I—"

"Her face told me everything." I cut her off, needing to let her know where my head was. "She found out who she was and came back to tell me." I shook my head,

unbelievably disappointed in myself. "She tried and tried to show me she was loyal, and because I'd been so well schooled by Nonna in the importance of the family and our oath, I couldn't see it. Now…" I swallowed hard, "she's up there in turmoil while I'm down here with Nonna's eagle eyes watching my every move."

"I'm so proud of you, Elio." I turned to face her head-on, wondering why on Earth she would say that now.

"I also believe Sienna had no idea who she really was, and so does your papa. Shame on Elenora for withholding such a secret, and shame on Nonna Greta for behaving in such a way." She reached for my hand. "I'm just so proud you can see this for what it is and not turn your back on someone who needs you now more than ever."

"I love her, Mama."

"I know you do, and that's why we are going to make this right, but it will require you having some distance from her."

"I'm not sure I can do that."

"Trust me, son, the last thing you need is your nonna meddling any more than she has." She gave me a knowing look, and I found myself wondering if Nonna had ever crossed Mama before. "I think it's best for Sienna to take some time away from the house, to clear her head. She needs time to digest this news even more than we do. Surely it can't be sitting well with her."

I nodded my agreement but loathed the idea of her leaving the house without me. I shifted my gaze out the door and caught Nonna watching me while she spoke to someone. Her gaze, which once brought me so much comfort, now brought only anger.

"Can you distract Nonna long enough for me to go talk to her?"

"No, figlio.*" She set her glass down and angled herself, so her face was hidden from Nonna's view. "Your nonna needs to think you're finished with Sienna. If she even suspects for one moment that you're not going to listen to her about her fears, who knows what she'll do. Don't underestimate her. Let me go to Sienna. I'll tell her what we've discussed, and as soon as there's an opportunity that's safe, you can go to her. But for now," she stood and ran a soft hand down my cheek, "stay away." I gave a slight nod of agreement and forced myself to sit back in the chair.*

I'm not sure how many times I tapped the screen on my phone to check the time. With every minute that passed, I felt my chest growing tighter, my blood pumping harder, and my foot vibrated against the floor.

Fuck it.

I texted Gain in spite of the fact I knew he was working in the garage. I'd sent him on a mission to set off Nonna's car alarm. Gain was a particularly trustworthy soldier and never asked questions, just did as he was told. Moments later, I heard the alarm, and the kitchen was instantly illuminated with flashing headlights. Abramo shot up from his chair and went racing outside with Nonna hard on his heels.

I hopped to my feet and charged down the hallway,

up the stairs, and into Sienna's room. Mama shook her head in defeat as I burst into the room, then smiled at me.

"I'll leave you two be, then," she said but leaned in as she passed me to speak quietly into my ear. "A plan has been hatched. Don't waste time discussing it, just reassure her that you love her. No more than five minutes." She eyed me as she said that.

Once the door was shut, I locked it and quickly moved across to her. I was glad the room was dark. She didn't need to see the pain and hate I was carrying on my face. She sat with her back straight and her legs over the side of the bed. She sniffed and wouldn't make eye contact with me. Her hair fell all around her face as I knelt in front of her and found myself unsure what to say. Instead, I took her hand and slid my family ring onto her ring finger then moved her hand to my chest, covering it with my own.

"We've spent a lifetime getting to right here, I will not let a name change that."

"I swear," she croaked, "I swear I had no idea."

"I know." I cupped her cheek with my free hand. I hated to see her hurting and how much this situation really did change things. She flinched slightly at my touch but didn't pull away from me. "I'm so sorry for everything, Sienna. I trust you more than anyone in this world. I was momentarily blinded by all our family rules. I want to spend the rest of my life making that up to you."

She let out a sob and leaned into me and pressed her lips to my neck. I wrapped my arms around her, wanting nothing more than to hold her tight.

"We will get through this, but—"

"I know." She took a deep breath and hesitated, and it reminded me that she and Mama had already hatched a plan.

"You should go."

She sighed and pulled back, but I grabbed her head and pressed my lips hard against hers. Again, she tightened at my touch, but a moment later she surrendered, and I knew as she relaxed and kissed me back that we were going to be all right.

Donte was leaning against the counter when I came in, and the moment he registered me, he shook his head and stepped back. His gaze swept quickly around at Nonna's new soldiers, who now seemed to hover everywhere now, and cleared his throat.

"Ah, boss, this was left for you." He pointed to the counter, knowing better than to have touched it. As I studied it, Niccola and Vinni came in and joined us. Then Mama, who looked as though she hadn't slept all night, emerged from behind them and gave me a slight nod to read it.

"She traced the words, *La Fine*." Donte's tone made me look up.

It was written in flour, which he knew meant it was for me.

"What context is this?" I grated.

"I told her about the story that Niccola used to share about you. About how you were in love with someone, and that's why you didn't date." He cleared his throat. "The look on her face told me everything. When I told her I knew it was her, she begged me not to tell a soul. That's Sienna, making sure everyone else around her is all right, even at her own expense."

"Donte," I warned, not needing a rundown on Sienna's personality.

"She's saying your story is over, boss. *La Fine*," he blurted then averted his eyes from me.

I turned away from them and broke the seal on the envelope she left. The necklace she always wore was curled in the corner of the fold, and I slid it out into my palm. My heart skipped a beat as I realized the bear pendant no longer rested against the crow. I grasped the chain and threaded it through my fingers as I tugged the paper out. The room went silent as her words flooded my head and my stomach sank.

Dearest Elio and Capris,

As a little girl, I dreamed of having a place I could call home, a room that was just for me, and parents who would tuck me in, kiss me goodnight, and chase the monsters away.

Then one day I met you by the pond. You earned my trust and slowly became my friend. You taught me what it meant to share life experiences, and I eagerly awaited each note you would leave for me tucked in the trunk of a tree. As the years went on, I fell totally in love with you and let my guard down enough to finally meet your family.

I never thought I would ever be so accepted by

anyone, let alone complete strangers, and to feel their warmth and love was overpowering. I'll admit I was nervous at first. Who could blame me? It was my first interaction with people who were so obviously happy and wanted to share it with me. You brought me that.

Then just as I became comfortable and felt a sense of belonging, my entire world disappeared. Nothing was left of you but a picture and a broken heart.

The only way I could cope with my loss was to put you in a box and seal it up tight in the fear that, over the years, if I slipped in a moment of weakness and thought of you, I wouldn't be damaged.

Moving on was the hardest thing I'd ever done.

Then life brought you back into my world.

I was tested, and I failed.

You chewed me up, swallowed me down, and spat me back out.

I thought I was doing everything right.

I thought my loyalty was enough.

I thought I was enough.

I never asked for this. I am not this.

But I know as I'm sitting here writing these words that this is it for us.

This is where we are supposed to say goodbye.

I can't—won't go through that again.

Instead, I will go.

Thank you for my memories. They will always remind me of what family should mean.

I'll be all right and will do what I do best—survive.

Because I've put you back in the box.

Because some dreams are just not meant to be.

Once yours,
Sienna Giovanna
Formally known as
Alessia Coppola

Once I finished reading the note, I handed it to Mama. Her body language and glance told me to listen. One of the new soldiers was on the phone reporting to Nonna that there was a note left from Sienna. I gave Mama a nod of understanding as I tucked the necklace into my pocket and headed for the front door. Papa, who I hadn't seen since the whole episode with Sienna, had just returned, looking darker than I'd ever seen before.

"Papa?" I stepped in his way, blocking him from the door.

"Deal with the warehouse then come see me right after," he growled.

"All right." I wanted to press more, but the clock was ticking. I headed for the car.

"Elio?" Papa called after me.

"Yeah?"

He rubbed his bottom lip and hesitated. I could see the storm inside him was brewing strong. "Watch your back."

"Understood."

He brushed by one of Nonna's new soldiers, nearly knocking him over.

"Now what do we do?" Niccola asked as he came

up behind me.

"Our job," I said as I dropped my sunglasses down and made my way into the sunlight.

"What about Sienna?"

One of my soldiers opened the car door for me while a few others stood at the bottom of the staircase per my nonna's request. I looked over the car roof at Niccola, who looked unsure where my head was.

"No one told her to leave."

"No one told her to stay either," he countered.

"She's a Coppola." I gritted the word through a tight jaw. "That alone is enough."

"People would kill for a love like yours."

"At least we get to kill." My tone gave him the warning to drop the topic.

"All right." He opened his door slowly. "Just seems wrong to me you didn't go after her."

I refused to comment and slipped behind the wheel. He dropped heavily into his seat and shut his door.

We had some people to deal with, and I needed her out of my head. I tore out of the driveway, leaving a dust cloud behind to drift over the new soldiers. When we were far enough away from the house, I made an effort to settle my temper.

"Elio, I just—"

"Do you really think I would let her leave?"

"Wait," the corners of his eyes lit up, "so, you're going after her?"

I glanced at him as I slammed my foot on the brake at a stop sign.

"When?"

"Mama and I already have a plan in motion." I shifted into first gear. "Right now, all eyes are on Sienna and me, and if things don't look legit, Nonna will know something's up."

He sat in silence, mulling over my words. "I feel like I don't have the entire story of what's going on here."

I sighed heavily, and he nodded and let it go. He quieted, and I knew his mind was still working.

Every second that went by, I burned with the urge to go to her, but I needed to play this out carefully. One wrong move, and things could go sideways again. I hated how blinded I'd been by my love for my nonna, that I'd questioned the one person in my life who had never given up on me. But Nonna had always been my rock in the family. She was the top of the hierarchy, one you'd never suspect of betrayal. No one in the family would ever question the motives of those above them. Ever.

"Does she know how you feel?" Niccola asked. "That you're not mad."

"Mama spoke to her last night, cleared the air on a few things. I went in afterward, and we're good. But I didn't know she was going to leave when she did."

"I don't blame her. I wouldn't want to be anywhere near Nonna right now."

"Yeah."

"And the fact that she's a Coppola?"

I glared at my cousin and shook my head, unable to go there just yet. He held up a hand to show he understood and let it go.

"I can't believe Nonna knew who she was before you did."

I let the anger that I had pushed aside moments ago seep back in.

Once at the warehouse, I felt my blood race like ice through my veins. The normal excitement I felt at these moments was absent. Today I fell into a darker place. As I hurried through the underground pathways, I could hear the whispers of those we held in our cells. We weren't total savages, but we kept our enemies for a while before we disposed of them. Sometimes the mere idea of being trapped underground, with an unknown death date, played on the mind enough to make a man squeal what he'd been hiding.

I stood in front of a wrought iron door and watched as six Coppola rats blinked back at me from the shadows. The whites of their eyes caught the low lighting and outed their locations.

Stefano was relentless with his army. Every time we turned around, more crawled out from between the cracks and tried to burrow their way into our lives. Lately, it had become even more blatant, and I couldn't help but wonder if he was becoming desperate or if it was just another distraction to draw our focus away from what was really going on.

"They were found sniffing around the market, near our wine vendors," Donatello joined me, "harassing the locals and kicking up dust about the explosion your girl was involved in."

I glanced over at him, puzzled. I had just assumed, given all that was going on, that the bomb that hit Sienna was a Coppola hit. Was it not? Or maybe they knew even before Sienna did that she was a Coppola, and wanted to remove the problem before she figured it out for herself.

"My thoughts, too." He nodded as he read my expression. "Anyway, I figured you'd want to be the first one to question them. I'll get out the tools."

My patience for the Coppola family had just about run out, but I needed to keep my cool now more than ever. One slip, and I could screw everything up.

"No, dip them instead."

"Sure, boss." Donatello motioned for the soldiers to take the men into the other room.

The first three men were handcuffed to a pully and lifted into the air, while the other three sagged against the damp wall, their eyes fixed on their fate. A motorized system transported the dangling bodies toward a pit I'd had my men dig a couple years back when I was feeling inventive. I lifted my hand to signal to Donatello to begin. The gears grated, then very slowly, each was lowered a little until they realized they were above a pit of tar.

"Imagine thick tar coating your lungs while pushing any air left up and out of your throat." I began to pace in front of them. "Your instinct is to kick and thrash, but you are barely able to move, leaving just your brain to fire off cold, pure fear. Finally, acceptance kicks in that you are slowly dying, drowning in thick, black sludge." I shrugged without any emotion. "To think you could have prevented all of this by simply telling me what I need to know." I twisted my cufflink while my words sank in. "I will make this very simple," I commanded over the sound of the gears. "Why were you asking about the bombing in the town?"

When none of them spoke, I flicked my finger, and the gears lowered them until they were knee deep in the tar.

"I'm not in the habit of repeating myself, and I think it's very clear that your fearless leader will not be showing up to save you. You are merely a number to him, a pebble in one's shoe." I stared at the one who looked like he might crack. "Speak now, and I might spare your life, or…" I glanced at Donatello, and the men were lowered to their waists.

"Because!" the one in the middle blurted and kicked out at his buddy as he snarled at him. He closed his eyes tight, clearly ready to lose his nerve.

"Because?" I repeated, taking a step closer.

"Because it—"

"Traitor!" one of the men against the wall called out and gasped as one of my soldiers punched him hard in the stomach. I pointed in the air, signaling to Donatello to release one of the men, and he dropped heavily into the thick tar. He wiggled and screamed briefly as he sank, but there was no hope. His hands were still bound, and the pit was deep.

"You were saying?" I encouraged the man who had spoken. He was now pasty white and dripping sweat. He looked over at me. The other men were silent, most likely in shock. I wasn't interested in them.

"Will you spare my life?"

"Depends."

"Stefano won't!" his partner shouted. "Tar or Stefano?" He spat off to the side. "I'll take the tar."

"Very well." A moment later, he too fell to his death. I was impressed; he didn't scream like the other one did. "Now, why were you asking questions?" Silence fell over the remaining man as he twirled slowly in the air. I grew annoyed. "Donatello." I turned to leave when the gears started to squeak.

"Because it wasn't our hit!" The man finally finished his sentence, stopping me in my tracks.

"Tell me more," I said over my shoulder, needing him to repeat what he had just said.

"We were told to sniff around because it wasn't our hit." He fought to catch his breath as the tar oozed over his shoulders. "Stefano is panicking because there is a third player after her."

The blood drained from my head as I stood like stone. Sienna was a Coppola, and that changed things, but if there was a third party in town, how did I not know about it? Or was it my nonna and her men who wanted to get rid of her on their own?

"What else?"

"Nothing. We get told very little, just to not come home until we know something."

"Did you find out anything at the market?"

"No," he shook his head, "your men got to us first."

I glanced over at the other men, who watched us intently.

"What about you?" I locked my gaze on one of them. After a moment, the light in his eyes faded and his lids lowered as he spoke.

"I stand with the Coppola family."

"Drop them all," I shouted as I turned and raced out of the room.

I didn't have time for pathetic pride or useless wails.

"Someone pissed off the devil," one of the rats called from one of the cells, so I pulled my gun and shot at him without missing a stride. I hoped his screams of agony would add fear to those who were left.

I lowered my sunglasses as I burst through the door to the outside. Anger coursed through my blood, making me see red. I was tired of the secrets and lies, tired of not knowing what the hell was going on until it was too late to do anything about it.

"Boss?" Niccola caught up to me, huffing. I held up a hand to keep him at bay.

"How could I not have known?" I boomed.

"None of us thought there could be someone else involved. We just assumed it was Stefano…" He paused and joined my side. He changed his tone. He knew there was so much more than this eating away at my core. "It's just a name, boss. She's still Sienna."

He lowered his eyes when I glared that he even went there.

He cleared his throat, knowing he was pushing all my buttons. "Don't let a name change a lifetime of feelings between you."

I wanted to lash at him for harping on a topic I didn't

want to discuss but stopped myself. I could ride this out alone or…I pulled out my wallet and handed him the paper Sienna had found in Nonna's car.

"What's this?"

"I think it's time you knew the truth about Nonna."

Chapter TWO

Sienna

The hotel ceiling had swirls that went off in different patterns. Since I was on a two-day cry binge, it didn't take me long to discover that it was a maze. With a heavy arm, I lifted my hand to trace the paths and found my way out. Now if only I could do that in real life.

I slipped into a memory.

I lay on my side, numb and cold with my eyes fixed somewhere outside the window. The murmurs from downstairs, which normally I'd find comfort in, now made me feel like I didn't belong. My head swam with the truth, and my heart fought to care to beat anymore. I flinched when the bedroom door opened and rolled my head to see who it was. The darkness kept the visitor hidden. That was until her soft, beloved touch brushed down my arm, outing who it was.

"Cuoricino?" She spoke softly as I shifted over to let her sit next to me. She brushed my hair off my face and wrapped me in her arms. "I'm sorry, Sienna, for the way we behaved downstairs. It just took us all by surprise."

"I swear, Andrea, I had no idea." I struggled through the knot in my throat.

"I know." She hugged me tighter. "Never once did I think otherwise."

"Do you look at me differently now?" I had to know to protect myself from the blow of losing this family again.

"I look at you the way I always have, like the daughter I've always wanted." She kissed my hair, and I let out a silent sob of relief. I should have known better than to think Piero and Andrea would ever think I'd keep secrets from them. Secrets were the root of all evil and never got anyone anywhere. But…

"And Elio?" I managed to get out.

"He loves you, Sienna. It's just…" She trailed off, and I squinted to look up at her, but it was too dark to make out her face.

"Just what?"

"Maybe it's time I shared something with you, and then I will explain what we are going to do."

A voice pulled me from my memory. "You need to eat." Ugo was at the edge of the bed looking down at me, concerned. I struggled to hold on to my memory, but it flittered away. I forced myself to recall what he'd just said.

"I will, I promise." I closed my eyes as tears prickled. I loved that Andrea had come to talk to me that night. Her love and her kind words made me feel a lot better. But the fact that Elio had come himself filled me up and helped a great deal to repair my torn heart. The truth, however, was what it was, and no matter how much they tried to put a good face on it, the shock of knowing the truth was incredibly unsettling, not only to them, but to me. I didn't blame Francesco. How could I? He'd kept me safe and brought me Elio; he gave me happiness. But my mother? How could my own mother hold such a secret from me? How could I know if that was even the last of it? Could there be even more hateful things I didn't know about? Would Elio and I be strong enough to get through any more?

"I'm not sure how long I can keep your location from your mother. She's growing restless." The mere mention of my mother made me see red.

"She's managed to not know it for nearly a decade." I rolled away from him. "I think she'll be fine."

"Sienna," he sighed, "you're putting me in a bad position here."

"And though I deeply appreciate what you've done for me, dear cousin, no one is holding a gun to your head to stay."

"Are you always this stubborn?"

"Yes."

"I'm giving you until tomorrow. After that—"

"After that, what?" I was like a robot, hollow and empty, working only because my mechanics did so with no thought.

"Just," he grunted, "just, get some more sleep."

When I heard the door shut behind me, I pulled my knees to my chest and held myself together as another wave of emotion ate away at my insides.

One more day, that was all I needed before I would decide. I almost welcomed the pain, as it made me feel something, but even it didn't last as I gave in to the cold darkness that consumed me.

I wasn't sure what time it was when the hotel door opened, but I groaned, not wanting to hear about food or my mother.

"Ugo, I'm fine."

Suddenly, the bed dipped. I couldn't see who it was because it was so dark in the room. As soon as I caught a whiff of his aftershave, I rolled into his chest, buried my face, and broke.

"You don't look fine," Wyatt whispered in my hair.

"No matter what," I forced the words past my lips, "you can't leave me."

"I couldn't if I wanted to."

I dragged my hand across my face, smearing the tears, and his eyes bulged when he took in my swollen, bruised face.

"Did someone hit you?" He peered at me in the semi-darkness, but with only the low cast of the outside streetlights, he couldn't clearly see.

"Mariano." I held up a hand to stop his anger. "Don't

worry, I got a few of his teeth."

"Teeth?" he shouted as he took a deep breath to calm his nerves. "Tell me what the hell is going on." He leaned over me and switched on the bedside lamp to see my face.

I bit on the inside of my lip. I knew my best friend would hear me out and say he understood, but there was tiny part of me that was worried. What if he turned his back on me?

"Sienna?"

"Seems I have monster blood running through my veins." His face scrunched in confusion. "Apparently, you're best friends with a Coppola." His mouth dropped open.

"As in…"

"Yup," I flopped my arm over my sore eyes, "as in the ruthless monsters who have been trying to kill me and take out the Capri syndicate."

"How?"

"Apparently, my ever-so-forthcoming mother had an arranged marriage to the Don of the syndicate."

"Here I was off chasing story leads, and you were here stumbling over a huge one of your own!" Wyatt's voice was incredulous.

"Aren't I lucky?" Sarcasm dripped from my lips.

"Wait, so you're the Coppola princess and Elio's the Capri prince. You two are the modern-day Romeo—" His voice was excited now as his imagination took over.

"Don't," I warned. "They both died at the end, remember, loving one another. Not me. I'll die alone, a stupid fool for thinking I could fit in their world. Now here I am, a part of their world, a part they hate."

"You know that's not true." He pretended to brush me off, which only made me angry, and when he saw I was pissed, he dropped his attempt to lighten the mood. "Sienna," his voice softened, "he called me looking for you the other night. He ran into trouble at the dockyard or I'm sure he'd be here. When he gets wind of all of this—"

"He has." I sniffed, hating that it wasn't time yet to share the truth about me and Elio being somewhat okay. Although Elio had assured me we were fine, the hurt of their reaction and their horrified expressions still hurt, and it pecked away at my self-confidence. The more I thought about that day, the less confident I felt that things would work out. When I knew we were truly solid, I'd share the truth. For now, I was too scared to say the words out loud.

"Really? Then, I'm sure it's just a misunderstanding."

"Wyatt," I dragged myself up to sit and brushed my hair away from my eyes, "Nonna Capri hated me because she knew who I was before I did." I skipped some keys parts about how I was kidnapped and run out of town. "When I wanted to leave, my mother finally shared the truth with me about who I really am." I turned on another lamp and reached for my purse. I tossed the heavy ring at him. He admired the bear then caught the dates of the family members engraved inside. "When I finally got back to Elio's," I went on, "to tell him what I'd learned, the entire family was there waiting for me.

She got to them before I could." I paused to get a handle on a threatened sob, remembering how they'd all looked at me and how I instantly felt chilled. "The look on Elio's face when he saw that ring of evil in my hand is not something I'll ever forget. I have the blood of the enemy in my veins." I let out a long breath, trying to pull myself together.

"Si, maybe he…" He trailed off when he caught himself siding with the maybes.

"As much as I love that you want all of this to be a misunderstanding, Wyatt," I covered his hand with mine, "I still haven't fully recovered from our last fallout, and I'm really not sure I can do it again, so I just need a little time to think all this through." I dried my hands on my pants and dropped back to stare up at the ceiling. "Andrea came to see me before I left," I blurted but stopped myself from sharing everything. It wasn't time yet.

"What did she say?"

"That she loved me no matter what, but that maybe it was best I took some time for myself."

"That's good."

"It is, and I love her for saying that, but," it was on the tip of my tongue, "things are changing, and I'm just not sure where I fit anymore." He reached out and rubbed my shoulder. "I'm so disappointed."

"You never asked for this, Sienna, but maybe you can be the one Coppola who isn't all bad."

His words struck a chord in me, and for a moment I stilled, wondering if that could be possible.

"If it's possible, I feel more alone now than I did living on the streets, before I met you," I admitted after a few moments.

"Luckily for you, you now have me." He held out his arms, and I crawled into them, loving that I had someone who would drop everything for me. We stayed like that for a while until I heard him quietly clear his throat. It sounded like he was getting emotional.

"I'd like a free pass on a question."

"Okay." I sagged, raw and open.

"Do you still love him?"

I hated how much that question affected me now. I knew I did love Elio, but still wasn't sure if who I was now was going to be a problem after all the dust settled. Would I ever be fully trusted in the Capris' eyes? And could I blame them if I wasn't?

Sounds from the shower in the next room came to me, and I let the white noise wash over my swimming head.

My eyelids grew heavy, and as I drifted off to sleep, I let the truth slip from my lips.

"It would be so much easier if I didn't."

The next morning, after I'd showered and changed, I stood on the balcony and pretended not to notice Wyatt and Ugo talking quietly about me in the parking lot below.

I had two choices right now—go home and wonder what could have been or take charge and grow a pair. After what I learned last night from Andrea, I thought I needed to grow a pair.

I went back into the room, sipped my coffee, and nibbled at an apple pastry as I hatched a plan of my own. I wasn't sure how long I zoned out, but I suddenly heard the hotel room door shut and the sound of the guys' muffled voices.

"Nice to see you eating." Ugo moved to sit across from me as Wyatt swiped the last of the pastry from my plate.

"Are you feeling any better?" Wyatt asked, checking his phone.

"Yes."

"Would you like to see your mother now?" Ugo's face looked relieved. "Or go home?"

"No," I let out a long breath with my decision made, "I have a different place in mind."

Ugo's face dropped, and Wyatt lowered his phone.

Present Day

Ugo tipped the bellman as the last of our luggage was removed from the room and packed away in his trunk.

"I'm gonna check out. Are you good here?" Ugo, who had been hovering since I told him my plan, looked worried.

"I'm fine." I forced a smile and pulled my mascara from my makeup bag. "I'll be down in a few minutes. I'll meet you in the lobby."

"All right."

I turned back to the mirror and leaned forward,

brushing the small black wand over my eyelashes. It was nice to see a little color back in my cheeks.

Just take it one day at a time.

The door opened, and I closed my eyes and lowered my head. Ugo was wonderful, but he was like a hovering mother hen. Between him and Wyatt, I could barely take a breath without them wondering what was wrong.

"I know you're worried about me and my idea, but I got this."

"Do you really?" His voice made my eyes pop open, and I whirled to find a vibrating Elio glaring at me from the doorway. His normal attire of a pressed shirt, tie, and jacket was not even close to what he wore right now. He looked disheveled, his shirt was partially unbuttoned, and his face was furious.

"We need to talk." He held up the letter I'd written and looked fit to kill. "Now!"

No.

"What the hell are you doing here, Elio!" I couldn't do this now.

A half an hour later, I took a deep breath and let anger pour off my body, completely ignoring those around me as I pushed away from the elevator wall and stepped out into the lobby, leaving those on the elevator glad to see us exit. Elio, whose knuckles were bloody from punching the wall upstairs, turned to glare at me. We both stood our ground in the lobby. We glared our loathing for one another, then without a single word, we flew off in opposite directions.

Ugo appeared in a flash and looked me over then took my makeup bag from my clenched fingers.

"Ah?"

"Don't," I warned him. "It's not worth it."

"Was that Elio?" Wyatt said his name, and I felt my stomach heave. "Sienna, what did he say?"

"Absolutely nothing."

"Come on, Si. You were up there for almost thirty minutes."

"He wanted closure, Wyatt." I laughed darkly, not caring who heard me. "And I gave him some."

"Did you at least tell him about what Mariano did? How he was working with Nonna Greta?"

"No." I spoke quietly in case Elio was still within hearing range. The last thing he needed right now was to go flying off the deep end. There were bigger issues to deal with.

"Why not?"

"Mariano's day is coming. I don't want the attention or a verbal lashing for not telling him sooner."

"Sienna, I really think—"

"Wyatt, just drop it, okay? I'm not part of that anymore." I whirled and handed the front clerk a small, padded envelope. "Could you please make sure this goes out in today's mail?"

"Sure thing."

"What was that?" Ugo was at my side.

"Proof that I was taken against my will by Nonna

Greta." I snarled, more pissed than anything as I thought of that moment.

Ugo looked over my head and then back at me. "All right, that's enough attention on us. Let's get moving."

Wyatt looked over his shoulder to try to spot Elio as we headed outside to the waiting car.

"There's no reason to look back, Wyatt." I threaded my sunglasses through my hair, shading my eyes. "I know I'm not."

Wyatt grabbed my elbow and stopped me. "Sienna, what's going on?"

"I'm not the woman I was two weeks ago. I refuse to be." My comment couldn't be any closer to the truth. Something in me had changed, and I really liked it. I looked past him and saw a blacked-out car and someone's silhouette. They appeared to be watching us. "I've got another chance to start over, and I'm taking it."

"And you think this plan of yours is the way to do it?"

"I do." I ducked down and disappeared into the cool breeze of the AC.

"Elio's going to kill you."

"And when that happens, I want a piñata at my funeral, filled with bees, so people are happy but not too happy. I read that on a meme somewhere."

He rolled his eyes at my attempt to lighten the mood. "It's not funny."

"Yeah, it is."

"Will you fill me in on everything now?"

"It's a lot, Wyatt. Are you sure you want to be

involved in it all?"

"So, help me God, Sienna."

"All right." I twisted in the seat and started from when I was dropped off at Elio's house and proceeded to share everything with him.

Wyatt stared straight ahead at the back of the seat. I could almost hear the wheels spinning in his head. He hadn't moved for a long while.

"You wanted to know." I shook my head and went back to my phone, studying what I needed to know. As we grew closer to the city, my heart crept into my throat and the toe of my shoe tapped the car floor. I would never admit I was terrified. If Ugo thought for a moment that I didn't have myself together, he would have turned the car around so fast.

"This is stupid," Wyatt suddenly muttered, as his eyes zeroed in on my fingers as they flexed and unflexed against the fabric of my dress.

"Maybe." I looked away, not wanting my best friend to see he was right. "But I need to do this."

A long stretch of silence fell over us before he rubbed his face and let out a long breath. "I know."

The car wove through the streets, in and out of vendors, around children walking home from school, so serene, so normal. Then it stopped. We had reached our destination. I braced myself for part one of our plan.

"Ready?" Ugo glanced at me in the mirror, and when I nodded, I heard him curse. He wasn't happy with me, but to my surprise, he was still going along with it. If I was to guess, my mother wasn't far away, but I would deal with that heap of a disaster later. First was this.

"Wyatt, stay here." I was proud that my voice sounded controlled.

"I have no problem with that." He squeezed my hand but wouldn't look at me.

"Hey," I tugged at his arm, "I got this." I waited for his timid smile then climbed out of the car, tugged my purse up tight under my arm, and straightened my back.

"This way." Ugo pointed and looked at me over his shoulder. "Remember—"

"I know," I reassured him and followed him around the corner.

Ugo gripped the top of my arm as I swayed in fear in front of a sign that read Dager's Den.

"Why here?" I couldn't look at him.

"Because," I heard the flex of his jacket as he rubbed his face, annoyed with my questions, "she's like clockwork. She'd never miss a day to flaunt her power to the other men."

Sweet Lord.

"I think I might faint."

He cut me a quick glance then shook his head and cursed.

My entire body froze with fear, and my eyes went wide at the sound of the handle being pulled. The door opened to reveal a woman with eyes as black as coal in a face with skin so white it almost glowed. Her dark hair was pulled tightly back into a bun, and a pair of glasses hung from the collar of her blue blouse. Her perfectly ironed gray slacks stopped at her ankles just above her small-heeled boots. Both hands rested on a glass ball that sat on the top of her black cane. I felt like I had been transported directly into a nasty scene from a Disney movie.

"Ugo." She only spoke his name then closed her eyes slowly, and when they opened again, they were on me. I stepped back, but Ugo pressed me forward, rooting me back in place. She was like a cobra only inches from my face. It made me want to run and scream at the same time, but my brain seemed to have shorted out at the simultaneous commands.

So, I just stared.

"Nonna Rosa," Ugo addressed her, and I felt him look down at me, "I want you to meet someone."

A cold chill passed through my body, and I became lightheaded as my heartbeat pulsed in my ears. "This is Theo's Alessia, your granddaughter."

She lifted her eyes to stare at him for a brief moment then turned those black pools back to me. Her colorless lips pressed into a hard line as she tried to see inside my soul.

"Prove it."

I stood frozen, completely unable to respond. She had awakened such a deep fear inside of me I was completely at her mercy.

Ugo reached for my hand and held it up to show her the ring.

She grabbed my hand between her icy fingers and held it close to her face. She closed one eye and twisted the band around and gave a low gasp.

Chapter THREE

Elenora

"Why aren't you more worried?" I glanced at Francesco as I sent off another text to Ugo, who promised me Sienna was just fine. She wasn't; I could feel it.

"Because she's a grown woman who just had her heart broken for the second time in her life. She needs space."

"Space is not what she needs."

"It's exactly what she needs." He stood and checked the time on his phone.

"But she's in danger."

"But she's with Ugo, right?" He arched one eyebrow, making his point.

"I'm her mother, and she should be calling me back,"

I fumed, annoyed no one else was taking this seriously.

"You are," he nodded as he came forward to block my constant pacing, "but you also just came into her life. Her natural instinct is not to call you."

"Then who?"

"I'm guessing that would be her best friend or, up until a few weeks ago, Elio."

"Don't," I shoved a finger in his face as fire festered inside of me, "mention that boy's name in front of me."

"That boy is a very well-respected man who loves Sienna very much."

"Is that why he turned his back on her and made her slip away in the wee hours of the morning?"

"Love doesn't come without it's challenges, Elenora. You of all people should know that one."

"Meaning?"

"You could have told her who she was when you arrived, but you chose not to. Just like all the rest of it you haven't shared."

"So, this is all my fault?" I shouted as I shot him a look not to go there.

"I'm saying we're all to blame for what happened. Many of us have a part in her story. But pointing blame at Elio, the only person besides Sienna who was truly blindsided by all this, isn't going to make the situation any better."

"None of this would have even happened if my brother hadn't been slaughtered by that *boy's* family in the first place. The Capris caused this."

"I'm not doing this again." He shook his head and

stepped back, needing distance from me.

"Maybe none of this would have happened at all if you hadn't picked the enemy," I muttered, hoping to sting him like he did me all those years ago.

A dark smirk raced across his lips, and he let out a sardonic chuckle. "I didn't pick the enemy. I chose my family. Let's not forget that your parents hated me from the very start."

"For good reason." I snickered, wanting him to burn inside like I was.

He cleared his throat as he stepped closer, trapping me between two chairs. He lowered his voice as he stared into my eyes. "Your brother's blood never touched my hands, and my family never had anything to do with his death either. But, as always, you'll believe what you want."

I let out the breath I was holding as he spoke and turned away. I refused to believe him, and I was infuriated that he still clung to the lie and refused to admit the truth, even to himself.

"And what about Noemi?" I said over my shoulder. "When were you going to tell me about her?"

"Need I remind you that I never met Noemi? I only knew her name. You told me about her but never showed me a photo, and I've never had any interaction with her. There's no way I could have connected those dots. Her family had zero ties to the Coppolas. I'm still reeling about it."

"I find that hard to believe." I glanced back at him.

"What's new?" He tossed his hands up, annoyed

with me. "This right here," he huffed, "is why we're not together. It's you and your hate. You can't let things go and just be happy, and you're dragging everyone you love down with you."

"I am not!" I snapped but felt like a child with my reaction.

"Good Lord, Elenora! You have a silver platter serving you your daughter. It's a second chance! Most would sell their soul for an opportunity like that, and all she wanted was the truth, and you couldn't even give her that."

"I did, and look where it got me!"

"Can you hear yourself? See the wake of damage you've caused?" His hands fisted into his hair. "You better tell her the rest, and while you're at it, tell me the whole story of Noemi. My family has had enough pain for one lifetime."

"I—" I stumbled with the truth on my tongue, wanting to shout it out loud, but I couldn't. It wasn't time yet. It was the only ammo I had left to take down the Capris. "I can't."

"Tea?" Oscar broke our moment, and I used that excuse to move across the room to the tray. I poured myself a cup as I waited for my heartbeat to slow. Francesco cursed then stepped out onto the balcony to take a call.

I allowed myself a moment and slipped into a memory that had pushed its way to the surface.

I opened the door to the little bistro that was only minutes from my place, as I'd spotted my broken-hearted brother sitting in the window like a statue. My stomach sank. It had been two months since Noemi had decided he couldn't give her everything she wanted and had left him, leaving nothing but a note on his desk. Later that night, he had reached out to her in desperation to try to fix things, but she simply explained she wanted more out of her life than he was going to give her. She said she'd known he was supposed to take over the family business someday, and she'd been excited about it. She imagined the life they would have had with lots of money to travel, perhaps even visit the Seven Wonders of the World. She had come to realize Angelo wasn't interested in any of that. He wanted the whole white picket fence, kids, and a minivan. He was a man who needed very little to be happy, and that life was not what she envisioned for herself. Once she realized it, she was out. He was left with nothing but the pieces of his own crumbled dreams.

"Hey," I sank onto the stool next to him and wrapped my arm around his shoulders, "how are you?"

"I don't know." He shrugged. "Here, I guess."

"Okay." I nodded like I understood. "Any word from Noemi?"

"No, just me calling and leaving voice messages."

"How many have you left?"

"I call every day—"

"That's not so bad."

"Every day on the hour. So, like, twelve times."

"Angelo," I groaned, "that's way too much."

"Don't women want the man to fight for them? Fight for their love?" He turned to look at me with

such confusion and pain that I wanted to cry. He didn't deserve this.

"Yes," I said softly, "when there's a chance the relationship can be mended. Noemi isn't after the same things you are."

"What, you think she's after a man with more money..." His voice trailed off, and he suddenly sat a little straighter and his face turned red. "Wait, what?"

I followed his line of sight, and my mouth dropped open. There was Noemi, arm in arm with the underboss of the Coppola syndicate, Theodore. We stared as he leaned down and kissed her cheek.

"Oh, my God," I muttered and pushed my hands down on his shoulders as he went to jump up to go after them. "No, Angelo, you can't. Theodore isn't someone you want to get tangled up with."

"You know his family met up with ours last week, right?" He tried to move again, but I was ready.

"Huh?" I held up a hand to stop him. "Why in the world would our family meet up with the Coppolas? They never let us go near them. Ever."

"My guess would be they want to chat about their money. They launder it through Papa's insurance accounts."

"Papa isn't doing that." Our father was a shark in the business world, but he would never be so stupid as to make a deal like that.

"No?" He looked me dead in the eye. "They came to some kind of an agreement years ago. I remember because there was a handshake and some drinks afterward." He

let out a long breath. "Or maybe Papa couldn't cook the books anymore, and it came time to pay out the Coppolas and there wasn't any money to give."

I stepped back, completely confused on what he was talking about.

"I'm not following."

"You really didn't know?" He shook his head like he was surprised I didn't know such a dirty secret about our family.

"Is this the face of someone who knows what the hell you're talking about?" I pointed at my face with both index fingers.

"Papa hasn't been making the bills since you were thirteen, Elenora. He made a deal with the Don to launder their money through the company in exchange for keeping Papa's doors open. Problem is that deal came with a cost, and now it's time to pay up, and the last I saw, we didn't have near what the payment was."

"That doesn't make sense. I saw the books. We're fine."

"No, you saw the cooked books, my dear sister." I shook my head trying to follow. "Honestly, I know you didn't know about it. He did it for us. He doesn't actually know I know either. His pride is too big for me to burst that bubble. However, now," he rubbed his face, "it's collection time, and I wonder what that will entail."

I sank back onto the stool and joined in on his blank stare at the happy couple. We both learned something new today. My papa lied to me, and my brother's heart just got crushed to dust for the second time in two months.

How could he be dating her?

The patio door opened, and Francesco pulled me from my unhappy memory.

"Let me guess." I set my teacup on the table. "You were summoned?"

"We have a possible lead on Mariano. I need to check it out." He gathered his keys off the desk, ignoring my tone.

"Well, when *family* calls…" I let all my unhappiness drip from my tongue, then waved him off. He caught my hand, holding it tightly.

"Hate is such an ugly look on you."

I looked away, not liking how raw I felt with him. We had so much history that it was easier to hate him than to continue to love him.

"Weren't you leaving?"

"One of these days it will be the last time," he muttered as he left, slamming the door behind him.

Instantly, I remembered the last time he raced out of a room like that and let my mind go spiraling back to when that hateful day landed at my feet.

"Mama? I'm here." I burst through the front door with an armful of the flowers from the garden that she had insisted I pick. Something about how tonight had to be perfect.

"There you are, Elenora." She kissed my cheeks and stepped back to admire my outfit. "I guess this will do."

"Do?" I moved to the sink to pour some water into the vase then began to place the stems neatly inside. "What is this all about, anyway?"

"Your father is entertaining some work friends tonight, and we needed you here."

"Oh, is it the gentlemen from the United States?" I knew Papa had made a huge deal with some American who was looking to expand over here.

"No." She turned on her heel and left me in the kitchen wondering why she was being so vague.

"Hang on. Where is Angelo?" I followed her out to the dining room. "Shouldn't he be here, too?"

"Um," she pretended to fluff the pillow, "he'll be here later."

That should have been the red flag. Papa always made sure Angelo was at all the meet and greets.

"Mama?" Just as I said her name, the doorbell rang, and my life as I knew it was about to change forever.

"Please, come in." Papa waved in the guests, and my knees nearly buckled beneath me. "Theodore, this is my daughter Elenora."

"Lovely to meet you." He extended his hand, and I looked at it in confusion. That was the very same hand that had rested on Noemi's hip not a week ago. Those were the same lips that had brushed her cheek as I sat by my poor brother and wanted to weep. "Or perhaps not." He rolled his eyes but smiled when my mama came up next to me and jabbed me in the side.

"She can be a little shy at first."

"I can?" I muttered as my mother gave me a little shake and a frown. Then she stepped forward and led the Don and his wife into another room, leaving me alone with him.

Theodore looked around the living room and seemed unimpressed with the decor.

"It's polite to offer a guest a drink." He swung his gaze over to me. "Or are you mute and deaf? Because if that's the case, maybe this isn't the worst situation after all."

That snapped me out of my daze. "I think I'm wondering why you are even here, in my parents' house."

"Ah," he scoffed, "she does speak."

"And hear too," I snapped back. "And what is this situation you speak about?"

"Oh," his eyebrows pinched together, "you don't know?"

"Know what?" I folded my arms and glared at him.

"You've been sold to me. So, that being said, I'll allow you to call me Theo."

I didn't remember much more than that. Dinner was a blur. Mama avoided my line of sight, and Papa was putting on quite the show, acting like a fool, showing off. That night, I was escorted to the bottom of the stairs and was told to pack my things and that I was going to be taken to the Coppola mansion in the morning. One of Theo's men stayed outside our home.

"I don't understand." Francesco had crawled through the window to find out what was going on. He sat on the edge of bed while I sat like stone on the chair. "They can't just sell you."

"Apparently, they can and did."

"You don't have to go, Elenora."

"Yes, I do." I stood, furious at him, furious at

Theodore, and even more furious at my parents. "They made it very clear that if I didn't do as they said that my parents would suffer. Death was an option."

"But why you? Why not someone with more money or—"

"Run away with me," I begged and dropped to my knees in front of him, taking his hands. "I'm already packed. We can leave and just find a little place somewhere in the tropics. We could be free of all this."

"Elenora…" He stopped himself, and I knew what was standing in his way. What was always standing in our way—his precious syndicate. His precious family. "You know I can't do that. You know I can't leave my family. Andrea just had her son, and they need me there. It's where I belong."

"They're not your family." I retracted my hands and stood, feeling lightheaded.

"They are." He struggled with his frustration. We both knew there was no way out of this hell.

"So, you choose them over me?"

"No, I choose both of you."

"There's no choosing both."

"Don't make me choose, Elenora. I hate this situation more than anything, and I'd fight like hell to keep you. You know that. But if your parents made a deal with the Coppolas for you to marry their son, I'm not sure what I could possibly do about that. There are rules in this world, ones you can't bend."

"So, you're giving up?"

"Good Lord!" He stood with his hands in his hair.

"No! I'm just trying to figure out a plan here."

"We run."

"I can't do that!"

I marched over to the window, folded my arms, and used my head to point to the door.

"You're kicking me out?"

"You did that to yourself."

"Elenora?" He went to grab my shoulders, but I stepped back. He'd shown me where his heart really was. With them.

He left, and I slammed the window and threw myself on my bed with tears streaming down my face.

"It's for the best." Mama was suddenly in the doorway. "You need to get away from Francesco and all the trouble that comes with him." She reached over and locked the window. How did she know he was here? "Though you may not see it right now, the Coppolas can offer you a life he can't."

"And if I don't want that life?" I tried to dry my cheeks.

"You will."

"I don't love him!"

"You will."

"Mama!"

She stood a little straighter and looked over her shoulder down the hallway. "You're too young to know what love is. You will do this without any trouble, Elenora. Do you hear me?"

"If I don't?"

"No, you will, my dear, or the family you love won't

be here tomorrow." She gave me a look not to push any further and closed the door behind her.

Chapter
FOUR

Elio

"I don't care about the price, just get me what I want." I hung up and tossed the phone on the desk then leaned over the back of the leather chair to calm my anger. I looked out at the garden terrace filled with ivy and potted sunflowers. I thought how it once brought me such comfort to look at it. Now it cut me like glass every time. Since Sienna came back, I hadn't needed my office in the city to escape and be alone.

But now, things were different, and we needed to keep a close eye on Mariano's parents, especially since Mariano had vanished. I knew he was most likely off somewhere snorting coke with some woman he'd met. He was so damn irresponsible. The news that Sienna was a Coppola had changed things. We were now forced to conduct all our business outside our home away from curious ears, especially Mariano and his parents. It meant any wining and dining of our clients and old family friends had to be done here at the office, at least until things were figured out.

My phone buzzed against the hardwood, and I glanced down, feeling my mood shift even darker.

Nonna: We need to meet and discuss a few things.

I pressed my lips together and rubbed below my nose, taking a deep breath. We hadn't spoken since that night she came to the house to share the news about Sienna's origins.

I closed my eyes and remembered that night vividly.

My phone vibrated.

"Where are you?"

"The dockyard. Donatello texted that he needed me here," I muttered, frustrated. "Listen, Wyatt, if you hear from her, please tell her I'm looking for her, okay? And I'm concerned my nonna might have something to do with her being gone."

"Why?"

His words sounded a million miles away as I focused on a sound behind me. I whirled to find Anna stepping off the office stairs. She tossed Donatello's phone on the ground and crushed it into the concrete with the heel of her boot.

"Elio, are you still there?" Wyatt's voice came across the line.

"I think it's time we had a little chat." Anna smirked

as she took a step back and looked over her shoulder. I followed her line of sight and saw Stefano with a baseball bat in his hand.

Oh, shit.

Like water trickling through the cracks of a seam, at least thirty of his soldiers emerged from all around me.

"Wyatt?" I whispered, slipping back into the dark corners of my mind. "Call Vinni."

Lowering my hand, I quickly sent the number eight on a group message and tucked my phone away, pulling the gun from under my jacket. Eight was the number for 'shit is going down, find me.' We've only had to use it one time before, and it wasn't this bad.

"I'm listening." I tried to buy some time as I eyed the men slowly encroaching on my space.

"I want him alive," Stefano called to his men, and I noticed he stood back like the coward he was.

"You were so blind," Anna chuckled loving every moment of it, "blinded by that bitch of a woman."

"I can see why you were threatened." I jabbed at her, wanting her to see she meant nothing to me. Most people would flip the script, give in to their instincts, and agree with the crazy woman holding the gun, but not me. Never once had I led Anna on.

"I'm not threatened, Elio. There's no reason for me to be. She's not even here anymore. She left on a one-way train ticket."

"Willingly, I'm sure." I swallowed past the lump in my throat. I needed to find her.

"Depends on how you look at it. Sure." She smirked

with a shrug.

"Where's Mariano in all of this?"

"Ugh," she brushed me off, "he wasn't even a good lay. He was just convenient."

"And this is better?" I pointed at Stefano. "Siding with the enemy?"

"At least my talents are being used for a good thing."

"I hardly think spreading your legs for the entire syndicate is a talent."

She glared at me and ran her tongue along her teeth as she snarled.

"It's a shame my father tipped off yours all those years ago. Piero would be worm food now, and maybe you could have seen who was actually behind it all."

My blood ran cold. I always wondered if Anna knew the truth, and my gut was right. She did.

"Open doors and kindness have always been, and will always be, the Capri downfall." She peered a few feet away. "I was hoping over the years you'd see that and perhaps be a better ruler, but now, after meeting your little pet of a woman, I can see why the DeSimones tried to take out your father all those years ago."

There it was—the truth. We had teamed up with the enemy. We had let them in. Their smaller syndicate needed help, and look where it got us. This was why we should trust no one. This was why, when I became Don, everything would change. My father seemed soft, but he had a core of steel. I'd seen his wrath, and it was time to unleash it again, starting with the soldiers who were supposed to be watching the DeSimones every step. Watching our back.

I pretended to laugh and dropped my head to check the time on my watch. Three minutes.

"Your syndicate will fall, Elio Capri, all because you men are blinded by the wrong women."

Huh.

I swirled on my heel and ducked low as I sent five bullets into the five men who were about to jump me. I spun around toward Anna and shot one over her shoulder and heard her yelp in fear. She bolted for the office while I got another seven shots off before I jerked from a kick in the back.

I pretended the hit knocked the wind out of me and grabbed my stomach, then suddenly kicked Stefano in the shoulder, causing the bat to fall to the ground. As he stumbled backward, I used the toe of my shoe to roll the bat and flick it upward into my hands. With all my might, I slammed it into a man's skull who had come at me from the side, then nailed Stefano in the ribs as he lunged forward.

"Elio!" Vinni's welcome voice called as I took another hit to the face. I fed off the pain. Any feeling was better than the hollowness that ate away at my insides.

Blood blurred my vision momentarily as more hits came, and I did whatever I could to inflict pain back. It wasn't until I heard Vinni's blowtorch being lit that I stopped and stood tall. I let a smile spread across my bleeding lips and relished their screams as their souls scrambled to disperse.

"Boss? You okay?" Vinni said quietly from the doorway, jolting me back to the present. "The lead was another dead end."

I drew in a breath and tried not to snap at my cousin for not being able to locate Mariano. No one could lately. After Sienna left, he vanished. My gut told me he was hiding out on Coppola land, but most of my resources were following Stefano. I wanted to send more, but that would only raise suspicion from other people.

I felt like things were slipping away, nothing was as it should be, and I was still trying to figure how I was going to wade through the dark sludge that filled my heart.

"Also," he took a step into the room, "I spoke to Niccola." I nodded with my back to him. "I can't imagine how hard this must be—"

I held up a hand for him to stop.

His phone made a noise indicating a message. "Donatello says the package arrived."

A ball of pain swirled around the pit of my stomach, and I dug my nails into the leather of the chair once again.

"Elio?" Mama joined Vinni. "Our company has arrived."

"Are you sure about this, boss?"

I grabbed the letter opener and chucked it across the room, drilling it into the center of the painting that hung above the fireplace. Mama jumped but didn't say a word as I stormed past them and down the hallway to the lounge where the guests were being handed drinks.

I just needed to know if she was okay.

"Ah, son," Papa greeted me with a weary expression that mirrored my emotion. "These are some friends from the south." He waved at the man who was surely my father's age and then some. "This is Mr. Leonardo and his wife Mirabella."

"I've heard a great deal about you." Leonardo offered his hand to me. "I would like you to meet our daughter, Carina."

Carina was tall, slim, and looked very bored.

"Charmed to meet you." She flashed me a grin, but it didn't stay for long. At least we seemed to be on the same page. It was all so tiresome but necessary.

"Come, let's all have a drink." My father sat in his favorite chair and wined and dined like all was normal. "Let's have some food and talk business."

I offered my two cents when needed, but my focus kept being pulled to a certain text message that still hadn't been updated.

"Elio," my father shot me a glance, "maybe you can show Carina the terrace."

I hesitated and watched the screen for a beat longer then pushed to my feet, attempting to hide my annoyance with his request.

I pointed in the direction of the double doors and forced a smile at the young woman. Carina stood and joined me.

"He has a lot to deal with right now." I heard my father's voice as he covered for my lack of graciousness in the situation.

"He seems just lovely," Mirabella said as she tried

to make Papa feel better.

I felt guilty and knew I had to make a better attempt for his sake, in spite of the billion things I needed to get finished.

"Another?" I held up my empty glass to Carina. I spoke with more cheerfulness than I felt.

"Why not." She handed me hers and turned to admire the flowers. "If I worked here, I'd move my desk outside. This place is really pretty. You barely feel like you're in the city."

"Mm." I handed her the drink and took a seat on the edge of a planter.

"Was this your idea?" She pointed around and eyed me as she took a sip. I nodded, looking around. I had spent so much time surrounding myself with Sienna that now wherever I looked she was here. How…how could I have seen this storm coming? I squeezed my eyes shut, stopping the loop from spinning again.

"So, it's a special place for you?"

Again, I nodded, appreciating her intuitiveness.

"Or is it a special place to remember a special someone?"

Too far. I looked directly into her eyes, holding her gaze and letting her know that wasn't a topic I was touching.

"Figured." She half smirked, reading me like an open book. "I have such a place at my home, too."

I checked my phone again, and still nothing from that number.

"It's tricky, isn't it?" I looked up, trying to recall

if I missed part of her conversation. "Loving someone you can't have." She leaned her shoulder into the ivy-wrapped pillar as she spoke. "I'm buying time, waiting for some people to be removed from my life. I want to be happy with who I want to be with and not who I'm being told to want."

I looked down in my glass. "I just wish that was my situation. I would have killed anyone that stood in our way."

"Is she still alive?" I barely nodded. "What's standing in your way, then?"

Acid washed over my tongue, and my body temperature rose.

"Blood." I tossed back my glass and downed the rum.

"I see." She moved to sit across from me. "So, she's forbidden fruit. Let me guess, you love her, but you can't cross that line?" She nodded as though I answered her question. "Funny how being in powerful families comes with such obligation. There are people watching you, right? Making sure you don't see her or making sure you're doing what you should be doing?"

"Something like that," I muttered.

"For me," she went on, "I'm pretending. Making up fake lovers so I can fend off the wolves, while my heart lies in the hands of another. It's hard to pretend, though. Most men..." She trailed off like something came to her. "I'm not into tall, dark, and brooding types." She pointed at me. "I'm more into the light and goofy guys, and something tells me I'm not your type."

Well, she nailed that one on the head.

"I think you have one type, and that's your girl. I don't know what your story is and if you even want her anymore given your one-word answer of *blood*." She dropped her voice to mimic mine. "But something tells me you need to look like you're not wrapped up in her anymore. I'm thinking you have zero interest in dating. So…"

I waited for her to go on.

"Seriously? Do I really need to spell this out for you?" She rolled her eyes. "Pretend with me. Be my cover story, and I'll be yours. It's perfect. My family and I visited today, we spent time together, I fell for your conversational skills," we both smiled at that, "and you fell for my ability to stay quiet." I couldn't help but smirk. "I need this, and I think you do, too?" She pleaded with me, and for the first time in a while I saw a way around my family's situation. If Nonna was focused on Carina and digging into her past, it would buy me time for my own digging.

"Does your silence also mean yes?"

"We keep it simple." I held up a hand when she went to speak. "Less is more when it comes to a lie."

She beamed. "Where do we start?"

Mama had insisted I come back to the house for dinner. She hated the idea of me being alone, when that was all I really wanted. Silence to think. However, I knew it was more about Papa and how we needed to fix whatever was happening in our family. It was something that couldn't get out. People might think we were vulnerable and not as focused on the enemy as we should be, and that would be dangerous for all of us.

Though the tension was thick, we maintained that we were stressed over Sienna and nothing more.

Papa handed me a padded envelope. We'd come into his office to be away from the hustle of the kitchen. He tossed his jacket across the desk, and I saw his shirt was unbuttoned at the top. He looked unusually frazzled.

"Papa, I think we should talk about Nonna. I feel…" I paused when I heard footsteps outside the door. Papa shook his head and checked the cameras. It must have been the house staff because he focused back on me.

"Open it." He waved at the envelope.

The envelope had already been torn at one end, so I looked inside then slid the contents into my hand. "Teeth?" I looked up with a question at Papa then back to the envelope. I pulled out the folded paper and read the words. "I wish it was proof of a hit. But take it as proof of my loyalty. I was taken against my will. –Sienna." I did a double take as I stared again at the teeth then shot my father a puzzled look.

"I'm not sure whose they are, but regardless, she obviously wasn't going down without a fight." He attempted a chuckle but was much too dark inside for the humor. He cleared his throat and turned on some music to muffle our voices. "You know Mama and I know the truth, son. We both know she would never have deceived us. Yes, the news hit hard, and we're still reeling from it, but we know that after a little time and some understanding, things will work out."

"Will it?" I challenged. "I appreciate that Mama went to speak to her, and that Sienna is taking some time for herself, but there's something else. Papa, I really need to share something with you."

"Hang on." He pulled his glasses from the top of his head and held them up to the phone screen. "Francesco says the lead on Mariano was a dead end."

"I'm sure he'll show up soon looking for Sienna." I snickered. "Are you sure Francesco is even looking?"

That made Papa lower his phone in a hurry. He stared at me with an expression I'd never seen before and knew I'd hit a nerve, but I was tired of not getting answers.

"Pardon me?"

"I'm living in a den of secrets, taking one hit after another, and Francesco knew all these years who Sienna was, and he chose never to share it. I guess I'm just trying to understand why he's still here."

"Are you saying you want him gone?"

"No, not really." I shook my head, feeling my own confusion for the painful things this life sometimes brought. "Papa, you want me to take over the family business, but you won't share why the man you consider to be your best friend kept one of the biggest secrets from us."

"I knew." He cut me off, and my face dropped. "Sit down, son."

I lowered myself into a chair while my ears rang painfully. I wasn't sure what I was about to hear.

"Well, I didn't know." He took back his words, and I was sure he said it that way just to grab my attention. "But I wasn't completely kept out of everything." He waited for me to nod for him to go on. "I barely remember meeting Elenora once years ago. She didn't seem to have much interest in us, so I didn't take much notice of her. I guess something happened between Elenora and Francesco, and he chose us over her. About two years later, he came to me and asked for a huge favor. He wanted a few months off, said if there was ever time to trust him with something it was then. When I asked what was going on, he said he couldn't tell me, but that it was about a child who needed help. Said he'd made a promise to someone, and for the safety of all of us, he couldn't share it."

"And you accepted that answer?"

"If Niccola or Vinni came to you with that, you wouldn't have trusted them?" He had a point, so I nodded for him to go on. "Regardless, if I knew who Sienna was or wasn't, he felt it was his duty to save her, and to be honest, I think I would have gone along with it even if he had told me." Suddenly, his gaze moved over my head, and I turned to find Francesco standing there with a pained expression on his face.

"I just wanted to let you know the DeSimones have arrived."

"Thank you," Papa responded.

"Elio." His face spoke volumes. Clearly, he'd heard some of our conversation. "I don't expect you to understand why I didn't tell you the truth about who she was, but just know this. I gave up my love to give you yours."

He left, and Papa shook his head.

"Like I said, son, I have and always will trust that man. Mafia rules or not, he's staying, because he's family."

Chapter
FIVE

Sienna

I sat in the corner of the little pub sipping a drink Ugo had ordered for me. It was bitter and packed a good punch, which helped ease my nerves. Wyatt had to return to his assignment, and there was a part of me that was happy he'd left. I had a feeling things were going to get a whole lot worse before it got better. I shuddered as I relived the last few hours.

Turns out all high-powered nonnas were utterly terrifying. Ugo had warned me that his welcome would be an unwanted one, since he'd left years ago in disfavor. Apparently, he was considered a traitor to the family, but now, since he had brought me to their doorstep, he hoped this good deed would be our ticket in.

I leaned back and stared out the murky window at the door Ugo was now behind. I let my head go back to the events of this morning in an attempt to ease my rattled nerves.

"If we're going to do this, Sienna, you need to know the truth about me," Ugo said hesitantly.

"I'm listening." I placed my espresso down and crossed my legs.

He stood and brushed his hands down his pants uneasily. "My mother is Theo's younger sister by seven years. Like most females in our syndicate, they are forced to the sidelines and do as they're told. Very different than the Capris," he muttered, *and I saw him wince at the mention of Elio's family. Though the wound was raw, it was something I'd lived with for years. I waved him to go on. "My mother was told who she was going to marry, a son from a family close to our syndicate, of course. It was all about the money. Despite the two of them hating one another, they were married three months later and lived in our main house, under my nonna's rule. If you thought Mariano or Nonna Greta Capri was scary, you're in for a rude awaking with my grandparents. Just be glad Nonno was murdered six months after your father was."* He shook his head as if the memory of his nonno still haunted him. *"Anyway, Mama loved a baker who worked in town. She'd slip away whenever she could and meet with him when her husband was away. I'm sure you can see where this is going?"*

"I can, but I'd rather not guess."

"I was conceived six months after Mama married.

Instead of keeping it quiet, Mama tried to use me to get out of her marriage. Nonno wouldn't have it and roughed her up pretty good. I still think he was trying to get rid of me, but I was here to stay. Soon after, my papa was found dead, shot in the head, down by the water's edge."

"Oh, Ugo, I'm sorry." I covered my mouth, feeling his pain as he shared his story.

"I regret that I never got to know him. I heard he was a good man, who worked hard and fought for what he thought was right. As the son of a bastard baker, you can imagine I had a hard time all through my childhood, living in that house. I was hated by all."

"I actually can imagine how awful it must have been for you." Ugo nodded, knowing my time spent at the De Vaio house as a child had been dreadful and continued his story.

"Mama never fully recovered from the loss of her lover and had moments when she would just stop and stare at the wall for hours, no doubt trying to recall a happier time. I knew she loved me, but staying with that family was easier said than done. Oscar was much older, and he took pity on me and helped when things got too hard. Then one day, when I was in my teens, this woman appeared at the house. She had dark blue eyes, her smile was warm, and her name was Elenora." He caught my gaze and held it as he spoke of my mother with such warmth. Warmth I was still waiting for from her.

"She was to be married to Theo, the worst of the two uncles. He had a nasty temper that could blow at any point. Your mother cried through the entire ceremony. I

remember her face was so pale, and her hands shook as the rings were exchanged. Theo barely even registered her fear. He was too busy looking at someone else."

"Do you remember who?"

"I do." He looked away. "It was Noemi, who is now apparently Elio's aunt."

"So, Mama was telling the truth."

"Indeed. Neither Theo or your mama wanted to marry, but Elenora's family owed money, and Theo needed a son to take over the family business. If he couldn't produce one quickly, his father's younger brother, who was already married, might have one first. It's like a race to the finish line. Children and money seem to be the major pawns when it comes to our lifestyle. Plus, by the two families joining together, the Coppolas would gain a lot of connections through Elenora's father's company, and that's no small thing. What I mean to say is, your grandparents were extremely connected. They were wealthy in the people they did business with, if not so much in physical money."

He dropped back down in the chair. "I'll skip over the rest. Your mama will want to fill you in on that, but things went from bad to worse when you came along. Baby girls are not nearly as valuable as boys. Elenora hit her breaking point and couldn't take it anymore, so she left. I walked in on Oscar soon after. He was packing his bag, saying he'd chosen a side and he wasn't coming back. I raced to my room and did the same, then we piled in the back of his car and left. We never looked back. That chapter of my life was over, and I couldn't've been happier."

"What about your mother?"

"I ran into her at the door. She took one look at my suitcase, looked over my shoulder at the car, and stepped aside to let me pass. She told me to have a better life than she'd had and to be free for both of us."

"Did you," I cleared my throat, "find your freedom?" I felt a tear slip down my cheek at how hard that must have been for the mother as well as the son.

"Yeah," he gave me a sad smile, "anything was better than being there in that house, treated like dirt. But," he paused, looking me straight in the eye, "me leaving was the ultimate betrayal, so getting you inside that house will take a little roleplaying."

"I think I can do that."

"It's not you I'm worried about. I will need to act like I left to hunt you down, and when I did, I brought you back home. Sienna," he leaned forward, "you deserve to know who you are and where you come from, but with that comes a level of evil that you haven't seen yet. You can never let your guard down, never trust anyone, and most of all, don't let them get in your head."

"I know what I'm doing."

"All right." He let out a long breath. "I really hope so because Elenora will murder me herself when she finds out what we're about to do."

"Let me worry about Mama."

"And your test results came back." He held up the sealed envelope and handed it to me.

"How? I mean, don't you need something from

him?"

"Yeah," he let out a long breath, "but it's not important how I got it. What is, though, is what the paperwork says."

I nodded and ripped the side of the envelope straight down, pulled out the papers, and peered at the results. As I expected, I was a 99.9 percent match, and no doubt was left. I was Theodore Coppola's daughter. I held it up to show him, and he smiled, knowing we had all the proof we needed.

"Can I get you another?" A man's voice pulled me from my thoughts, and I blinked up at him, trying to recall what he said. "Another?" He pointed at my glass.

"Oh, no, thanks."

"Are you new to the city?" He looked around, making a show of searching for someone. "Because I'm here a lot, and I would remember someone like you." I wanted to roll my eyes and hoped he'd think I was annoyed and leave, but at the same time, I needed to play off who I was now. Appearances were everything.

"You could say that." I forced a smile.

"Is there another way I could say it?" Oh, boy, he was flirting, and I was like stone inside.

"You could say I'm back after a very long trip."

"How long?"

"Mm," I closed one eye as I thought, "twenty-some years."

"That's a long trip."

"It was."

"I bet you have a ton of stories."

"Not many worth mentioning." He gave me a smirk, and I could tell he wasn't going to leave very easily.

"Are you normally so cryptic?"

"Yes. It's my specialty, actually."

He laughed and held up a hand to show me he'd back off. "Look, are you here alone? Because when that sun sets in an hour, you don't want to be out there alone."

"Why? Are you planning to stuff me into your trunk?"

He chuckled. "You have a dark side."

"I'm just positively unoptimistic." I pushed down the feelings that wanted to spring up.

"You're funny."

"Glad my dark side entertains you." I took a swig, the last of my drink. "I have a friend due to arrive any moment."

"Good," he nodded, "because unless you pay for protection, it's a war zone out there."

"I'll be sure to watch my back." I wanted to ask what he really meant, but my guess would mean paying off my family.

"Maybe I'll see you around?"

"Maybe."

"Well, in that case, I'm Salvo."

"Sienna." I sat a little straighter when I saw Ugo open the door. When I turned back to address my new friend, he had his back to me and was talking to another guy.

"Well?" I stood when Ugo approached.

"It took a bit of convincing, but after the story, I

shared the DNA results. There's now a car outside waiting to take you to the main house. They'd like you to stay with them."

"Now?" I started to panic inside. I knew this was what I wanted, but it was happening too quickly. "Are you coming?"

"Yes." He rubbed his face like he might be sick. "I wasn't given an option. I think they'll be watching us very closely, so from now on, we are who we came up with last night."

"Did you call —"

"Not yet." He cut me off when the driver stepped into the bar and made a show of watching us. "Time to go."

Chapter
SIX

I tapped the steering wheel with my thumb as I stared at the ivy-covered house. I leaned forward and looked up at the little window nestled between the green vines. It was the one Nonna normally would be staring out from. When she decided one day that she no longer wanted to leave my uncle's house, they converted the entire upstairs for her to live comfortably. She had a window on all four sides of the house. It allowed her to keep an eye on people's whereabouts. I never thought much about it…until now.

Grabbing my keys and phone, I slipped out from behind the wheel and made my way around the side of the house and up the back stairs. Voices stopped me before I reached the top landing, and I stretched my body to peek around the corner.

"You know what it means when someone of my stature requests your services, correct?

"Yes, Ms. Greta." The Finder stood in the sun, while Nonna stood, nearly hidden, under a shade tree. Her rosary beads swung as she handed him a thick envelope.

"Abramo says you're the best. Let's see if that's true."

"It is," he assured her as he looked inside, fingering the contents. "Am I to watch just Sienna, or your grandson as well?"

"Both." She handed him what looked like a photograph. "I want to know everything you find out. Nothing is too small."

"Understood."

As I watched her step toward the house, my temper soared and the white heat of it burned. I almost felt lightheaded. She was as conniving as a fucking Coppola. The nerve of this woman having Sienna and me followed! I pushed off the wall and burst through the door, nearly knocking down the maid, who was shocked to see me.

"Mr. Capri," she quickly followed right on my heels, "Lady Greta is in a meeting right now. If you could just wait in the other room—"

I totally ignored her and continued. As I turned the corner to the study, I saw Aunt Noemi on the phone.

"What do you mean?" Her voice told me something was wrong. "Why would she do that?"

"Grandson." Nonna's tone made me whirl around

in white hot rage. *Hold it together.* "I see you are up and doing well. I didn't get a call that you were conducting business here today, so what brings you by?" I knew she could probably feel the anger that poured off me, but she didn't comment.

Don't snap.

"I…" I tried to contain myself. Now wasn't the time to bring things to a head. Not yet. "I need a few things from the barn."

"Oh?"

"Yes, we have two men at the warehouse who seem to know something about the bombing."

"Please tell me you aren't still fishing for answers over a girl who could have ruined your life." My fingers drew into a fist. "She's a liar and one of *them*. Don't waste your time on something that's no longer your problem."

"A bombing happened in my town." I stepped closer, vibrating with anger. "No one gets away with that, regardless of who's involved." She looked up at me, and her eyebrows lifted at my intensity. "That is, after all, what you taught me."

"This's true. I just want to make sure your head's in the right place."

"And where do you think it might be, Nonna? With Sienna, or with the note you left years ago on my car windshield stopping me from going back for her?" I couldn't hold it back. The corners of her mouth dipped for a hair of a second, but she quickly regained herself.

"I would advise you to check yourself here, grandson. You're accusing me of something I'd never dream of doing. Your happiness is everything to me. But I warn you, I'll step in if you go after her again." My heart pounded in my ears, and my mouth went dry. "I've cleaned up enough of your messes in the past. Don't make me take care of her too."

Messes? When had I ever made a mess and hadn't cleaned it up myself? If she was referring to Sienna, I should snap her neck and drive her head onto a spike. That would certainly send a message that I was about to take over our syndicate and things were going to change. It was all I could do not to reach out and do it. Any love I ever had for her had drained away when I heard her and The Finder making that deal. The itch to kill was strong, so I turned and headed quickly for the door. I didn't trust myself and wasn't sure how much more I could take from her.

"Elio," she called in her sharp, commanding voice. It made me stop, but I didn't turn. "Don't forget which family you belong to."

I slammed the door behind me and pumped my arms on my way back to the car. Once on the road, I slammed my foot on the pedal and watched the numbers jump as I sped away. I took the corners tight and drifted in a few spots. I needed to feel something—anything but the urge to kill my own nonna. She lied right to my face, threatened me, and threatened Sienna. Regardless of our past, Sienna didn't deserve this from my family.

Suddenly, I slammed on the brakes and skidded to a stop just a mile from the gates. The Finder was leaning against his car as if waiting for me. I leapt out and crossed the street. He held up a photograph as I advanced toward him, drawing my gun from my waist.

"I need to tell you something."

That slowed my step and helped curb the murderous anger. I slipped my weapon back in place.

"Somehow, your nonna got wind of who I am and has hired me to keep an eye on you and Sienna." I snatched the photo from his hand and recognized it right away. It was taken at Vinni's birthday party. My arm was wrapped around Sienna's waist.

"What else?"

"She paid me this," he tossed me a wad of cash, "and told me she'd pay that much again if I brought her anything."

"Is that so?" His honesty and obvious loyalty had me rethinking his death.

"What do you want me to do here?"

My mind was working fast. If I was going to take Nonna down myself, I needed to find out all she knew. I'd need to regain her trust to do that. Having The Finder as the one she hired definitely worked in my favor, but at the same time I wondered if she'd also hired someone else. I certainly wouldn't put it past her; she was a smart woman. Could this be a test? Did she really not know that we had been—and still were, I corrected myself—friends and working associates?

"You're going to do your job." I handed him back the photo. "Wait a bit, then tell her that I'm seeing someone else. Tell her Sienna is out of the picture and is just fine, wherever she is. You'll report to me and share your conversations. I want to be in the know at all times. Understood?"

"Of course, but Elio, I should warn you."

"Of?"

"Her mother, Elenora, is still in town and asking a lot of questions about Sienna's whereabouts. If you don't want her meddling in your plans, you might want to address that."

"I figured as much." I nodded, thinking Francesco needed to jump on that.

"One more thing." He lowered his voice but then shook his head like he decided not to say it.

"My time is valuable," I warned.

"Just watch Tieri, okay?"

"Meaning?"

"He's had his eye on Sienna ever since she and Mariano came into the office that day. When he learns she is fair game, he might make a move."

"Let him." I turned on my heel and left, leaving him to do his job and me to burn off some rage. The less involved in our plan the better.

The workout did nothing to help, and now I was just sore as well as pissed. I'd showered and dressed, but my muscles screamed beneath my suit, and I wished I had another way to work off my tension. I squeezed my eyes shut and leaned over the fireplace with my hands on the mantel. As much as my heart was wounded by who Sienna was, it was no fault of hers, and I still felt that familiar craving to find her, strip her down, and bury myself deep inside her. No matter what was happening, when we were together, I felt I could figure anything out, but now…

Stop.

My fingers tightened and I ground my teeth, feeling the anger pump through my veins. It was almost painful. My body craved hers, and my head was slipping. I needed to find a better outlet.

"Son?" Papa's hand landed on my shoulder as I stared into the fireplace.

I wondered if I should just toss the notes into the fire and ignore the truth. No…I couldn't. I would be betraying our family's motto. The word *loyalty* carved in the crest above the wall caught the light, and fate told me what I needed to do.

"What's happened? Are you all right?"

"No," I shook my head slowly, "I'm really not."

"Elio, no one would blame you if you needed to take a vacation, clear your head."

I reached over and pressed the white noise button we often used when we needed to speak privately. Papa looked at me, questioning the reason for the privacy. I studied his face and held up a finger to give me a moment. In spite of the fact that Gain had told me that Mariano's parents were out in town this evening, I wasn't taking any chances. My actions told Papa that I was about to disclose something very sensitive. I nodded at Francesco, who had just entered the room, to come closer.

"First, Francesco, I'm sorry." I felt the need to apologize. It wasn't something I did often, so when I did, they knew I meant it. "I may not fully understand your reasons for doing what you did, but if you hadn't done it, I wouldn't have someone I truly love. Are we okay?"

"We are." He shook my hand but held on to it as he stepped closer. "I want to say the storm has passed, but I don't believe it has. Please understand there are still a few more secrets lingering around that I don't have the answers to."

I saw red but recognized he was coming to me with something before it smacked me in the face later.

"All right." I tucked that information aside and focused on what I needed to share.

"Papa," I looked into his eyes and knew my face spoke volumes, "here." I pulled out the two small notes and handed them to him then watched his face scrunch in confusion.

"This is the photo and note from years ago, the one you found on your car?" I nodded. "Okay, I recognize that one, but what is this one?" He held up the other small piece of heavy paper. "It looks to be the same card stock."

"Sienna found it."

His head jolted up to mine. "Where?"

"The back of Nonna's car." A series of emotions washed over his face as he digested what I was saying. Papa was a smart man, and I didn't need to say too much for him to put the pieces together.

"Are you sure?"

"I wouldn't have showed you if I wasn't."

"Son, are you aware of what you're saying?"

"Yes, I am." I cleared my throat uneasily. "I would never accuse anyone in our family, especially my nonna, if I didn't feel certain. I tread carefully. I knew we were all hypersensitive on this topic. Think about it, Papa. Since Elenora showed up and started creating waves, suddenly Nonna breaks her strike of staying cooped up at Uncle's house, after nearly a decade."

"She has been spotted a few times in the city," Francesco commented. He had said nothing to this point, only stood quietly, listening. Listening was a big part of his job within our family. He spoke slowly and knew to tread very carefully with Papa, too. After all, Nonna was his mother and the matriarch of the family. "If it truly was her and she did try to keep you from leaving all those years ago to find Sienna, do you think she knew who she was all along?"

"Maybe," my father answered as he rubbed his head, "but we did yearly background checks on Sienna, and nothing ever came up. Certainly nothing that ever hinted at who she was."

"Alessia's prints wouldn't have come up in any database." Francesco glanced apologetically at Piero to gauge his reaction to his words. "Elenora and I covered all the bases years ago when we changed her name to Sienna. Those were the good old days, when you could be erased and live as another person." He gave a dry smile.

"Then maybe Mama didn't know." Papa sighed, not

wanting to believe it.

"Then how was it she came to the house before Sienna even got there to tell us the news?" I challenged. "How did she know who Sienna was?" I moved to the bar and poured myself a stiff drink. "None of it makes any sense." Francesco picked up the notes and studied them.

"Actually," Francesco tucked his hands in his pockets, "she may have known something. Elenora used to tell me about an older lady who she'd seen watching her before in a restaurant and somewhere else. She noticed her because she held a bright-white set of rosary beads. The first time she noticed her was when she met Noemi, and the second was right around the time we broke up. I didn't pay much attention, just figured it was one of the elders vetting Elenora because of who I was to the family. But now I wonder…"

"Do either of you have any other proof?" Papa tried to make sense of it all, and I understood his frustration and pain.

I lowered my voice. "When I confronted her about it weeks ago, she slipped as she denied it. I never told her where the note was left, but she knew where it was. I don't think she even realized she outed herself." I closed my eyes and took a deep breath, calming my nerves. "And then today I saw her meeting with The Finder."

"The Finder? As in the man you worked with as the Santoro Brother?" I nodded at Papa. "What did she want with him?"

"She hired him to keep an eye on me and Sienna."

"What?" His hands dropped to his sides. "I know she's stopped running a lot of things by me since the night all this came crashing down, but I can't imagine that she would go that far."

"She's watching us. She's making sure I stay away from Sienna." I felt instantly hot with the thought of someone trying to run my life. "Whether or not I'm with Sienna, it's no one's business but mine. I won't be her puppet. I work my ass off at this job, and I'm damn good at it. I will answer to no one."

"The nerve of her."

"She threatened me, too, and forbid me to see Sienna."

"Really?" I saw his change in mood and knew we were now on the same page.

"At the risk of overstepping here, Piero," Francesco rubbed the back of his neck, visibly uncomfortable, "this isn't the first time your mama has played dirty." I watched my father's face twist as something came to him. "Let's not forget about the night before your wedding."

"Papa?" I stepped closer, and he avoided eye contact with me.

"Pardon me." One of our newer soldiers stood in the doorway.

"Did you return the favor?" I snapped, hoping at least one thing was going right.

"Yes, Savage is dead, and Lynch and Grant both know it."

"Good." Cavalier and Savage were taken care of. "One less fucker to deal with. "Make sure the girl gets home."

"Yes, Jordon already is home."

Good. "You're dismissed."

"Of course, boss."

Papa looked at me and tucked the notes into his pocket. "Well, it's sad, but I guess it's a good thing Sienna is tucked away right now. She doesn't need to be caught up in this mess."

I pressed my lips together and blocked his way as he went to leave.

"What is it, son?"

"You should know I went to see Sienna at her hotel."

"And?"

"You might want to sit down for this."

SEVEN

Sienna

Ugo played his part well, making a point to ignore my nervous small talk and my obvious sighs whenever I asked too many questions about nothing. I needed to play the nervous, lost child from years ago, at least at first. Later, I would allow myself to gain confidence. He needed to portray an annoyed ass who had little time for me. The hardest part was we had to appear as if we were strangers.

Rome was a gorgeous city at night and a place I had always wanted to spend more time. Wyatt and I had driven through it while chasing a story, but we were always on a deadline and never got to stop and explore.

The climb up the hill seemed to go on forever, but

we finally reached the top and stopped before a pair of gates with armed guards out front. One of the men flashed a light in my eyes when the driver held up an ID and demanded they open the gates immediately. As they slowly pulled back on their tracks, I leaned forward to get a better look at what seemed like a castle. It sat in the middle of an open area that was all covered in concrete. A few trees were placed here and there, but someone seriously lacked a green thumb. As we moved around the driveway, I saw there were little buildings at the back. I wondered if that might be where the staff was required to live.

It certainly wasn't the same kind of feel the Capri property had, except for the fact that it was also behind secure gates and had soldiers everywhere. It was much more intense. The Coppola property was in the heart of Rome, however, and not on the outskirts like the Capris property where they had lush, green grass, trees of all sorts, and gardens and wineries for miles. This place reminded me more of a prison, or maybe my view was just tainted since I knew what Stefano Coppola, the Don of the syndicate, was capable of.

"Sienna?" Ugo tapped my arm to get my attention when the driver hopped out. "Look, if anything happens, anything at all that makes you think your life is in danger, there are tunnels under the house that lead underneath the gates and out into the city. When you can, call me, and I'll find you or arrange a pickup, if I can't get away."

"Where was this conversation last night? Or a week or two ago?"

"It's been a long time." He undid his safety belt. "Things have slipped over time."

"How do you know they are still there and not sealed off?"

"I don't, but the Coppolas are paranoid people. They'll always have an escape route."

"Care to tell me where one of these entrances is?"

"There's a small room across from the second bathroom on the main floor. It's a laundry room for the staff. Behind the ironing board, there's a small door that leads down to the first tunnel. When we're alone next, I'll try to sneak you down. Don't look for it on your own. Wait for me to show you the way. It's confusing, and you can get lost pretty easily."

I nodded to show I understood the risk.

"All right, let's go." He opened his door and slipped out, while I took an extra minute to calm my pounding chest. This was my idea, but it didn't mean I wasn't a half a second away from pulling back and running. The only thing keeping me here was the thought that if I was going to leave the Capris with anything, before I disappeared back into my old life, was that I am and have always been loyal to their family. This would be proof that I was always on their side, no matter what it took.

The driver moved ahead of us with our bags, and I tried not to stare at the scary-looking sculptures that lined the walkway up to the front door. It didn't help that the lights that shone on them cast shadows in all the wrong places.

I stopped a few feet from the door and looked up at

the four-story, very old mansion looming above me.

Deep breaths.

Once inside, I was greeted by a staff member who took my sweater and my bag then ushered me into a massive common room filled with people who all stopped and stared. Ugo joined my side, and I felt a bit better knowing he was right there. A soldier with a tattooed row of crosses along his neck stared at me. He gave me the creeps. I stood tall but leaned closer to my cousin.

The silence was deafening until I heard the click of a cane, and the crowd slowly parted to reveal Nonna Rosa Coppola, dressed in nearly all black with only a little pop of color in the blouse she wore under her masculine jacket.

"Alessia. Welcome home."

Run.

"Everyone," Nonna Rosa addressed the room, "I would like you to meet Theo's daughter, my granddaughter, Alessia Coppola, and by birthright, our mafia princess."

The hairs on my arms stood as she reached for my hand and held it up to show off my family ring. There was a collective gasp as the crowd sucked in a sharp breath, while mine whooshed out as I tried to look confident. Then three older men slowly approached me, all similar in height and build. They took turns as they admired the ring up close. Each nodded as though satisfied it was legit. The smiles and looks at my face were brief as they completed their task, then they all huddled, muttering together. Who in the world were they?

"Thank you, Nonna Rosa." I finally found my voice as I tried to remember my manners and all that Ugo told me to do. I straightened my shoulders. "If it's all right with you, I'd rather be addressed as Sienna."

Nonna Rosa's eyes bugged out as she gave a quick glance to the three men, but I didn't care. I wasn't Alessia. She was someone else, and I wouldn't let them take the only name I'd known from me. Ugo did say to show a little confidence when I could, and this seemed like the best time.

"Well." Nonna Rosa shot me a stiff smile, and her hand, which still held mine, squeezed painfully. As I looked at her, her small eyes bored into mine like I just murdered someone in front of them all. "We will address that later. Come, now, child."

I shot her a look. I wasn't a child, and when I actually had been, I was hardly allowed to be one.

"You have lots of people to meet before you go to bed tonight. We will discuss your new life in the morning." She took my arm and cleared her throat at the three old men. They all stood tall and seemed to try to read me as they eyed me from head to toe.

"Alessia, these three gentlemen and I are the elders of the family, the oldest ranking members of our syndicate. I'm not sure how much knowledge you have about our family's lifestyle, but if you remember even one thing from tonight, it's this. Nothing happens in this family without all of us knowing about it. If there's a problem, we all figure it out together. No one outranks the others." I noticed her face went to stone at that last part.

"Lovely to meet you…" I waited for their names.

"You may call us," the one on the left pointed to himself then the others in turn, "Pippo, Betto, and Lotto." He ended with the man on the right who looked like he might be the youngest.

Seriously? How was I going to keep that straight?

"Where have you been all these years?" Betto fired at me without so much as a greeting.

"Not here, that's for certain," I said, deadpan, and heard Ugo clear his throat as a warning not to push them too far. I couldn't help it. Who asked that only ten seconds after meeting me? It was, after all, a long story and not one I was willing to jump into without a lot of thought.

"Perhaps that should wait for another time, Betto." Nonna steered me away from them, and we stopped at another group of people.

I wasn't sure how many people I met, but there wasn't one name that stuck with me. Colors and sounds were a blur, and by the time I was shown to my room, I was utterly exhausted.

"Is it always like that?" I asked Ugo, who stayed behind after one of the staff made sure my bed was turned down.

"Oh, just wait." He moved about my room, opening and closing jewelry boxes, little cabinets, and closets. "This place will wear you down to a nub, and when you don't think you can take it anymore, the real fun begins."

"Such as?" I yawned kicked off my shoes.

"You may wear the ring and have their blood, so

they can't deny you being here, but they will be watching your every move, making sure you are who you say you are. Believe me, they know all about you and Elio, and they'll pump you for as much information as possible without you even realizing it."

"I'm ready for all of that."

"Right," he rubbed his head, leaning against the desk, "but that's just that part."

"What does that mean?"

"Want me to be blunt?"

"Yes."

"The three men you met tonight, the elders."

"The ones with the matching names?"

"Yes, them." He sighed. "They are my grandfather's brothers, my uncles. They and Nonna are like the counselors, the hierarchy. What they say goes, and those three will protect you."

"You think Nonna would hurt me?"

"I don't trust anyone here not to hurt you, Sienna. Your return will flip the family upside down. You must watch out for everyone. This house is steeped in money, power, and greed."

"I can do that. I'm pretty good at looking out for myself."

"Good, because you're a female wearing a ring meant for a male. No syndicate like the Coppolas wants a female ruler. It's a man's world, and in their eyes, it can't happen."

"Nonna Rosa isn't a man, but she certainly seems to hold a lot of the power here."

"Yes and no. Yes, but only because her husband was the Don. She outlived him, so she is considered one of the elders. The elders hold a tremendous amount of power in the family because they've been here the longest. Nonna can't make a move on her own without the uncles' agreement. However, she's very smart and has found ways to work around them at times. Still, because she is a woman, she could never take over completely, and it is always a frustration for her. Unless, of course, she was a woman who had that." He pointed to my ring. "So, what do you do when your gender gets in the way of your evil plan?" He lifted his brows and made a questionable face.

"You bring in someone you can control?" I guessed.

"Right. Enter Stefano. He is male and he is a Coppola, so she needs him to be head of the family, but mostly because he's stupid and easy for her to manipulate."

"But wouldn't he be the next in line to take the seat, anyway?"

"Bloodline, yes, but if the uncles got wind of how reckless and bold he really is, especially the things he's pulling with the Capris, they'd remove him and appoint someone else. It's why Nonna keeps him away from the uncles as much as possible. Don't get me wrong, the elders want nothing more than to see Piero burned at the stake so they could get what's his."

"I know Piero has more land than the Coppolas."

"It's not just about the amount of land, it's also that they have very rich soil and grow the best grapes in all of Italy. They also have some of the best ports in the county. Not to mention their contacts in America and other countries. Piero and Elio have done an extremely good job of absorbing territory. They also keep out of the media, which is smart, and most of all, they are charming. People really like them, and they do a lot for their community."

I closed my eyes, missing Elio. We had a long road ahead of us. I wished we could just leave and be alone to live together in peace.

"Stefano's father died of cancer, right?"

"Yes, but I don't think his father's cancer was what killed him. It was too fast."

"Are you saying Nonna killed her brother-in-law?"

"I wasn't here." Ugo shrugged. "It's just what I've heard from other people. But he pushed back on Nonna even before Theo disappeared, so I'm sure when he took over, things didn't go smoothly with her. He wasn't as stupid as his son is."

"Crazy." I finished putting my clothes away and pulled out shorts and a tank to wear to bed. The room was nice and had a small balcony, but it felt cold and bland.

"Ugo." Nonna Rosa was suddenly in the doorway. *How did I not hear her cane?* "I think it's best if you return to your room and get some sleep." My stomach dropped, wondering how much she heard, if anything.

Nonna turned to address me with an attempt at a smile. "You will have a big day tomorrow, and in a few days, once you're settled, we will prepare a party to welcome you home."

She eyed Ugo and waited for him to leave. Once we

were alone, she closed the door behind her and sat in a chair by the small table.

"Come here, dear." She motioned for me to join her. Somehow, I willed my feet to move and sat across from her. I pulled up my legs and placed my hands between my thighs to hide my nerves. "You really are quite a pretty woman."

"Thank you." I tucked my hair behind my ear.

"Why don't you tell me how Ugo found you."

Thankfully, I had this part well-rehearsed, as Ugo had warned me it was coming.

"It was the article I did in *Fab Magazine*."

"Yes, I understand that created quite the buzz."

"I guess." I shook off her comment.

"You strike me as someone who doesn't like a lot of attention, so why would you do such a revealing article?"

"I was trying to find my mother and also to share my story that you can come from nothing and still be something if you want it badly enough."

"Very true."

"Ugo told me my mother wanted to meet me."

"Oh?" Her face gave her away. Just as Ugo predicted, that information caught her interest. "Your mother is alive?"

"Yes, she is." I pretended to brush a tear away.

I could tell by the hitch in her breath that she was either piping mad or had just realized a piece to the missing puzzle regarding our disappearance all those years ago.

"Where is she now?" Her casual tone didn't fool me.

"I have no idea, but if you do find her, please don't share that I'm here."

"Oh, dear." She rested her cool hand over mine. "Did you two have a falling out?"

"You can say that." I sniffed and shifted as though uncomfortable with the topic. "Let's just say when I asked her about my past and begged her for information about where I came from, she refused to tell me anything much. She just hedged around and put me off. When I finally told her I was leaving and wouldn't play her games anymore, she tossed this ring at me, and finally the truth came out."

"Which was?"

Lord, she was almost out of her seat with her need for information.

"That I was the daughter of Theo Coppola and that he sent us away years ago, just because I wasn't born a boy." I watched her pupils contract. "Of course, I know, being a journalist, that there are always two sides to every story, and given the fact that she left me on someone's doorstep when I was just a child, there had to be a lot more to *my* story."

"Smart girl. Yes, there is," she muttered, deep in thought. "So, Ugo knew where your mother was all along?"

"I highly doubt that." I shook my head. "She seemed irritated that he hung around during the short time we were getting to know one another. It was like he was watching me, and the moment he got confirmation on who I was, he changed. He's not that friendly, is he?" I faked a sad smile, and she made a noncommittal sound. "Then one day, when I had enough and went to my mother to demand details from her about where to find my family, the Coppola family…" I smiled timidly at her but got no reaction, so I went on with my story. "When I got there, her hotel room was empty. No note, no call, nothing. I went to Ugo and asked if he knew what was going on, he said he didn't have a clue. But then he told me he knew how to find my family and offered to bring me to see you. That's how I ended up here."

"Good for him." She seemed to buy my story. "And your mother hasn't reached out since?"

"I think she got all the information that she needed."

"Which was?"

"To know I wouldn't fall for her lies and that I chose my father's family over her."

The wrinkles that bordered her eyes smoothed out as a smile crossed her face.

"You chose wisely, my dear granddaughter, though we have much to catch up on. I think it's best you get some sleep now."

I stood and waited for her to do the same. She was old, but she was quite fit and had no trouble getting to her feet without so much as a wobble.

She turned just as she reached the door. "The man you're dating, the son of the Capri Don. Is that over?"

I felt as though I had been sucker punched in the gut. I knew she knew—of course she did—but I wasn't ready for it. My face registered my surprise, and she seemed to take pleasure from catching me out.

"Very," I assured her.

"Good," she squinted as if trying to read my mind, "because that would be a very big problem if it wasn't."

"I understand."

Chapter
EIGHT

Elenora

Why do I get the feeling you know what's going on?" I asked Oscar, who hadn't looked me in the eye all morning. "We've never withheld anything from each other before, so why start now?"

"I'm not purposely trying to be mute about something. It's just that *that* something isn't mine to share. Also, if I did, I'm not at all sure how you'll react about that something." He rolled his eyes and sighed as if he heard himself.

"So, you're saying whatever Ugo is about to tell me, I won't be pleased about it."

"Let's just say, I know I'm not." He looked over my shoulder, and I saw relief flash across his face. Ugo must have arrived.

"I apologize for being late." He waited for me to nod for him to sit. "I missed the train this morning and had to wait for the next one."

"Train?" I asked, curious as to where, exactly, he was hiding my daughter.

"Yes."

"No." I leaned forward and lowered my voice. "One-word answers won't work this time, Ugo. I want details on what's going on and where my daughter is."

"I set this meeting up, Ms. Elenora. I wasn't trying to hide anything from you, but I must respect your daughter's wishes when she asks me to do something for her."

"Which was?" I didn't like his tone.

"For me to give her a little time while she figured out what she wanted to do next." He glanced at Oscar, and I grew even more impatient.

"It's been almost three weeks. What has she figured out?"

"That she wanted to meet her father's family."

It was as if someone had poured freezing cold water down my back. It pooled in my lungs and sucked the air down. I was numb to the core.

"Tell me," I cleared my throat heavily, needing a moment to steady my breath and get hold of my temper, "that you didn't just drop my daughter off at the Devil's doorstep."

"There's a little more to it than that."

"Answer my question, Ugo."

"In a nutshell, yes, I did."

Oscar suddenly leaned forward and removed the espresso cup from my hand.

"Do you have any idea what you've done?" I felt the rage bubble up inside of me. "Do you have any idea what they'll do to her? What they are capable of?"

"Yes." He nodded. "Don't forget, I grew up in that house. I lived a lot longer in that hell than you did."

"Careful," Oscar warned, but Ugo dismissed him.

"Elenora, your daughter, my cousin, is much stronger and smarter than you realize. She's not going to the Coppola mansion to join the family. She's going to learn about where she came from, yes. But she wants to worm her way behind enemy lines so she can implode the Coppola syndicate from the inside out. She's doing this for herself, for you, for…" He stopped himself, and I held up a hand.

"Finish that thought."

"For all of us. She's doing this so we can all be free."

I knew there was more, but I needed a moment to digest it all. I pushed my chair out and slowly wandered over to the window. I felt Ugo and Oscar follow me.

"How long has she been there?"

"A few days."

"Good Lord," I muttered and pulled at my necklace, feeling the terror race through me.

I closed my eyes and remembered when I'd first arrived in that house…

"This is your new room." Theo's caporegime struggled to hold all my bags. "Get moving. These are

heavy."

Somehow, I forced my leaden feet to start moving and swallowed past the impulse to scream and kick up a fuss. Maybe if I did, they would see they made a mistake, that they chose the wrong woman. But then my parents' faces flashed in front of me, and I knew their fate rested on my shoulders. It was a heavy load.

"Bed there," he pointed, "toilet and bath in there, balcony, sitting area, closet, and whatever the hell that is." He motioned toward the vanity. "If you need to go anywhere, you come to me, so remember my face. Understand?" I nodded, and he pointed at my bags. "Get unpacked."

Then I was left alone, in a quiet room, with no idea what was expected of me. The room was dull and lacked any sense of decor. The furniture was outdated, the curtains smelled funny, but at least the bedding seemed new. I opened one of my suitcases and pulled out Francesco's sweater and wrapped it around my shoulders, needing to feel him with me. My heart ached for him, but he'd hurt me, and I wasn't good at letting that stuff go.

I skipped unpacking and leaned back and closed my eyes. In spite of my heavy lids, tears ran in streaks down my cheeks. I hadn't been that close with my parents; they weren't exactly warm and fuzzy. Hugs and kisses were rare, but they mattered, and I thought they loved me. The fact that they had sealed my fate with their mistakes was unforgiveable. I wondered how I was going to get through this.

I spent the next two days in my room, unsure of where my place was in the house. The staff brought me food but barely glanced in my direction. Surely, someone would wonder about me. Not even Theo had shown himself. I started to grow annoyed with their complete indifference. Anger began to simmer, then my temper began to rise. I was going to do them a favor by sleeping with their whore of a son, just so he could win the race of having the firstborn son. I was sick over the thought of his hands touching me.

When I was finally brave and pissed off enough to venture downstairs, I came face to face with the lady with the cane. Her clothes were just as dull as my room. She smelled like bean sprouts, and her paperwhite skin reminded me of undercooked dough.

"Elenora?"

"Yes."

"You will address me with, 'Yes, Nonna Coppola.'" *She pointed to a wooden chair. "Sit." I did, and she sat across from me. "You are here merely to produce an heir. You will not be given the same rights as the other women here until you've earned my trust. You will not leave the property for the next two weeks, and when you are allowed to leave, you must ask for permission and will always have an escort. You will respect Theo and the others in this house. If you don't, there will be consequences that, I can assure you, you won't like."*

So, she's blunt. Ouch.

"Do you understand?"

"Yes, Nonna Coppola," I said quietly when I was

really cursing at her inside as I plotted her death with that stupid cane. She didn't even need it. She sat tapping the foot she pretended to need the cane for. I'd seen her hop up and walk perfectly fine. I wanted to roll my eyes, but I also needed her to not hate me. It was, after all, the first time I'd met this woman in person.

"You may tour the grounds today, but when Theo arrives home from his trip this weekend, you will attempt to conceive immediately."

That explained his absence. Wait, what? "But we're not even married yet!" My mouth dropped open. I hoped I had some time before that would start.

"Then perhaps we need to move up the wedding, if your moral compass is struggling."

She played dirty, and I saw I needed to amp up my game if I was going to survive this.

"Does Theo have a favorite color?" I went for a sweet demeanor. "I would like to make sure I dress appropriately for the occasion."

"Speak with his capo. He can fill you in on his likes and dislikes." She made way too much of an effort as she pushed to her feet and stared down at me. "You are not here to fall in love, Elenora. You are but a means to an end. I know all that goes on inside and outside of these walls. If you think of disobeying me, I will know, and you will not be the only one who suffers." She was referring to my parents.

"Yes, of course. I understand."

When she turned her back, I flipped her off and decided I'd go find the capo. As I got up, I heard a chuckle from the other side of the room and found a man around my age laughing at me. He wasn't really handsome but certainly wasn't hard on the eyes either.

"You have a death wish." He smirked. "If she caught that, you'd get the belt."

"Maybe I'd be less desirable with lash marks on my back," I muttered.

"You clearly haven't spent much time with Theo," he muttered darkly then extended his hand. "I'm Oscar, and I will most likely be your only friend here."

"Elenora. And I can be likable." I felt the need to defend myself.

"I'm sure you can be, but they aren't. The housemates, the staff, and our various daily visitors hate you already. You are about to marry the almighty Theo."

"They can have him. I don't want him."

He tilted his head as he studied me. "You really have no interest in being with him?"

"I'm nothing more than payment for the dirty deals my parents have made. The moment those doors open, I'm outta here."

"You won't get far. Everyone is paid off, and there are incentives for those who tell on one another." I let out a long breath, trying to consider any options that I might have left. "Maybe I can help you?"

"I'm listening."

A chair scraping on the floor brought me quickly out of my memory, and I blinked back the horrific feeling of being trapped with no way out.

"Tell me, has Elio Capri forgiven her for who she

is?" I heard him flex in his suit.

"No. In fact, he came to the hotel to speak with her, and she told him to get out of her life."

"Has he so far?"

"Yes."

"Good," I said over my shoulder. "Ugo?"

"Yes?"

"I want to see my daughter."

Chapter
NINE

Sienna

A few days later, I was starting to feel a little more comfortable with my surroundings. Nonna Rosa had been tucked away in her office for most of my time here. I guessed by the comings and goings that something big was going on. She kept Ugo away from me, and that was hard, as I had no one to talk to. I knew he was supposed to act aloof with me, anyway, and it was easier when he wasn't nearby. I did overhear the staff talking about how tonight's dinner was going to be interesting. I wasn't sure what they meant, but it was something to look forward to, nonetheless.

I spent the day on the west side of the house. There was a little study that had a hidden balcony where I could be alone. It looked over the hill, and you could see a panoramic view of Rome. It was the only place I could pull out my phone without feeling like someone was watching me.

Once my phone powered on, I saw several missed messages from Wyatt.

Wyatt: I'm still not on board with this plan, but how is it going?

Wyatt: I just need one message from you, so I know you're okay.

Wyatt: Tell me you're not locked in a dungeon somewhere.

Wyatt: I want to visit. I need to know you're okay.

My poor friend was worried sick about me, but I didn't want to risk anyone hearing me use my phone. Not yet, at least. Perhaps a quick text.

Sienna: Sorry, just trying to fit in. The place is different. No one really talks to me yet. I think everyone is unsure what to think. Ugo left for a day, and now he's back. Nonna has kept him away from me. Nonna asked about how I was found and about Elio. I suspect more questions to follow. I think someone is coming to dinner tonight, so I'll fill you in on that when I can. I'm always listening and watching but have nothing to report yet. We will have a story that will shock the country, Wyatt, I just know it. I miss you so much, and I will tell you all when I can see you again.

I read over the text message again. It was risky sending texts, and I wanted to be sure I'd left nothing out.

Ugo assured me my phone was protected by something he'd installed, but it still worried me. My gaze slipped over to Elio's name once more, and I felt a jolt of loneliness. *Focus*. Maybe in our next life we would get this love thing right, but for now we had many obstacles to get over first. I cleared the emotion from my throat as I felt the phone vibrate in my hand.

Wyatt: We will have the best story, but just don't make it cost you time that you can't get back. Dinner sounds interesting. I'll be looking for a message about that. Keep in touch. I'll see you soon.

I powered down my phone and leaned back, letting the cool evening air brush over my face. Maybe I needed to set an end date here. Ugo and I had discussed this a little, but I needed one for myself. Wyatt was right. How long was I going to play this game? How long should I put my life on hold again? Deep down, I wondered if there was a part of me that was unsure if I could handle my old life anymore. Maybe I just needed to see this for what it was, a chance to gain some power back, wipe the slate clean, and start embracing who I really was, the daughter of a mafia Don. Yes, I was done with running, with trying to guess my past. I needed to focus on the future. If I wanted to be free of all things dark, this was the only way to do it.

"Have you seen Alessia?" Nonna Rosa's weathered voice broke through my thoughts, and I leaned over the balcony to see her talking to one of the soldiers. "What do you mean, no? She should be dressed and ready for dinner by now. It's your job to keep an eye on her."

Oh! I pushed back and scrambled to my feet. I raced through the room, out the door, and down the long hallway toward my room. I was quite sure no one had seen me. The click of the cane on the stairs told me I had maybe a minute before she'd be walking in, without even so much as a courtesy knock. I hid my phone behind the dresser, stripped down, and shimmied into the dress I'd planned on wearing for dinner. I slid my feet into my leather heels and quickly sat at the vanity. I had just reached for my earrings as the door opened.

"Good evening, Nonna Rosa." My image smiled at her from the mirror, and I begged my flushed face to settle. "How was your day?"

"Good." She looked around like she expected there to be someone else in the room with me. "Have you been up here all day?"

"Mostly, yes." I threaded my earring through the tiny hole in my ear. The dark blue beads matched my dress. "I'm terribly sorry. Am I late for dinner? I found a book and got caught up in the story." I prattled on as I waved at the book I had found in the living room earlier.

"Yes. You are late. Come downstairs the moment you are ready, and don't dally." She closed the door behind her, and I sagged with relief.

I stalled for as long as I dared, but when I heard voices I didn't recognize, I knew it was time to go down.

"Excuse me," I stopped a housekeeper on the stairs, "have you seen Ugo?"

"I believe he's downstairs, where you should be," she whispered sharply and stepped toward me. Her jet-black hair swung at her waist. "The elders are here, so tread very carefully."

"Oh, yes, the three *rhymers*." I grimaced and wanted to ask about who else was here, but she stepped back and hurried away. *No small talk there.*

The very long staircase had a slight curve to it. As I made my way down, I saw a few people mingling. Suddenly, something strange passed through me. I should have listened to my body and not kept walking. Ugo caught my gaze from across the room and made a point of nodding at the elders who stood holding fancy glasses and cigars. I noticed people kept their distance from them, probably not comfortable mingling with the *all-powerful*. As I reached the bottom of the stairs, a sudden flash of movement bolted toward me.

"What are you doing here?" Stefano wrapped his arm around me and lifted me to my toes as he pressed the tip of his gun to my temple. Everything went in slow motion. I blinked slowly as a flinch traveled through my core and exploded through my chest, sending prickles up my spine. Ugo appeared in front of us, and I held up a hand to stop him. Guests yelped in confusion, and the staff scattered from the room.

"Drop the gun, Stefano!" Ugo hollered, but Stefano ignored him. His lips touched my ear, and I shuddered.

"How dare the girlfriend of my enemy be in my home without me knowing!"

"It's not what you think." I tried to get my footing, but he yanked me around like I weighed nothing. "I'm one of you."

"Lies!" He tossed me to the floor, and I landed on my wrist with all my body weight, and my cheek bounced off the floor. *Ouch!*

Stefano's face flushed red with anger as he turned on Ugo. "I don't know why you have returned, cousin, but you are not welcome here," he snarled. "And you," he spat at my feet, "you just won't die."

"Stefano!" Nonna Rosa shouted from across the room, and everyone went silent. I noticed the three elders had moved forward, and Nonna kept them in her sights as she swiftly approached and placed a hand on Stefano's arm. "Forgive me. I wasn't aware you had returned home. This," she peered down at me as she spoke clearly, "is your uncle Theo's daughter, Alessia. I know you must be confused to see her here, but it's all right. Ugo has brought her back to us." She lifted her hand and brushed a soothing wave at the room. "We'll explain everything that's happened, but please allow your cousin to stand."

You could have heard a pin drop throughout the room, and it was as though everyone held their breath to see what their Don would do. One of the male guests took the liberty of leaning down and offered a hand to help me to my feet. My wrist throbbed as I pressed my hand against my hot cheek. My eyes went from Stefano to Nonna Rosa, but I kept my lips sealed to see where all this would go.

"The enemy must be filling your head with lies, Nonna Rosa," he snarled as I stepped back and took a moment to straighten my dress.

Nonna slammed her cane on the floor, and the

chilling sound echoed against the stone walls. "I am still your elder, Stefano." Her voice was quiet but held steel, and I was close enough to see the warning in her eyes. "We will talk about this after dinner. I have invited a few people to meet Alessia." She turned and addressed the room. "All right, everyone, dinner is ready, so please, let's all put this unfortunate misunderstanding behind us and enjoy our meal. Ugo, please escort Alessia."

She took Stefano by the arm and led him toward the dining room as she talked to him in a low voice.

Ugo took my arm and looked down at me. "Are you okay?"

"Yeah." With a trembling hand, I touched my cheek and winced, trying to hold back the urge to flee.

"Maybe we shouldn't do this." He looked worried.

"No, we can do this." I turned away, taking a deep breath.

"Sienna—"

"I said I'm fine." I sniffed, avoiding another awkward stare-down with the soldier with the neck tattoos. He just plain made me uncomfortable. "Dinner is waiting." I grabbed his arm. "Come on. Nonna Rosa said you should escort me, but remember, don't look too happy about it. You're supposed to act like you don't give a damn about me." I practically dragged him into the dining room.

"I need to slip out and make a call," he said quickly once we got close to our table. He pushed my hand away and hurried off. I continued on my own.

"Alessia," Nonna Rosa called as she stood behind

a chair at the head of the table, "your chair." Stefano dropped his glass on the table, and she glared at him. I stood straighter and walked the length of the mile-long table and slowly sank into the hard chair. Ugo returned a few moments later and sat on the side at the opposite end, far from me.

My mind spun as I ate. I was thankful it was my left wrist that throbbed as it rested painfully on my lap. I knew it was swelling up, even as I sat there. There was no time for tears as I struggled to figure out my next move. One glance at Stefano and his angry face built my resolve to stay here if just to spite him.

I picked up on the low chatter around me and tuned in and out of the voices to see if I could catch anything worth listening to. I knew everyone would be very careful around me, but we were all human, and humans were prone to slipping up.

"She's beautiful," a woman said quietly nearby. "I can't believe she was dating Elio Capri."

"I don't get it," her friend said. "What's appealing about her? She has nothing to offer him."

Sticks and stones, I reminded myself.

"Dessert?" A waiter smiled as he leaned down with a dish of chocolate gelato in his hand. It was attractively arranged with a sliver of orange peel on the top.

"Thank you." I tried to smile. "That looks lovely".

Nonna tapped the table to get my attention, and she shook her head at me.

"Don't talk to the staff," she mouthed.

Seriously? I instantly thought of Donte and how I

valued our friendship. I felt bad for the waitstaff here. Most of them seemed more scared than happy to have a job.

I didn't touch the gelato. I hadn't much of an appetite, anyway. I hardly remembered what I'd eaten to this point. Soon, everyone retired outside for drinks and cigars while I hung back, making sure I stayed away from Ugo. I went to a sitting room and studied some photos on the wall and along a piano. I found one of my father. He was sitting in a restaurant with his father and brother. The journalist in me had me looking up photos of him soon after I found out who he was. These pictures were better and clearer than any I had found. I studied them more closely and realized I looked more like my mama than him. I held the framed photo closer to my face to study his features. He was handsome, dressed well, and had a nice smile. I tried to picture what he was like back when the photo was taken. Was this just a family meeting or a guys' night out?

I wondered what he would have been like with me. Would he have been kind or mean like Mama described him? Had he truly not wanted me? Could you not love a part of you? I couldn't imagine not loving your child. Abandonment seemed to be something that followed me everywhere. Perhaps, with my parentage, I should wear that as a badge of honor instead of a dark rain cloud.

"Your manners need some work." Nonna Rosa came into the room, and I put the photo down and blinked back my emotion. She looked from me to the photo but didn't comment. "If you are to be a part of this family, you will need to follow some guidelines."

"All right." I entwined my fingers and waited for her to go on.

"Our guests tonight came to see you, and you hardly spoke two words to them."

"After the way the evening began, I felt a bit uncomfortable."

"You and Stefano will need to get along."

"I wasn't the one holding the gun." I held my tongue from running.

She moved closer, tapping her cane as she did. "There's a way to smooth this situation over."

"How?"

"Give Stefano your ring and step down." *Here we go.* "It's not a position you'll want anyway, Alessia."

"It's Sienna," I corrected her, "and you're asking me to give up the only thing I have that connects me to my father."

"I have things of his you can have."

"I don't want *things*, Nonna Rosa. I want to live the life he did so I can know my roots."

She looked away and sighed like she was frustrated I wouldn't just give up.

A small piece of power slipped into place inside me, like a blacksmith soldering a knight's armor after a battle. I found myself standing a little straighter.

"As I'm sure you know by now," she started again, "the Coppolas have never had a female step into the role of the Don. It will be a big adjustment, and frankly one that I don't see happening. You don't have any experience, you weren't brought up in this house, and you don't know how we operate. I fear it will all be too much for you, even if the uncles did agree."

"You're right, I don't know much about the Coppola life." I stepped forward and took a moment to play this part perfectly. "But I do know an awful lot about how the Capris live." I watched the corners of her mouth fight not to lift. "I know how they run things, what their books look like, and," I paused for emphasis, "who their next target is." I lowered my voice to make my words stick. "You see a woman with a ring looking for answers, but what you should be seeing is a woman with a powerful ring who has firsthand knowledge on the enemy."

"Would you really share such details of the people that took you in and on the man you say you once loved?"

"Love is merely a feeling, Nonna." I stared straight into her cold eyes. "Blood is what gives you life."

Chapter
TEN

Elio

"We had a deal," I snarled into the phone once he finally picked up.

"I know. I'm sorry, but—"

"No, there's no but. You call on time or this is over." I pulled the phone away from my ear but quickly put it back. "If you don't, I strip you of your skin."

"Understood."

I hung up and stepped away from my car. I was about to blow the whole thing. I needed to settle my nerves but knew there were only two ways that could happen.

Sex or bloodshed.

My mind spun, my blood pounded, and my chest felt tight. I'd never felt this uneasy in my entire life, not even when we fled all those years ago and we barely escaped the faceless killer looking for my father.

I turned on my heel and stopped short as I saw Wyatt standing by the walk.

"Hey." He looked uneasy. "Vinni helped me past the gates. Got a minute?"

I nodded, knowing whatever he had to say that had brought him all this way was for my ears only. I motioned for him to follow me away from the soldiers who were watching him. The gravel crunched under my suede shoes as I walked. The sun that hung low in the early evening sky still had warmth to it. Autumn was here, and I was thankful the heat would be backing off for a while.

Wyatt stayed quiet until we were deep in the vineyard. I turned to face him and noted his hands flexed at his sides. He was nervous, and I knew I wasn't going to like this.

"Thanks," he finally said and licked his lips.

"For what?"

"I know you're a busy man, and I'm sure all of this can't be easy on you, but I appreciate you taking a moment to speak with me."

"Of course." I tried to read his face, and as he struggled to start, I squinted at him. "Wyatt, you didn't just come all the way here to see the vineyard."

"No." He let out a long breath. "Sienna is going to kill me dead."

That caught my attention.

"If you don't spit it out, I might beat her to the punch," I warned.

"You've been looking for Mariano, right?"

I tucked my hands in my pockets and eyed him. "Yes. He hasn't been around since we found out about Sienna. But apparently, he checked in this morning with his mother. He said he'd be back this week."

"And you've had guys tailing him?"

"To a certain point, yes."

"When did they start and stop?"

"Instead of piecing the puzzle together on your own here, Wyatt, just tell me what you know, and I'll connect the dots myself."

"Oh, God." He blew out hard. "Elio, I know something, but I don't want to make your situation any worse. But at the same time, the fact that you're letting Mariano come back to the house means that, whatever the hell happened in the hotel room, Sienna couldn't have told you this part." I shook my head, trying to follow his rambling words. "Did Sienna mention anything about Mariano after you were jumped at the dockyard?"

"No." My jaw ticked.

"And you didn't notice anything about what she looked like when she arrived at the house that night?" I shook my head as I tried to remember just what she looked like that night. I remembered her face was red and puffy from crying, but everything else was a bit of a blur at the moment. "When was the last time you spoke to her?"

"The hotel." I felt like stone. "Wyatt," I warned, "you have five seconds to explain, or my 9-millimeter will be between your eyes."

"Your grandmother got Mariano to grab Sienna from your house that day. The day everything blew up." His words came out in a rush. "He was at your house waiting for her. He grabbed her and threw her into Abramo's car with your grandmother." I stopped breathing as hate pumped through me. "She fought hard, but she wasn't strong enough to fight them both off. I just think you should know Mariano was the one who did it. He was working for her. For your grandmother," he repeated as he looked at me hard.

I held up my hand to stop his words. I needed a moment to process.

"Mariano hurt Sienna?"

"Yeah, he roughed her up pretty good, too. But like I said, Sienna did a good job defending herself." He tried to smile, but his mouth gave up on the effort and he shrugged.

"Go on. What else?" I could feel my blood pressure skyrocketing and knew I needed to hear the rest before I blew.

"Sienna told me your grandmother dumped her outside of town, then she rushed to your place to tell everyone the story about who Sienna was. There's more to it, obviously, but the point is Sienna got there too late to tell you herself. Then, I guess, your grandmother did a good job of spinning her tale in the worst way, because when Sienna walked through the door to tell you all what happened, she was basically dismissed by all of you."

"That's not what happened."

"Maybe not from your perspective, but look at it from

hers." He looked away when I glared at him. "Listen," he took a deep breath, "two times now you've broken my best friend's heart, whether you meant to or not. Every time you turn your back or question her it shreds a little off her core. So, the fact that I'm here, alone, telling you this must mean something to you. I would appreciate you not killing me either." He tried to make another joke, but it was clear he was more terrified than anything else. I admired him for showing up, but my head was racing.

I worked like hell to steady my breathing as the events of that night came back to me. I had screwed up countless times now, and for what? The Don seat was mine whenever I wanted it, but none of that mattered if I didn't have Sienna.

"Boss!" Vinni called as I slammed the door shut. "Boss, wait!"

"Don't," I shouted over my shoulder.

"Hey," Niccola was suddenly in front of me, "I know that look. It means you need to spread some blood, and I'm game, but hold up." He held up a hand when I went to move around him. "We've got company."

The door opened, and Nonna stood above us with her rosary beads swinging.

"What happened to you?" Nonna demanded harshly, looking startled at our appearance.

"Stefano's men jumped us at the dockyard," Niccola said as I vibrated with anger.

"Oh, no. I think I might know why they were there." She stepped back and motioned for us to join her inside.

"Oh, my God." Mama raced toward me, and my

father stood there, his face a picture of concern. "Are you okay?"

"I'm fine." I folded my arms and gently pushed Mama aside. "Nonna, what do you know?" I took the napkin Mama handed me and pressed on the cut above my eye, feeling the swelling coming on.

"Yes, Greta, why are we all here?" Mama handed me a bag of frozen vegetables Donte had raced in with.

"I'm sorry to say, but Abramo stumbled across some troubling news."

"Which is?" Papa stood impatiently.

"You've let a Coppola into our home." Silence blanketed the room as we all absorbed her words. "Sienna is the daughter of Theodore Coppola."

"Nonna," I felt the air being sucked from my lungs, "tread very carefully here."

"Grandson," her gaze swung over to me, "she's been lying to us, to you." She waved a hand at me. "She's a spy, and you just opened the doors and invited her in. Have I taught you nothing?" she scoffed at both me and Papa. "She was planted years ago." She glared at Francesco, who seemed about to lunge at her, but Papa held up a hand to stop him. "She fed on your weakness and wormed her way into your heart. If you don't believe me, then ask her."

"Ask what's in her hand," Abramo said as he suddenly appeared. He threw a glance at Nonna, who looked unsure for a moment. "One of the guys called and said he saw something in her hand, and she seemed to be crying over it."

"Whose hand?" Papa asked then stopped talking when the door opened and footsteps could be heard. Nonna moved to stand behind me. I put a finger to my lips in case it was Mariano, and Mama quickly changed the topic.

"And where are Anna and the notebook now?" Mama asked to quickly change the subject.

"No clue." I winced at the pain that shot through my ribs.

Sienna slowly rounded the corner, and her eyes widened at all of us. Her hand slid behind her back as she spoke. "What's happened?"

Abramo made a show of holding up his fist behind Sienna, and Mama cleared her throat.

"Sienna," the hurt in Mama's voice nearly broke me, "where have you been?

"I…" She paused and glanced around. "I was out."

"Show me your hand." Mama pressed on, but Sienna made a fist, which made the hairs on my neck raise. "Sienna, sweetheart, please show me what's in your hand."

I wanted to reach out and demand that everyone leave her alone, that it wasn't true—it couldn't be. She was mine. We'd known each other a lifetime, and despite the doubt that was planted in me, I knew who Sienna was, and she wasn't a Coppola.

"Sienna," Papa said softly, "please do as she says."

Slowly, with terror in her eyes, she uncurled her fingers, and resting on the palm of her small hand was a Coppola family ring.

"Oh," Mama cried, and I felt like the world just dropped a bag of bricks on my chest.

A loud ring hurt my ears, and my muscles cramped as I ripped my gaze away from her and sank into the chair behind me.

"This is why you shouldn't question me," Nonna hissed behind me.

"Elio?" Sienna's desperate voice begged me to say something, but I was stuck on pause. I barely felt Nonna's hand land on my shoulder when she addressed Sienna.

"Proof is proof."

I heard a small sob from Sienna as she raced out of the room.

I made a move to get up, but Nonna's hand pressed hard on my shoulder. I looked up at her, and her face held a stern warning. Before I could react, my phone began to vibrate, and I fished it out of my pocket. I checked the number then answered it.

"What?"

"Elio? It has to mean something, that I came to you." Wyatt's voice brought me back to the present, and I cringed as I heard Bria cackle from somewhere nearby.

"Yes, it does mean something, and I appreciate you coming to tell me." I rubbed my mouth as I tried to think.

My phone buzzed, and I glanced at it. Niccola was warning me that we were about to have company.

I stepped closer to Wyatt and lowered my voice. "Look, Wyatt, a lot's happening, and I can't explain right now. We have to be in Fiano Romano two nights from now. Stefano's been spotted there with two of his capos.

We have to make some big moves fast. You need to get out of town now. Your face has been seen, and it'll be reported, so you can't return. You aren't safe, not even here. Don't talk to anyone."

He pulled out his keys just as the soldiers approached us. He caught my warning. "Yeah, so, thanks for the talk, Elio."

Normally, I would have shot one of them in the face for even looking my way, let alone interrupting me while I was talking privately with someone, but I wasn't ready to start this war just yet. Not until all my chips were in place. So, for now, I'd let Nonna think she was in control.

"Mr. Capri," the taller soldier looked nervous, as he should be, "I apologize for this. But, sir," he directed his comment to Wyatt, "we've been asked to escort you off the property."

"It's a good thing I was just leaving, then." Wyatt left without looking back. I knew I'd need to do damage control with Nonna over Wyatt's visit. She knew he was a good friend of Sienna's.

"If you ever," in a flash I grabbed the soldier around the neck, squeezing just enough to let him feel my strength, "do that again, I will kill you and everyone you care about." I glanced at his buddy, who lowered his head and submitted. "Understood?"

"Yes." The man struggled for air. I held on a moment longer to drive my point home, then I let go and tossed him backward. I knew she'd sent them, and I knew they were confused as to whose orders to follow. They needed to know I was the one they should fear, not her.

I headed back up to the house and signaled for Francesco, as I stomped by him, to follow me straight into my father's office.

"Get out," I muttered to Gain, and he left without hesitation.

"What's going on?" Papa looked up from his laptop. Francesco leaned against the wall and waited for me to begin.

I leaned down toward Papa, pressing against his desk with my fists. I needed to calm this murderous rage. "Papa, it's time to make our first move."

He leaned back and removed his glasses to study my face. He seemed to make his decision and nodded slowly.

"All right, *mio figlio*. Let's do this."

After a long night of planning, I finally went home, worked out, then showered. I removed the crystal top from the decanter and poured myself a stiff drink and took it with me to the bedroom.

I sat on the edge of the bed and used my free hand to massage my sore shoulder. Aldo had stepped up his game since I had doubled my workouts with him. Not that it had helped my head at all.

As I sipped my drink, something in the floor-length mirror caught my attention. I walked over to the closet door and tugged it open. It was her dark blue silk teddy. It must have fallen from somewhere when the maid was here. Instantly, everything inside stilled. I knew it wasn't smart, but I held it to my nose and breathed in her scent. Every single nerve in my body fired off at once. Like one big, uncontrollable spasm. It hurt so badly. My heart begged me to go to her.

Reaching back for my phone, I brought up a voice message she'd left a while back. I tapped the speaker button, letting her voice fill the silence.

"Hey, so, I'm sitting here on the pool steps staring up at the sky. The stars are shining, and there are little peepers singing in the bushes next to me." She sighed like she had something on her mind. "It got me thinking, remember when we used to sneak out to the pond at night? I think I was what, maybe eighteen?"

"Eighteen and a half," I answered like she was actually on the other end of the call.

"You would do this thing where you'd reach back and pull your t-shirt off with one tug. I'd always sneak a peek at the way your arm muscle would harden, like iron." She giggled softly. "God, I was so captivated by you. I guess I still am, even after all these years. Only now it's a sexy suit and one hell of a…what does Wyatt call it? Oh, yes, a five o'clock shadow." There was a small pause. "Do you think of me when you're away?"

"Yes," I closed my eyes, "every damn minute."

"Well, I suppose I should get dried off. Andrea invited me to join her for a walk. Hurry back. We have so many things to catch up on, and most of them include you and those arms of yours. Goodnight."

The call ended, and I tossed the scrap of fabric away from me and practically ran out onto the balcony, desperately needing to be far away from it. She was my greatest addiction, one I needed to stay away from for now.

I spent the whole night out there on a lounge chair refusing to allow my heart to rule my head. I stayed hidden with my murky thoughts until the next evening.

Mama, once again, outdid herself. I couldn't help being amused. She was such a perfectionist; she left nothing out. The table was set beautifully, music flowed from the speakers embedded in the ground, and little paper lanterns dangled from trees. They cast a soft glow between the branches.

"Wow," I smiled as Mama came out holding a dish, "you look lovely."

"Thank you." She did a little spin to show off the new dress she had bought for tonight's dinner. "It's not every day you get to clean house, so to speak."

"It's been a long time coming." I kissed her cheek then sipped my wine, feeling my own body relax a little. I was looking forward to this myself. I noted, as he walked toward us, that Papa had dressed in his best three-piece suit.

"You look sensational, Papa."

He smiled at me then looked down at his wife, and, for a brief moment, I felt a snap to the heart knowing I'd only looked at one woman that way. "You as well, Elio."

"Yes," I looked down at my suit, feeling rather excited myself, "it's not every day I'd wear my Kiton." I brushed my hand down the front of the suit Enzo D'Orsi had handmade for me. Enzo was the crème de la crème when it came to making custom suits. He'd fly anywhere in the world if he chose to accept the order. I knew he only made roughly fifty suits a year, and I was very proud of the fact that he had agreed to do one for me.

"It's lovely, dear." Mama kissed my cheek then turned as she heard our company arrive. Papa winked at Mama as he made a show of placing a small bag by his chair. Then he took her by the arm, and we all went to greet our dinner guests.

"Everything looks," Bria, Mariano's mama, looked around in her usual bored way, "the same." She cleared her throat then gave an artificial smile. "My, you look quite handsome this evening," she purred and gave me a sleazy look. I bit my tongue.

"You as well." I took in her over-the-top leopard print blouse, diamond tiger brooch, bright red lipstick, and teased hair. She looked like someone from one of those American reality shows. I quivered at the thought of being with someone like her. I tore my injured eyes away, only to have them land on her husband's stomach. It was fighting and winning the battle against the buttons that strained to remain closed on his way too small shirt. His Todd Snyder suit was out of date and badly cut in the first place.

What was wrong with these people? A man's suit spoke volumes about who he was. Wearing a store-bought suit might have been acceptable to some, but not to a Capri. Call me a snob, but I took great pride in my appearance, and so did my family.

"What's on the menu tonight?" Roberto asked as he plunked himself into a chair. He pulled the napkin out of his wine glass and tucked it into his shirt. He didn't even so much as acknowledge my presence or mention the wonderful job Mama had done with the table. I hated how much Mariano took after his father's mannerisms.

Mama refused to answer him and took her seat as Papa held out her chair. He shook his head, unimpressed, and waited for Donte to pour us some wine. Bria watched him. I was sure curious as to why our chef was waiting on us and not our usual waitstaff. The fewer eyes, the better tonight. We settled into our places, Papa stood and lifted his glass for a toast. Bria rolled her eyes and snorted as she pulled her already lipstick-stained wine glass back from her mouth.

"I'd like to take a moment to say something." Papa directed his comment at Mama then eyed the table as we all lifted our glasses and looked at him.

"This should be interesting." Roberto snickered as I slid my steak knife under the table. My hand begged to jab it into his fat thigh.

"Our friendship hasn't always been easy, Roberto, but when you called me that day to request a meeting and gave me your word that we should join forces, I felt we had something very special. For years now, you have stood by my side, as a loyal friend, and worked closely with me and Andrea. We may not have seen eye to eye, but at the end of the day, just look how things worked out. We asked you here tonight to show you just how much you and your family mean to us. So, if you can take a moment to raise your glasses, let's send cheers to the future."

"I would have preferred a trip somewhere, but a dinner it is," Bria muttered as she took a sip of her wine. Mama shot me a quick glance.

"Elio," my father's voice caught my attention, and I flexed my hand over the handle of the knife, "shall we eat?"

I nodded once, and everyone turned their attention to their food. I tried counting from ten so as not to ruin the evening. I had looked forward to this meal all day, and the panzanella looked delicious.

"Oh," Bria eyed the dish in front of her, "this again?"

"You know…" I stood and held my wine glass up to the light then took a sip and savored the flavor before continuing. "If you all don't mind, I think I'd like to say a little something as well."

Roberto cursed under his breath and dropped his fork on the side of the plate, unimpressed I'd stopped his gorging.

"We've had our fair share of secrets that have come out recently, some more damaging than others."

"Like how your girlfriend is a Coppola?" Bria snorted as she shoved a forkful in her mouth. Rage burned through me, but I kept my cool.

"As a matter of fact, yes, that was a shock." I nodded. "But we had a good talk, and we're now stronger than ever." I watched her eyes widen in disbelief.

"Elio, you can't possibly be serious. She's the blood of those who're trying to kill your family!" Roberto barked.

"My syndicate, my rules," Papa said with a shrug.

"Funny you should bring that up, Roberto," I went on, "because when I got lured down to the dockyard a few weeks ago and was met by Stefano, Anna was with him." I held his gaze as he squinted to read my mind. "She told me who was really behind Papa's hit years ago, the same hit that separated Sienna and me."

Roberto's gaze shifted over to Bria, whose eyes had gone wide.

"Well, dinner is getting cold. Shall we enjoy it now? Cheers to a lifetime of loyalty and friendship." I grinned and took another appreciative sip from my wineglass. I glanced at my father, who acted like he knew nothing about what I was referring to.

An uneasy silence fell over our guests while Papa complimented Mama on how tasty the food was. I continued to smile, savoring the moment, and was pleased to see a bead of sweat form near Bria's temple.

"Any news from Mariano?" I asked after a bit. "He seems to have just dropped off the map. Like he's hiding from me or something." I chuckled at my own amusement. Again, I watched Bria shift in her seat while she tried to swallow. I imagined her throat felt a bit dry at the conversation, and I wondered if she was bright enough to know where I was going with it.

"No," she attempted a smile but refused eye contact, "he tends to disappear from time to time."

"Well, cocaine will do that to a person." I didn't miss a beat and gave a sorrowful look at Roberto, who shot me a wary look back. "Mama," I directed my attention to her, "you chose the perfect night to host this dinner. I only hope that when I drill a hammer into Mariano's chest and rip out his heart, it'll feel as satisfying."

Roberto took too large a mouthful, and when my words sank in, he began to cough and sputter as he tried to swallow it down. Papa got out of his chair and worked his way around the table until he was standing behind Roberto.

"Take a breath, old friend," he cooed as he caught my eye.

"Yes, slower bites," Bria said, in a trance while she stared at me.

"Bria?" I raised my voice loudly enough for all to hear.

"What?"

"Before I murder your son, I thought you might like to witness this first."

In a flash, Papa whipped the OB wire around Roberto's neck and with all his force yanked hard. Roberto's fat head dropped on the table with a heavy thud and rolled toward her.

Bria's hands flew to her mouth as a high-pitched scream was released from her throat.

"Gain, would you please pour me another glass of wine?" Mama held up her glass and smiled, completely ignoring Bria's total meltdown.

"Oh, allow me, darling." Papa poured her a healthy glass.

"Thank you."

"You see," I lowered my voice and kept it friendly as Papa took his seat and picked up his fork, "we do know who placed the hit on Papa all those years ago." She sucked in a deep gulp of air but said nothing.

"I also know your son saw a photo of Sienna in my room the night we first met. You asked Mama a lot of questions about who I was and who I was dating, so I know it was you who arranged to bring her back into my life. Was it to distract me?" I looked at her over my wine glass. "It almost worked, you know." I raised an eyebrow at her pale, stunned face. "But, typical Mariano, he got stupid and cocky. He let himself be taken over by drugs, and he overplayed his hand." Sweat beads broke out over her waxy face as she tried to keep herself together. "Now, look what you've done." I waved slowly at her husband's headless body. "This could all have been prevented, if you'd only been loyal."

I gently brushed the napkin over my mouth and tossed it next to me.

"You—you've got this all wrong," she managed to sputter and turned to Mama. "Please, Andrea, you have to know it was all Roberto. He had his hands in so many pockets. I begged him to stop, but he wouldn't listen to me." Mama continued to eat, so she awkwardly twisted in her chair to avoid looking at Roberto's torso. "Piero, we have land, money, and-and-and—."

"We now own your land, your money, and now you." I placed the DeSimones' deed and the papers to their syndicate's trust and pointed to where Roberto had signed it over to the Capri Syndicate. He'd had no choice but to sign it the week prior when I threatened to oust him for attempting to sexually assault a member of our house staff. Donte, who was still simmering over the sexual assault of one of his people, slammed the glass down in front of her and roughly poured the water with a curse.

Bria's face fell with confusion, and I knew she was freaking out inside. It only made this moment so much sweeter.

"Mama?"

"We should show a little grace because, after all, she did reunite you with your love." She folded her napkin into a neat square as she went on. "How would you prefer to go?"

"Please, please, Andrea," Bria held her hands up like she was praying, "I thought we were like sisters."

"You tried to kill my husband."

"It wasn't—"

"I suggest you start running now," Mama warned, and Bria glanced at me as if she'd misheard her. "Bria, go."

With shaky hands, she pressed her palms onto the table and stood, wobbling in her cheap heels. Her mascara ran in dark paths down her cheeks. She looked up then suddenly raced off toward the trees that led to the road.

"Allow me." Papa handed Mama a gun and stood behind her to keep her steady. "Line her up and…"

Bang! Bria's body jolted forward then tumbled to the ground in a heap.

"Perfect shot, Mama," I gave a happy nod, "straight

through the rib cage. Hopefully, it clipped the heart just enough for her to feel the pain."

"I have never been prouder." Papa leaned down and kissed her for a long moment.

"Well, if this isn't the best anniversary gift, I don't know what is." Vinni clapped his hands.

I felt my phone vibrate in my pocket, and I pulled it out. It was Donatello.

"Yeah?"

"Boss, I'm in town, and I was just talking to the minister. Apparently, his church was broken into last night. He was hit with something, some cash was taken, but he's all right, just some bruises and a black eye."

I moved away from the table and turned my back while anger festered deep down inside of me.

"Who was it?"

"Mariano."

Chapter ELEVEN

Sienna

"As much as I appreciated the trip to town and the shopping spree, Nonna Rosa, it really wasn't necessary."

"It was, actually." She slid her finger over the screen of her phone as she read something, and I was left to mull over what she meant. We sat in a sweet little café where Nonna Rosa said the food was good. We planned to have a quick bite before we returned home. It was a place I knew I'd have enjoyed if I was with a friend, instead of sitting here with this evil old woman, far away from Ugo.

I decided to question her. "Why?"

"Why what?"

"Why was this necessary?"

She looked up, placed her phone on the table, and leaned back. I was pleased she was wearing sunglasses, because her eyes made me uneasy.

"We have a lot of company coming over the next few months, and I need you to look your best. And, though you have an eye for fashion, your small suitcase only held so much. If you are to be head of this household, you will need to dress the part. How you dress says a lot about you, and in this life, everything counts."

"Fair enough." I tapped my finger on the table and slowly counted to six. I had to make sure I didn't rush this next part. "Fiano Romano." I said, as though distracted. Then I waited another beat, knowing I had her attention.

"What did you say?" She studied my face.

"Tomorrow night. Elio, Vinni, and Niccola will all be at the north end of Fiano Romano."

"How sure are you?"

"Sure enough that I brought it to you." I remained relaxed, as in that moment I had the upper hand, and she knew it. All I had to do was hope they showed up.

"Very well, I will pass the information along." She went back to reading, then stopped. "Sienna, where is your phone?"

"At the house." I wasn't prepared for that question and knew I couldn't lie. It would have sounded suspicious to say I didn't have one.

"I would like to see it when we get home."

"And why would that be?" I didn't like where this conversation was going.

"Do you have something to hide?"

"Do you have something to ask me?" I knew I needed to tread carefully, but she wasn't getting my phone.

Her lips tightened, and I could tell she was thinking over her words.

"No, I suppose not." She suddenly shifted gears. "I think it's time we left. We can't be late."

"Late for what?" I stood and gathered my things.

"We are celebrating your return home this evening. Everyone who is anyone is coming, so you'll need to look your best."

Oh, Lord. Kill me now.

"That really isn't necessary."

"Of course it is. It is very important, especially to the family."

My stomach rolled at the thought, but I knew it was an important part of establishing my position as a possible Donna. My mind spun as we drove, and I wondered if I was ready for where all this could lead.

Nonna Rosa was out of the car and up the steps before I could even open the car door. She certainly was spry for someone who needed a cane. The driver opened the trunk for me, and I looped as many of the shopping bags over my arms as I could and headed up the steps. I entered the house with the driver behind me struggling with the rest of the bags. We piled the things on the table inside the door.

I smiled my thanks, but he simply turned and left without a word.

A woman approached briskly and began to gather up some of the bags. She headed up the stairs with them, so I grabbed the rest and followed her to my bedroom.

"The guests will be arriving in a few hours. Mrs. Rosa insists you are to be ready and at the top of the stairs by six, no later."

"Well, if she insists." I tried to hide my intrigue. I liked the idea of people knowing I was here and ready to step up to the plate. The more people who knew about me, the harder it would be for me to disappear if a certain nonna didn't get her way. If this was what it was going to take to dig deep into the lives of these people, then bring it on. Besides, I was really getting good at putting on a great performance. I caught my smile in the mirror and relished it, straightening my spine. Oh, yes, tonight would be divine.

I didn't hear his footsteps come up behind me, but the moment he spoke, I broke out in a cold sweat.

"Do you really think you can come into this family after all these years and take over, just because you hold a melted piece of gold on your finger?"

I felt my face heat and my heart race. It was time to put my dear cousin in his place.

"No," I kept my back to him while I pulled a petal off the bouquet in front of me, "I'll take over this family because I'm better at it than you."

He chuckled then cleared his throat. "Even if you did manage to work your way up to gaining the uncles' trust, you have to get through her." His fingers played with a piece of my hair, and I tried everything not to cringe and pull away. "Let's be honest, Sienna. We all know who pulls the puppet strings around here."

"Stefano!" Rosa made me jump, but her evil eyes were cast his way not mine. "Move it along."

"See you around, Sienna," he muttered before they both left me alone.

I shivered and shed the unwanted feeling, not letting him get to me.

After everything was put away, I pulled out what I was going to wear. I'd settled on a simple black dress and heels. Often less was more. Since I still had some time, I decided to take a stroll around the grounds. I wanted to get my head ready for the evening.

"Well, imagine my surprise when my good friend tells me his cousin has returned from the dead." A familiar face and a sardonic smile spoke to me.

"Salvo," I greeted the man from the bar the other night, and I knew exactly who he was. Salvo was more than just Stefano's good friend. They were like brothers, and though Stefano had been assigned a *consigliere* by Nonna Rosa, Salvo was always around keeping tabs on things. The ears of the city. Thankfully, Ugo had Oscar dig deep into the family and was able to fill me in enough so I could start to understand the family webbing. My mother would be furious if she knew how much Oscar helped us, but she'd get over it.

"Good memory, Sienna." He made a show of remembering my name. "So, where are we going?"

"Going?"

"You look like you were heading somewhere."

"Well, not far, given these sixteen-foot prison walls." I waved my arm about. He chuckled, amused, once again, by my lack of positivity.

"Yes, the Coppolas tend to be a bit paranoid." He mused over my humor.

"They might as well have a moat, draw bridge, and guards in full armor."

"Nah, the armor is too restrictive," he chuckled, "but I'll suggest the moat at the next meeting."

"I'm still learning the ins and outs of the family, but if they have more than one home, why not live outside the city instead of this cold, old place?" I turned my nose up at the lack of things to look at on the grounds.

"You can't keep your finger on the pulse of the people if you're hidden away in the countryside. Here, they can keep an eye on everyone and everything."

"You mean look down on everyone."

He made a face as though he was thinking about what I said.

"I understand you're here to prove your place within the family as head of this syndicate. Don't you think you should embrace life here? The Mafia is, after all, a life of crime, and aren't you trying to step into the seat of power?" He eyed my ring.

"Yes. It is my place." I lifted my chin but looked around, knowing that someone was always listening. "I just think things should be brought into present day, that's all."

"Such as a female being Don?" He smirked.

"It's a start." I reached up and twisted a piece of my hair between my fingers. "But I've many ideas and a plan in mind."

"Now you have my attention."

"Yes, yours and many others." I glanced around at the soldiers hovering nearby. "As I'm sure my dear cousin has filled you in, I once dated Elio."

"Yes, that was brought up a few times."

I laughed. "I'm sure. During my time there, I learned a lot about their life."

"That was then, and I'm not saying it won't be useful, but what about now? Do you still talk to him?"

"Not since Greta Capri banished me. The whole Capri family made sure I knew I had no place with them, and especially not with Elio. They made that point very clear." I grimaced dramatically.

"Then what kind of information can you offer about them if you don't have contact anymore?"

"Just because I left doesn't mean I don't have contact." I glanced up at him and pictured Wyatt. "I just heard from someone this morning, and I know exactly where Elio and his two cousins will be this evening. Fiano Romano."

"And are you planning on telling Stefano this?"

I stopped and turned to look at him straight on. "I just did." I gave him a knowing smile. This was a move to see if Stefano would share the news with Nonna Rosa, and if he didn't, which I was banking on, I hoped it would start the game of doubt.

"Stefano painted you so differently."

"Stefano doesn't know me. He only sees the side I want him to see."

"I hope I get to know you, the real you."

"Don't stick a gun in my face, or try to blow me up, and maybe you will." I chuckled, curious to see if he'd react to the bombing comment.

That was still a mystery to me. Who had, and why had that bomb been placed there? Could it have been Stefano or perhaps Greta Capri?

I shook the thoughts away as I leaned over to check the time on his watch. "I need to go. Apparently, I have to dress up and meet a lot of people."

I gave him a wave as he laughed and headed inside to get ready. I caught my smile on the way upstairs in one of the pictures hanging on the wall. I rather liked this newfound confidence. I could get used to this new me.

I took in a long, slow breath once I managed to squeeze into the dress I'd found on the bed. The one I had chosen had been placed back in my closet. According to the maid, Nonna had insisted I needed to wear a more lavish dress this evening. I had to admit it was stunning.

The gown was black, but underneath a shimmer of gold could be seen through strategically placed slits when I moved. Hardly what I expected here, especially at a party where I was to meet a lot of people. I stopped my train of thought as Ugo came into the room looking dressed to impress.

"Nice to finally see you again."

"Yeah, Sienna, we need to talk." He quickly glanced back outside the door.

"Look, I'm not complaining." I dismissed his demeanor and turned to look over my shoulder in the mirror, holding a shade of lipstick up to my lips. The back of the dress was open all the way down to my tailbone. My whole back was exposed. I was surprised Nonna would pick such a revealing dress for this event. I stood, considering her choice of clothing. Lord, the way she dressed made a nun seem risqué. "Who doesn't love dressing up in a beautiful gown, but all this *just* to introduce me into the family?"

"No." His tone dropped. "Sienna, there's a lot more to it than that—"

"My, my." Nonna Rosa made us both jump as she nodded approvingly from the doorway, "Don't you look lovely." She was in a red and black dress which, as I predicted, was very modest, unlike mine.

For someone who usually used a noisy cane, she sure moved without sound when she wanted to.

"Thank you."

"Time to go." She quickly shifted her gaze to Ugo almost as if warning him of something. "We don't want them thinking the guest of honor is running late." She motioned at me, and I slowly followed her out.

"Remember," Ugo whispered as we reached the top of the stairs. I turned to look up at him. He shook his head like he wanted to say something but didn't. "You are a Coppola. This is the moment to make your mark. Stand tall, and dazzle them with your wit, charm, and smile."

"Did you just say dazzle?" I smirked, and he scowled

at me. "Trust me, Ugo, this is where I plan to shine."

I started down the stairs after Nonna Rosa and suddenly felt my stomach bottom out as I saw the sea of people staring up at me.

Here we go.

Nonna Rosa stepped down and waited for the crowd to simmer to a low buzz before she introduced me, using my birth name, and I fought my sigh that wanted to huff out. The crowd greeted me with a cheer and smiles for as far as I could see.

I gathered my dress in my hands, hoped to God I didn't fall, and dug my heels into the thin carpet.

Ugo disappeared again, and I was met by a handsome young man with a killer smile.

"Welcome to the party, Alessia." He offered me a hand to help me down the last two stairs. "I'm Leonardo."

"Please call me Sienna. Lovely to meet you, Leonardo."

"Trust me, the pleasure is all mine." He reached back and snagged a glass of bubbly from a waiter's tray. "Something tells me you will need this to get through the evening."

"Are you trying to win brownie points with me?" I sipped the refreshing prosecco orange and soda water brew.

"Well, I don't know. Did I earn any?"

"Oh, yes." I shot him a wink, knowing all eyes were on me.

"Are you hungry?"

"No," I waved a hand, "I need to let my nerves settle

a little before I can eat anything.”

“Alessia?” A man, who looked to be twice my age, smiled as he rubbed his white-laced beard. “I’d love to steal a moment of your time to tell you about my law firm.”

“Law firm?” Another man laughed as he came up to us. “Let’s not put the poor lady to sleep. Why don’t I tell you about my ranch? It’s just outside the city, and I would love to show you my thoroughbred horses and beef cattle.”

“How about this,” I held up a hand to slow their invites as I gave them each a big smile, “I do want to hear it all, so why don’t you start first?” I pointed to the bearded man.

As they took their turns trying to impress me, I made a show of tossing my head back to laugh and made sure that all the eyes that watched me saw just how at ease I was with everyone. Especially those at the main table. If Nonna Rosa was going to toss this many people at me at once, I was going to let her see I could hold my own. I memorized names, where they were from, what they did, if they had children. I even made a point to remember the one who had just lost his dog. I offered comfort, advice, and shared likes and dislikes. I made sure everyone who stopped to talk to me knew something about who I was. It needed to work both ways, and I knew I was a hit. A few times I caught Ugo watching, and once he gave me a secret thumbs up to let me know our plan was working.

“*Mi scusi, signorina.*” A man approached looking just as friendly as Leonardo, who still hadn’t left my side as he made sure most men never got too close. "Any chance you'd like to dance?"

I turned to Leonardo and placed a hand on his forearm as I leaned up to speak. "Don't go too far."

"I'm not going anywhere." He smiled.

I took the hand of the new man and let him lead me to the dance floor. People immediately parted to give us room. I was thankful for Ugo's lessons in the hotel room a while back because I had never been one for the dance floor. Instantly, I saw Elio's face and pushed it away.

Focus.

The man tugged me into him, and I nearly fell in my heels. Yikes! I liked a man who knew what he wanted, but he needed to earn my trust first. He snagged my hand with one of his then let his other rest way too comfortably on the bare skin of my lower back.

"Are you having a good time?" he asked as we fell into the swing of the song.

"I am. Are you?"

"I am now, but you're a hard woman to get to."

"There certainly are a lot of people here."

"Yes, and now I have you all to myself, so I plan on taking full advantage of it." His gaze dropped down to my cleavage, and I fought the urge to shift out of his hold.

"Why don't we start with your name?"

"Gabriel."

"And what do you do, Gabriel?"

He chuckled like I was asking him if the sky was blue. "I'm the owner of one of the largest shipping manufacturers in all of Italy."

"Good for you." I tried to remember if I'd ever heard of him before, but he'd only mentioned his first name, and I wasn't sure if I should press any further.

"I'm guessing you've never heard of me. It's a wonder you haven't. I mean, after all the time you stayed with the Capris. My name must have come up at some point. Colombo Oil."

Oh… I'd heard of them. I remembered a conversation between Elio and Piero and how Colombo Oil had tried to make some dirty deals over in America a couple years back. They were second only to the Capris when it came to shipping. The Capris' business was much bigger and more far-reaching.

"No, I'm sorry. But then I've lived a very different life from the one I was born into." I tried not to step on my dress when he sent me out for a spin. "My time spent at the Capri house was merely because they took me in without knowledge of who I was."

"You don't really believe that, do you? It's one thing that you didn't know, but for them not to seems highly unlikely."

"That's what I believe, and what I believe is my business. I am not a person to be swayed by anyone else's opinion." I brushed him off, feeling the room become smaller by the minute.

"Brains and beauty are rare to find in one package," he remarked, and I couldn't help but chuckle at his audacity.

"It's only overshadowed by arrogant men who think

they can wave money in front of a woman and believe that's all she'll see." I smiled sweetly at him and watched his face twist in anger. "If you wanted to impress me, Gabriel, you should have done more research on who I was and not been blinded by rumors and fairytales." I stepped back from him when the song ended and gave a little bow for show, knowing we were being observed. I looked around, hoping to spot Ugo, when another man stepped in front of me.

"I'm Tommaso." The man kissed my hand and gave me a seductive smile. "I own my own business and would like to tell you all about it if you'd grant me a few moments of your time."

"Oh, ah…" I fumbled at the sudden change of men. Gabriel stepped back up and put a hand on the new guy's shoulder, his face still angry from my earlier comment.

"Hey, fellas, we're here all night," I held up both hands to stop whatever the hell was about to happen, "and—"

"All right, boys." A taller man came to my rescue. He placed himself between the two men and me, then turned and spoke directly to them with a big smile. "Let's give the little lady a breather." He handed me a glass of wine and ushered me off the dance floor.

"Thank you for that." I took a breath, happy that someone had come to my aid.

"Are you okay?"

"Yes, of course. Though they were a little intense. I appreciate your help in diffusing the situation. Thanks again for that."

"It was the easiest money I've ever made." He winked then turned and walked off, leaving me to wonder what he meant.

As soon as he left, I spotted Tommaso heading my way again, so I shook my head at him.

"I just need to use the ladies' room. Give me a few minutes, and I'm all yours." I quickly began to move through the crowd, searching faces for Ugo. I spotted him across the room. He was standing on his own and caught my eye. He gave me a nod and pointed to the hallway as he held up five fingers. I nodded back and began to make my way slowly in that direction.

It wasn't easy to move quickly through the crowd, as I couldn't look like I was in any hurry. I made sure to stop and chat briefly whenever someone spoke to me. I filed away their names in my already overcrowded memory and laughed loudly when I could. Quick, funny lines popped into my head, and I had people laughing here and there as I made my way across the room.

I stopped as a few women asked about my dress and my hair. I felt that I played my part to everyone's liking, and though I was exhausted, I was proud of the image I was casting. They loved me, and I knew it all would trickle back to Nonna and the uncles.

My heels clicked on the floor as I turned the corner, leaving the hungry crowd behind, and leaned against the cool wall, taking a much-needed minute.

You can do this. You can do this. Just take a breath and focus.

"There you are." Salvo appeared out of nowhere, and

I found myself relieved to see a familiar face. "Trying to escape?"

"Don't tempt me. I just needed a moment." I laughed and acted like I was overwhelmed when really I was looking for my cousin to get a report.

"Can I get you anything?"

"I'd love a water if it isn't too much trouble."

"One water coming up."

"Thanks, Salvo." I squeezed his arm and smiled kindly.

I scanned the room after Salvo left and spotted Ugo. He inclined his head for me to follow as he slipped into a room off the hall. I quickly hiked up my dress and made my way toward the door.

"Why did you leave me with the wolves?" I exhaled with relief as I stepped into the room, happy to be free of everyone, if only for a few moments. "Ugo?"

A hand slapped over my mouth and pressed me close to their body. For a split second, I wondered what in the world Ugo was doing, but my senses told me it wasn't him.

"The urge to kill," Elio's warm breath brushed over my cheek, "every man who touched you this evening is overwhelming." I was momentarily paralyzed at his presence. His fingers brushed down my arm as he breathed me in.

I stepped away and locked the door behind me then turned and studied his face for a moment, then I jumped into his arms and slammed my lips to his. His lips matched my intensity as my mind clouded with emotion. His hands were in my hair, around my waist, then touching me everywhere he could reach.

I had missed his touch, his taste, his smell, and my senses were flipping out, needing more. He slid his arms down and lifted me off the floor, taking a few steps to carry us behind a barrier to be out of view if the door opened. Suddenly, my back was to the wall, and he was kissing me harder. I knew his body and his behavior as if it were my own, and something must have happened, because he wasn't thinking clearly.

Wait. I wasn't thinking clearly either.

"Elio?" I whispered when he finally let me come up for air. "You can't be here! It's too risky!"

"Stop," he warned as he went for the ties on the back of my dress. I wanted to give in so badly, but…I reached back and grabbed his frantic hands, pulling them away from my dress.

"There isn't time for this. Stop. Someone might come in."

"Let them." He licked from my collarbone to my ear while his hands flexed on my hips, then he moved them up to palm my breasts through my corset. I gasped as my body reacted to him, but I knew I had to stop this. I was the guest of honor and would be missed.

"Elio, stop." I pressed my hands on his chest and pushed him with all my might. His eyes burned with desire as he covered his mouth like he was about to lose it. "What happened? Why are you here?"

"I can't," he blurted but stopped himself.

"Can't what?" I wanted to hear him out, but I also

needed him to get the hell out of there.

"I can't control myself. My mind is spinning, and nothing is right. There are only two ways I can get control, fucking you or murder."

"It better not be murder because I need these people right now, so the body count will have to wait," I joked darkly, but he didn't find my humor funny.

"I should never have agreed to this."

"You didn't have a choice," I reminded him and didn't back down from his scary glare. "How did you get in here?"

"Ugo," he answered. "He's been giving me updates. And Wyatt filled me in on a few things, too." His eyebrows rose. "Did you give them the location?"

"Yes." I closed my eyes as everything clicked into place. "Of course," I sighed. "So, he filled you in on Mariano?"

"You should have told me."

I wanted to breathe fire at the two of them. At my best friend for sharing something that wasn't his to share, and at Elio for risking everything because he was struggling with us being apart.

"You promised you told me everything." He stuck a finger in my face.

"And you promised you'd never ever hurt me again. So, let's not pretend that we're playing the truth game anymore." I stepped back as he reached for my hand. "Look, the past is the past. It can't be changed, but we can learn from it. We came to an understanding, Elio, an agreement, of how this entire thing would play out, but don't mistake what this is for something it's not. We are nowhere even close to being okay."

"We'll discuss that later. You need to hear me out, Sienna."

"No, I don't." I lifted a hand when he went to take a step toward me. "Seriously, Elio, the damage that you've caused me is enough for three lifetimes."

"I never meant to hurt you."

"Regardless, you did."

He let out a frustrated breath and clenched his fists as he thought. "I'm sorry, Sienna."

"I know." I took a deep breath. "And I know not all of what happened before was your fault. You were being manipulated by your nonna, someone you trusted and loved dearly. It just hurts you couldn't hear or trust me through all that."

"Okay, let's do this now." He flexed his jaw and nodded a few times while he tried to sort out his thoughts. "I've only ever loved you. We fell into love so easily that things just worked. I think we can both agree none of us saw this storm coming. So, we need to pivot and start from the beginning again. We need to, I don't know, learn how to love with obstacles?"

I smiled at his words and allowed my tightly folded arms to relax. I could feel my defenses slowly dissolve as he struggled to make me understand what was in his head.

"I've made my fair share of mistakes, and I'm going to say the wrong things when I mean to say the right things. It's been ingrained in me to listen to my elders since I was a little boy. I can see my position has hurt you and probably might again, but call me selfish, I still want you." He came closer as he went on. "I'm sorry, but I love you in the worst of ways. I rely on you emotionally, physically, mentally, and fuck, I don't care." He took a deep breath.

"Elio." I wanted to stop him, but he held up his hand, and I stopped talking.

"The fairytales, romance books, great movies, whatever, are based on a version of love that only very few people actually find." He made a low growling sound that jolted my body awake, alerting me he was primal tonight. "You consume me in ways that make the very air I breathe meaningless. To me you're *that* love. I can't let that go—I won't let go." He relaxed his shoulders and looked at me with such raw emotion it held me hostage. "So, here I am. Asking one last time for forgiveness. I want it to be just us from now on."

I looked at him as he stood there breathing hard. His body was wound like a spring.

"If you ever question me like that again, that's it."

"I know." He cleared his throat, visibly uncomfortable.

"I'm scared to let my guard down again with you."

"I don't blame you, but," he slid a warm hand around my waist and pressed me into his hard body, "you will never find a man who loves you as much as I do."

"Maybe not," I warned as he leaned down to capture my lips. "Elio," I said his name as his lips touched mine, "I can't take another broken heart."

"You have my word." He kissed me, hard, and I struggled to keep my head on straight. I knew tonight was different. I knew this was it, and he knew it too.

"Speaking of trust," I stepped back, suddenly realizing where we were, "I need to get back there. I've a lot of people to meet."

"You mean a lot of men to meet."

I laughed. "Men and women."

He tilted his head back and whispered something I couldn't understand. "Sienna, do you even know what this party is for?"

"Please don't think so little of me. It's an introduction to the family."

He chuckled. "It's to find you a husband, to control you. Didn't Ugo warn you?"

"What?" I looked toward the door while I fought through the fog of having Elio here in this very room with me, in the Coppola house, no less. There were a ton more men than women out there, and I suddenly pictured their expressions in my head. I should have seen it, and I felt stupid for not realizing what was going on. Ugo had been about to share something before we got interrupted by Nonna Rosa.

"Welcome to an old school mafia family." Elio shook his head, annoyed with the entire situation. "They are nervous of your intentions and want to make sure you are controlled by a man," he went on. "I wonder how long before they realize you're uncontrollable."

"Excuse me?" My temper flared.

"It's one of the many things I love about you, Sienna,"

he growled and stepped forward, "but no man—I repeat, no man—will have you but me."

"We have some work to do on our relationship, but know this. I'm not interested in anyone but you." I spoke the truth.

"Sienna." He tugged me close, and unlike the man on the dance floor, when Elio did it, I wanted it and more. My hands fell to my sides, and he leaned in, inhaling my hair with a moan. "If I could only go back to that day we met at the pond. I would take you and never look back. I would give up everything I have to undo the pain I caused you. I can't think straight, I can't work, I can barely breathe when you're not around, and now things are so…" He paused as his forehead hit mine. "I just need you." His hands tightened on my hips, and I was so turned on. I wished I wasn't, not now, but I was.

"Elio, I've changed a lot these past few months. I'm not the same woman I was when I left the Hill House. I'm stronger and—"

We both froze when we heard the click of the door handle. Then the sound of a key in the lock.

"And you've never been sexier." He finished my sentence and kissed me, then gave me a little push ahead and swung to hide behind a partition.

"There you are." Salvo held up a bottle of water. "I've been looking for you everywhere. Someone told me you had come in here." I recovered quickly and moved toward him as I fought the urge to look back toward Elio. "Are you okay? You look a little flushed."

"Yes." I spoke clearly. "I just needed a few moments

to myself. I have a lot to think about."

"I should think so," he smiled warmly, "but Nonna Rosa is looking for you. Don't you think you should get back?"

"Of course." I smiled at him as he opened the door. I nodded for him to lead the way, and as he turned his back, I glanced behind the partition and saw that Elio had vanished.

Chapter
TWELVE

Sienna

Salvo hovered as I stood among the men. They formed a horseshoe around me as they all tried to get my attention. I couldn't believe I'd missed all the signs before. Every so often, I shut my eyes and focused myself as I homed in on Elio's scent that still clung to my skin. I wondered if anyone else could smell him. When one of the men touched my arm, I almost quivered, remembering who had touched me there last. Elio was right; we needed to be together physically just as much as mentally. Now I found myself flustered and needing release.

"Those are lovely earrings." Leonardo reached up, and his hand brushed by my already sensitive skin.

"Thank you." I forced a smile as I caught Nonna Rosa looking my way and gave her a nod.

Yes, look at me, doing the one thing you'd hoped I'd fail at. Keep swinging, Nonna, because I'm determined more than ever to tear down your kingdom.

"Nice job," Ugo muttered as he joined me at the table. I'd finally given in and allowed myself to sit. "You outlasted the very last guest."

"I've never been more tired."

"Let's get you up to your room, shall we?" He went to offer a hand but stopped himself, looking around. "Follow me up," he said without smiling and started ahead of me.

"How long do I have?" I asked once we were inside my room.

"Until?"

"Until I'm expected to marry one of them." I kicked off my shoes. "Elio filled me in."

"Yeah," he sank to the table, "I'm not sure, maybe a few months."

"Can we pull this off by then?"

"We can." He blew out his cheeks, showing how tired he was. "We'll just need to dig deeper and faster."

"And if we don't?"

"Plan B." He half smiled. "Basically, a lot of guns."

"I see." I slipped behind the partition and changed out of the dress. I sagged as my ribs thanked me for the room to breathe again. "Thank you, Ugo."

"For what?"

"For this, but for also keeping Elio in the know. I

appreciate you're willing to get along with him, unlike my mother." I stepped back around to find him slumped in a chair.

"Look, Sienna," his tone made me still, "your mother means well, but she carries a lot of hate inside her. I don't agree with how she's withheld things from you, but I also know there's even more she hasn't shared."

"Like?"

"I don't know, but I think Oscar may." He rubbed his head. "It might be worth confronting her because if we're going to pull this off, you need to know everything."

"Yeah," I sank down onto the bed, "you're right." I hated the idea of seeing my mother, but Ugo was right. I still wondered who'd sent her the magazine all those months ago.

"I'm tired. I'm going to bed." Ugo groaned and opened the door, looking both ways.

"Night, Ugo," I called after him, knowing he couldn't hear me. I was exhausted and forced myself up to prepare for bed. Tomorrow would be an interesting day, and I knew I needed my sleep if I was going to face it head on.

"You certainly seemed to enjoy the party," Nonna Rosa greeted me at breakfast. I sat outside on the patio to appreciate the warm sunshine.

"I actually had a lovely time. I really enjoyed spending time with Leonardo." I smiled at her. I was pleased I'd made a connection with someone who was actually interesting and hadn't tried to force himself on me or bore me to death.

"You did seem to win over quite a few guests." She nodded approvingly. "Did any stand out to you?"

"A few." I nodded. "Leonardo, Gabriel," I lied, seeing if she'd offer up anything about him, "and Salvo seemed nice."

"Salvo is a good man. He's been with the family for a long time. He and Stefano have been friends for as long as I can remember. Gabriel is all business and a lot older than you. I would be concerned about his ability to have a son."

"Nonna Rosa," I lifted a leg to tuck it under me as I turned to see her better, "with all due respect to the family, I don't need a man to become the Don. I can do this on my own. I've been through more than most have in one lifetime and still managed to come out on top."

"You have, and you're very much like your father in that respect. But rules are rules, and until my generation is gone, it's still a man's world. So," she looked out over the grounds, "if you want to rule, you'll need to find a man." She looked at me with a knowing expression and hesitated for a few beats. "A man you can control. A front, if you will."

Oh, what I wouldn't have done for Stefano to hear Nonna say that.

"Understand?" She eyed me.

"Not really, but I see what you're saying. Behind every man is a powerful woman. I just hate that it's necessary." I sagged back into my seat, feeling annoyed that they couldn't move with the times. Although, what did I care? I was just waiting for the right time to help bring this sexist old syndicate to the ground.

We sat there for a while as I enjoyed my coffee, then she tapped her nail on the top of her cane.

"How are you adjusting to life here?" She leaned in, and her creepy cane-for-show caught the sunlight as she studied my face.

"Where to begin?" I half chuckled then sighed as I hugged my warm drink. "That's like asking me to fill a jar one grain of sand at a time." I let her see me swipe a tear away. "I don't know, I guess I just thought by coming here I would get to know my family, get some answers, find my place. Instead, I'm viewed like an enemy by Stefano and, I must say, I felt like I was being paraded around like a prize in my new dress last night at that party." I glanced at her, and she quickly guarded her expression.

To my surprise, she nodded like she understood. "I suppose I jumped a little quickly with your arrival. This has been an adjustment for us, too." She glanced at me. "But you're part of my son, and therefore part of me as well."

"What was he like?" I sniffed, dropping my guard slightly as real emotion took hold. I missed Andrea terribly. I missed her warmth and our easy talks.

"Strong. and smart." She paused. "A bit wild at times. He was a good Don. We were very proud of him, and he ran our syndicate in the proper way."

"What's the proper way?" I tucked my feet up tighter and looked at her.

"With an iron fist." She looked straight into my eyes. "You need to take a hard line. Family first. Don't waste time trying to save souls. No soul is more important than your own."

"Seems pretty lonely."

"Gain, pain, sacrifice, triumph, those are the words the Coppola family live by. We don't need anyone else to make us happy. We can do that on our own. But what we did need was a son."

"And you got me instead." I felt unwanted all over again, especially when she didn't say anything. "Did anyone even love me?"

"Love is not what's important. You have to understand. It's not that we didn't love you, but we needed a son, and Theo needed to try again. But your mother sabotaged any chance of that happening."

"What do you mean?"

"Elenora insisted on bringing her brother to live with us while she was pregnant. Some nonsense about needing her own family, as if we weren't enough. He stirred up all kinds of trouble and often got between my son and your mother, where he had no place to be. Then he wanted someone who was Theo's. She was pregnant, too, for Pete's sake. Then, apparently, your mother got herself mixed up with the Capris' consigliere." She scoffed in disgust. "As if her brother wasn't trouble enough. He had entirely too much control over your mother. What a lot of hoopla it all was. He needed to leave before he twisted her head any more than he already had."

"Leave?" My skin broke out in goosebumps, and the hair on my neck told me to get up and walk away, but I didn't. I listened to the story that unfolded in front of me like a train wreck. "Did you…" I couldn't find the words. "Was it…" Again, I fumbled.

"We are Coppolas." She turned her head and met my gaze straight on. "When someone stands in our way, we deal with it. Your mother was stressed enough with just weeks left before your birth. So, we dealt with it." She gave a light shrug like it was nothing.

*Whoa…breathe…*So she knew my mother was interested in Francesco. That must have been why they blamed my uncle's death on the Capris, so she'd stay away from them. I couldn't get over the level of evil these people would lower themselves to.

"What's best to take away from this story, Alessia, is that I know everything that goes on in this house. Just like I knew everything that went on in your mother's. Her parents tried to fix the books, thinking they could put something over on us. They were lucky we didn't take them all out. Crooks, the lot of them. Elenora should've felt blessed to be here. It was only her slim frame and eye color that drew Theo to her. We weren't the only ones who saw her family for who they were. There were others coming for them. We were kinder than they'd have been."

Kinder…killing my uncle was kind? Stripping my mama of everything and taking her away from all that she knew was kind? It took everything in my body not to react to her words. Francesco didn't lie; it was the Coppolas who killed my uncle.

"Do you have the stomach, my dear, to take over such a powerful syndicate and deal with situations as they come?"

It took a lot, but I pushed what I had just heard aside and answered. "I do."

"All right." She motioned for one of the soldiers to step forward. "To rule, you must be able to take without so much as a thought." She pulled out a handgun and set it next to me. "Babies are born every day, but true leaders are rare to find, and—"

Bang!

I pulled the trigger, and the soldier jerked backward as he grabbed his chest in shock then fell to the ground. I flipped the gun around with my fingers and handed it back to her as the man still twitched in the fetal position.

"I have the stomach for it, Nonna, and my moral compass was compromised years ago." For the first time, Nonna Rosa smiled her approval right up to her eyes. I leaned back in my chair and pressed my fingers together so as not to reveal my nerves. The thought that occurred to me in that moment was how odd it was that killing had become something I could separate in my head quite easily. I wasn't sure how I felt about that yet. Not wanting to pull at that thread, I shook it off. "Have the Capris been spotted yet?"

"Yes. Stefano confirmed it."

"Excellent." I nodded approvingly and avoided the heap of a body in front of me. "I hope we can start to add trust to my list."

"Mm." I could tell she was trying to figure me out. *Good luck with that.*

"I'll send someone to clean that up." She stood and walked from the table. I waited a beat then hurried inside to my room.

As I sat on the bed against a couple of scrunched up pillows, I allowed myself to slip into the memory of how Elio discovered my plan to come here. My head still spun with the choices I'd made.

"What the hell are you doing here, Elio?" I shouted as he stood fuming in the hallway of my hotel room. "I don't have time for this. You need to leave now!" He looked like he was about to kill someone with his bare hands.

"Me? What the hell are you doing, Sienna?"

"I've got this, Elio." I tried to push by him, but he swung me around by the arm and pushed me into the wall. "Let me go."

"Sienna. You're going to hear me out whether you want to or not!"

"No, Elio."

"You will or I'll tie you down and make you fucking listen." He caught my chin and stared deep into my eyes. "I know you didn't know who you were. We discussed that, but you weren't supposed to leave yet."

"You think I'd stay in that house? With your nonna who wants me dead? Of course, I left!" I tried to wiggle free, but he outweighed me by a lot and was built like a friggin' tree. "She's insane and tried to run me out of the

city. She dumped me off in the middle of nowhere with nothing but a train ticket to Rome."

"I know," he gritted through clenched teeth, as though he had the right to be angry with me.

"Then why turn your back on me? Why let me think you believed your psychotic nonna?"

"Because only moments before I learned the truth about her, that she knew who you were before any of us did."

"Well, that's great, Elio, really." I dripped with sarcasm, knowing it would piss him off. "I'm glad that life is one big chessboard for you and your family to play on."

"You think I wanted this to happen?" he shouted. "To be separated once again from the only woman I ever loved? I needed her to think I hated you, so that I could flip the tables on her and take over what was mine. Remember, I risked everything to see you in the bedroom that night, because I love you more than anything or anyone. But before I got the chance to tell you my plan, you left, and then I find out from Ugo what you were planning to do!"

"Okay, okay. I'm listening to what you're saying, but I need to do this. I've got this."

"Are you mad? Sienna, one wrong move and they'll kill you! Not to mention what'll happen when Stefano finds out who you are."

I breathed deep to calm my own fuming anger. I knew us getting mad at one another would only end one way, and though I craved this man, my heart couldn't take another tug of war. "I need you to hear me." I slapped my hand over his mouth as he went to speak. "It's my turn to talk now, okay?" His eyes squinted into an angry glare, but I knew he was listening.

Glad I finally had his attention, I removed my hand and kept my voice even and logical.

"This isn't some plan we hatched overnight. This has been carefully mapped and thought out. Ugo and Oscar have done their research. They still have allies within the Coppola household, and the uncles still stand firmly behind the family rings. This," I held up my hand between us and wiggled the ugly ring, "is my ticket in. I will gain their trust, play their game, and when they least expect it, I will implode the syndicate from the inside out."

"It's suicide," he grunted.

"No, it's smart." I felt my confidence kick in. "Think about it. The Capris have been fighting the Coppolas for how long? Think of all the lives that've been lost. Now, a child from one of the families was taken from the pack and raised unknowingly by the enemy. What a plot twist that is." I smiled, feeling the excitement. "So, imagine their confusion when I return wearing my family ring with a DNA test in my hand, ready to take over the family business."

"And how will you ever gain their trust? They know we're together."

"They knew we were together," I corrected, and his face scrunched in anger. "And I'll tell them the real truth, that I had no idea who I really was, and as soon as I did,

I left and came back to them."

"It's not enough." He pushed off the wall and covered his face like his world was crumbling around him.

"Elio," I sighed, "you know this is a great idea."

"It's a brilliant idea," he snapped. "With the right plays, this could work. This could be the end of the Coppolas."

"Exactly!"

"But not for you." is

His shoulders fell. "I can't let you do this."

"Oh, Elio," I shook my head at the man who killed for a living, a man most people feared, and laid it out for him. "It's just not up to you anymore. Despite our painful history, this time around I'm coming out stronger and wiser. My monster blood is the key to ending this lifelong feud to join the two syndicates. The family will have the Don they deserve to have, you. You can't see it because you're blinded by your need to keep me under your protection, but I see it clearly, and it's the best move we have left."

"No, it's not."

"So," I ignored his last comment, "I'm going to do this."

"But why?"

"Because when this all comes to a head and your family rises to the top, there won't be any doubt of where my loyalty belongs. And I could go back to my life with my integrity intact and know I did right by all of you."

"Go back?" His head did a quick shake. "You can't

possibly think I'll allow you to go back to your old life. You belong with me."

"I wish you could set aside your alpha male quality for a just a moment and hear what I actually just said to you. Could." I repeated the word, not wanting to end what we had either. He just needed to know this move was important for me too.

He closed his eyes and took a second to calm himself. I fully expected him to come at this from a different angle and try to dominate me, but instead, when his eyes opened, I could see acceptance. He knew I wasn't going to budge.

"I've known you a lifetime, so I know this is something you are going to do with or without me." His words were almost chilling as he gave in. "So, I'm going to help you, but if you want this to work, you have to play their game better than they do."

"I'm listening."

"I know they'll let you in. Their curiosity will get the better of them, but it's getting past the grandmother that will be your biggest hurdle. The elders have a lot of power."

"No kidding," I muttered, but he ignored me. I could almost smell the smoke as his brain worked overtime.

"I could slip you my location now and then via a third party. That way, you can prove to them that you can be useful. You can start to gain their trust. But," he stepped closer, "you need to know they'll test you in unspeakable ways. You'll have to react fast without thought. Any hesitation and they'll see right through you."

"I can do that."

His hand slipped into my hair, and he pulled my head back gently so I'd look at him. I was thankful I'd just finished covering up most of the bruises left over from Mariano.

"What happened after you left my house with my nonna? Did she hurt you?"

His eyes showed me a glimpse of the storm raging inside him. The truth was on the tip of my tongue, but I couldn't say the words. "Just some threats, if I returned to the house."

"Is that it?"

"Yes." He nodded, and I realized he was spinning out with everything else, so he didn't spot my lie. I left out the part about how Mariano attacked me because Elio had enough on his plate right now. I could deal with my coke-snorting want-to-be lover myself.

"All right." His tongue touched his lips as he thought. "The number one thing is we can't see one another. We're over, you hate me for everything I've done, and you're more than ready to educate the Coppolas on the Capris' way of life."

"Oh, Elio." I hated this. I wished our lives were anything but this.

"We can't communicate, no phone calls or texts, completely cut off." His lips hovered over mine, and I drank in his scent, preserving this moment like the addict I was. "Nonna's got soldiers everywhere, including the lobby of this hotel. Always know you're never far from listening ears. The Coppolas pay good money for gossip, and Nonna's looking for any excuse to prove that I can't let you go."

"Okay." I barely got the word out.

"I was followed here, so if this is the end for now," his jaw ticked like the words ate at his soul, "we'd better make it look good." He dove down and caught my lips with his as he moved my hands to the jacket of his suit. "Hate me Sienna, show them we fought."

I let my mind go to all the painful emotions that had pierced my heart and reminded myself that this life was meant to be painful. It wasn't the happy fairytale we were promised in storybooks. I pulled my hand back and slapped him across his face. He growled then grabbed my hand and turned my ring around, so it was facing inward.

"Again," he ordered, but when I hesitated, he shook his head. "You see, that's the problem, why you can't do this. You can't think, you just need to react."

Slap!

He lunged forward and grabbed my head and stole my breath as he forced my mouth open, kissing me with such force that I yanked on his shirt and sent the top two buttons flying across the room. I jumped in his arms and wildly tousled his hair with my frantic hands. He massaged my thighs as my legs squeezed his hips. We were savages.

We weren't okay, but we needed to sell this, and I wasn't about to let his nonna win. No one was going to win but us.

Suddenly, he put me down then fell to his knees, hiked up my dress, and disappeared underneath.

"Elio!" I moaned as I lifted one leg up over his shoulder, and his tongue split my folds. "This wasn't part of the plan." I tried to steady myself, but he wasn't wasting any time. He dove his skilled tongue deep inside me, circling my sensitive nub. My head clouded, and my body temperature rose to the point of pain.

Anger, frustration, and need hit me all at once. I was becoming crazed in the cocktail of emotion. My stomach tightened, sending confusing signals to my head. Once again, my heart tossed caution to the wind, and my mind was left to stand guard solo.

Stop thinking... *I begged myself*...just have this moment. Say goodbye now so we can say hello again another time.

My legs started to quiver, and that lovely ball of excitement grew. Hunger hummed low in my pelvis, warning me I was close. "Yes," I almost screamed, "more, Elio."

Then he was gone, and I felt everything inside me jerk back into a tight coil.

"What the hell!" I snapped when he stood. "Why did you stop?"

"Two reasons. One, if you're going to be pissed at me, you need to act like it."

"I already was!"

"A sexually frustrated woman is more believable. And two," he hovered over me, and I could smell my arousal on his breath, which it was oddly intoxicating,

"just remember who belongs down there and who doesn't."

"Screw you," I snarled.

"Oh, Sienna," he groaned pressing his erection into my belly, "anytime." He smirked then went back to his scowl. "Grab your stuff, and let's go."

"Sienna. Sienna." A sudden shake had my eyes blinking as I fought to hold on to the memory. Ugo was by my side, looking frantic. I shook the memory off and gave him my attention. "You have to come. Your mother's in town, and I can't hold her back anymore."

"Oh, shit." I rubbed my head, knowing my day was only going to get worse from here.

Chapter

THIRTEEN

Elenora

I glared at the man who stared at me from across the dingy bar and wished Ugo had chosen another place to meet. This place was on the outskirts of town, and the smell alone would have kept most people away. The table was sticky, and the chairs made me think I'd have to burn my dress after we left. I used a napkin to try to brush some of the crumbs from the surface, but they only stuck to something that had been spilled earlier.

"Elenora," Oscar stood next to me like the loyal bodyguard he was, "they're here."

Sienna looked better than I expected, which meant they hadn't been too hard on her yet. I knew it would only be a matter of time before they'd wear down her spirit and suck her dry of any life.

"Mama," she greeted me as she approached.

"I'd stand, but I'm afraid my dress wouldn't come with me." I raised my nose at the place and made a face.

"No need for that." She eased into the chair and looked for a clean spot for her purse. She settled on her lap. "How have you been?"

"Don't." I wasn't in the mood for games. "I'm so furious with you I can barely sleep."

"Well, nothing like ripping the bandage off." She glanced at Ugo, who hadn't dared to look at me.

"You didn't give me the courtesy of knowing what you were up to before you made such a horrible decision, so why should I play nice?" I shrugged, still annoyed that my own flesh and blood would think so little of me.

"Mama," she said calmly, "I wasn't trying to go behind your back."

"But you did."

"Wow." She shook her head and looked up at the ceiling, "no one ever questioned my actions back when I was growing up and trying to survive, but now I have to run my every move by you and everyone else?"

"No one said life was fair," I muttered in frustration.

"Oh, trust me, I've learned that countless times already." She held up a hand when I went to cut in. "It took me almost dying for you to tell me my father was dead, and then I had to be abducted before you told me who I really was. I'm so tired of having to piece clues together to figure things out when everyone else around me knows my truth."

"Don't be dramatic, dear. That's water under the bridge at this point, and it's not the reason I'm here. This little charade of yours…"

"Mother," she cut me off, "this little charade, as you call it, is going to be our best way out. It was my decision to go to the Coppolas, not just for answers but to also make one of the biggest moves that a syndicate has ever seen. So, you can sit there and be upset all you like. I'm living at the Coppola house for the time being while I gather as much information as I can."

"It's just not safe."

"No, it isn't. But I'm smart and know how to play the game, and I've already learned a lot of things about myself, which I'm tired of waiting to find out from you. By the way, I've also learned some powerful information about you from Nonna Rosa."

"Nonna Rosa knows nothing about me." I leaned forward with my face twisted to be sure she knew that woman was wicked.

"Nonna Rosa had your brother killed. It wasn't Piero. She knew you liked Francesco, and she blamed the murder on the Capris to make sure you wouldn't leave Theo for him."

I pressed my hand to my chest in frustration with what was happening here. The evilness that draped over that family was slowly seeping into my child.

"Did she admit to you that she pulled the trigger? Did she actually say she killed Angelo?"

"No, but she told me the story—"

"Why can't you see the writing on the wall, Sienna?"

"What?"

"She's playing you to see if you'd come to me and tell me that. She wanted you to flush me out so she can kill me. Just like she's done to so many others."

Sienna shook her head, confused.

"Why would she make up a story about killing your brother? Who does that?"

"A very smart woman."

"I just don't see it."

"That's because you're so naïve."

"Wow." She pulled her sunglasses out of her purse and tugged it over her shoulder, preparing to leave. "As always, Mother, this has been a warming experience."

Oscar stepped forward to stop her, but I shook my head. "Where is Elio in this whole thing?" I tossed at her. "I thought at the very least he was protecting you from them."

"We're not together anymore." She looked away and cleared her throat.

"I thought you loved him."

Her gaze snapped over to mine. "Imagine his surprise to find out that I'm the daughter of their sworn enemy. Thanks for the heads up on that, by the way."

"You think I'm proud of who your father was?"

"Proud?" She scoffed. "I don't care if you're proud or not. You played puppet with my life, while you ruined yours."

"Excuse me?" How dared she make light of the fact that I'd given her life?

"Mama," she took a deep breath, "you're living in

the past, dwelling on things you can't control anymore. You're letting the man you've loved your entire life walk away because you don't want to see the truth. You hold a grudge over Piero for something he didn't even do, and now your only daughter is standing right here in front of you telling you I've been forced to find out about myself in the only way I can." She paused and took a step closer to me. "And when I've figured out all I want, I'll dig deep and rip out the very heart of the syndicate that hurt you and everyone else around me. There'll be nothing left but bone dust."

"Sienna," I grabbed her arm as she turned to leave, "it's not safe. There's a—"

"Mama," her tone made me snap my mouth shut, "do you still have copies of your father's cooked books?"

"What?" My head rocked back in confusion. How did she know about those?

"The books," she leaned closer and lowered her voice, "the ones your father kept for his company, do you still have them?"

"No," I lied.

"If you did, I'd really like to see them."

"Well, I don't." I hated that she knew that about my papa. I'd never forgiven my parents for what they'd done, but nonetheless, they were my parents. She never knew them, so what right did she have to cast judgement? "Need I remind you that what you're hearing there isn't—"

"The time to play my mother has passed. Please, just be supportive of this decision."

I licked my lips, feeling outraged that we'd gotten to this place, but I caught Oscar's face and slowly released her from my grip.

"Mama," she pulled on the collar of her jacket to put it back in place, "I must know, is there anything else I should know about you, my father, or anything that might come up that could blindside me?" She stared at me as if reading my mind. "I'm begging you as your only child, spare me any more pain and let the truth come from you. Please, Mama?"

Images flashed in my head, but I couldn't put them into words. How could I when she was in love with a Capri and living at the Coppolas'? "I wanted to give you the world, Sienna, and look what you did with it." Her face stretched as if my words cut her like glass. "You decided to be a part of both the worlds that brought your mother the most pain."

"And you, Mother, just chose your own hate for them over your only child." She shook her head in disappointment. "Please don't contact me again."

"Ugo," I sneered once she was out of hearing range, "if anything happens to her, I'll kill you."

"I know." He nodded, standing a little straighter, then he left behind Sienna.

I tapped my fingers on the table as I felt the lack of control fester inside.

"Elenora—" Oscar began, but I cut him off.

"Get the car."

"Where are we going?"

"To figure out what the hell is going on up north."

How could Elio, the man who claimed to love my daughter so much, have let her go into the enemy's house? Did he even know? Well, he was about to.

"Very well." He left, and I tried to fight off the memory, but it took hold anyway.

I curled into a ball on the window seat and watched the rain pour down onto the grounds of the Coppola house. My head hurt, and my stomach rolled liked the perfect storm. Theo had his way with me for nearly two months, and though it was consensual, and we had what I thought was a good talk before we began to make a child, it was what happened afterward that bothered me the most. His total disdain. He would make me promises and then break them. He told me my brother could visit from time to time, but when I would bring it up and ask when, he would act like he had no idea what I was referring to. I felt used and cheap.

"What's wrong with you?" Theo stepped into the room with his towel wrapped low around his hips. His hair was still dripping from his shower. He admired himself in the mirror, and I wanted to roll my eyes at how vain he was. He was nasty toward me and often belittled me in front of others, but because I didn't care about anyone here, I just dismissed it.

"I'm just wondering why you lied to me."

"Which time?" He snagged a shirt from the hanger, and I wanted to toss a candlestick at his head.

"You promised that if I went along with this whole baby thing that you would let my brother stay for a while. I miss him, and you know what they say about a woman

trying to get pregnant."

"That they are a pain in the ass."

I loathe you.

"That a happy woman is more apt to get pregnant than an unhappy one." He shook his head with a laugh. "Well, I don't know about you, Theo," I made a disgusted face, "but the idea of more sex with you isn't very appealing. So, why don't we make every effort to make this work?"

He slammed the dresser drawer shut and thought for a moment.

"Fine. Tell him to come, but if he steps out of line in this house, I won't think twice before kicking him to the curb."

A huge smile broke across my face even as a wave of nausea washed over me. I'd keep that quiet until I was absolutely ready to share. I hated the sweat that broke out along my forehead. It brought back memories I had swallowed back and repressed. I hated my life here.

"Make sure he stays out of my way and keep him the hell away from Noemi."

"That's something I just don't understand."

"Shocker you don't get something," he snapped in his normal jerky behavior.

"Why me when you love her? Is it because she's dating that guy while still seeing you?" I had overheard Theo on the phone a few days ago freaking out about who she was dating. I figured that her dating someone else would make him less interested, but I was wrong.

"It's not up to me who has the child. There's more

to it than you know." He glared at me from the mirror, and I knew I was getting too personal again. He barely ever shared any of the family dynamics with me, so I was always shooting in the dark for information. I simply couldn't help it; I felt so alone here. "Besides, you're merely here to pay your family's debt, and maybe I don't want my woman all stretched and unattractive like you'll be...well, are."

"Because you're something special." I dripped with sarcasm, and he whirled around, shoving his pistol in my face. I was way beyond finished with his arrogant ways, so much so that I stood and held my arms open.

"Go ahead. Undo two months of lousy sex and fake orgasms."

"Listen, you stupid piece of shit," he grabbed a fistful of my hair and yanked my head back so hard it forced me to cry out and scratch at his arms to pull myself back upright, "you'd be so lucky to carry my child. So, hope to be so lucky that when this is over, I don't bury a bullet in your head."

"Pardon me, sir." Oscar once again was there to stop Theo from going too far. My mouth often got me into trouble, as Theo had a temper and could get abusive with me. Generally, he was just verbally abusive, but today I thought I went a little too far. "Ms. Noemi has returned from her weekend trip and is looking for you. Shall I escort her to the dining room where she'll join you for breakfast?"

"Yes," Theo grunted and tossed me to the floor then checked himself again in the mirror. He barged past

Oscar as he left. Yes, go to the woman who probably just spent the weekend with another man. That's not desperate.

"Ms. Elenora," he came rushing to my side and lifted me to my feet, "are you all right?"

"Yes," I huffed, wanting nothing more than to get hold of the gardener's rat poison and dump it all over his toothbrush. My hand went to my stomach without thinking, and his gaze dropped while his mouth opened in shock.

"Are you?"

I looked away and fought the tears, but his hand covered mine, and I looked at him, unsure how to take his affection.

"Just a few weeks, I think." I didn't want any attention until I'd processed it myself, and the longer I could keep it from the family, the better off I'd be. "Could you help me with something, Oscar?"

"Yes," he stepped back, "anything."

"Can you help me get my brother here? I'm not sure I can do this without him."

"Of course." He sat me on the bed. "Like I said, I'll do anything you ask."

A hand suddenly landed on my shoulder. Oscar brought my memory to an end, and I blinked the images away. "The car is ready."

"Thank you," I answered with such emotion that his face scrunched in confusion. I patted his shoulder and led the way out of the nasty dive of a bar.

Chapter FOURTEEN

Elio

I was tired and hungry, but all things considered, things went in our favor. I unlocked the front door and tossed my keys on the side table. I shrugged out of my jacket and rolled my sleeves up my forearms as I headed for the bar, needing anything to take the edge off.

"Hey, there." Papa pulled off his glasses and closed one of Sienna's journals, placing it on the table. "How did it go?"

"Good." I tugged the crystal top off the rum decanter and poured a double for him and the same for myself. I handed him one, and we tapped glasses. I took a seat on the couch across from him. "They played right into it. We drove the car into the courtyard, and Roman played his part perfectly. Just as the transaction was done and the car was pulling out, one of Stefano's Jeeps showed up."

"Was he there?"

"No, it was Salvo." Papa made a sound of disgust. Salvo was a snake, though he was better at hiding it than Stefano. We'd had a few run-ins over the years, and I knew enough not to trust anyone who was associated with him. Especially the women he kept close. "The Jeep followed our car, and they led them on a long, wild chase up north. They only lost them about an hour ago."

"Do you think it worked?"

"Time will tell." I leaned forward and rubbed my stomach, hating the uneasy feeling that sat directly in the center of my gut.

"How was she?" he finally asked after a few moments had passed. I had shared Sienna's plans with my father and Francesco. They needed to understand what was happening so we could all plan accordingly.

"I don't know." I rested my hands behind my head and leaned back. "She sure wasn't falling apart, but Salvo has his sights on her."

Papa chuckled as he sipped his drink. "What I wouldn't do to see her go head-to-head with him."

"Or head to sheets." I couldn't help my gloomy tone.

"Oh, son," he shook his head, "that's the Capri curse you're battling with right there."

"The what?"

"The male side of this family lets jealousy run amok when we're in love. I've never seen you jealous of anyone but her, and I understand that feeling firsthand. I've taken out my fair share of men who've so much as looked in your mother's direction."

"Is this supposed to make me feel better?"

"Coppola blood or not, Sienna loves you. Yes, she's upset, but she's still here after everything that's happened, and that alone speaks volumes."

"She mentioned about going home after all of this."

"Yeah, she's hurting, again, and I'm shocked she even wants to do this. You know she's still in love with you."

"I know, but what am I supposed to do with all those men sniffing around what's mine?"

"Fight for her." He held up a finger. "But no one can know that you are. So, you need to get creative. Nothing could ever stand in the way of my love for your mother, but if I was being tested like you are, I'd go to great lengths to show her how I felt."

"You're right." He *was* right, if we were going to spend our life together, I needed to start to repair it now and not wait.

"Son, we all love that girl. Do you think, if she was anyone else, we'd let her live after what we found out? No. She'd be dumped in a river somewhere, joining the other members of her family."

"I don't know, Papa, she's getting in really deep with them."

"Which is what she needs to do."

"Yes, but what if she needs me?"

"She'll let you or Ugo know if she needs you." He

smiled. "I can't wait to see that family fall. I'll bask in the rubble when she takes them down."

"Yeah." I nodded, feeling so burned out on things I couldn't control. "So, let's see, we have no notebook, Anna and Mariano have slipped through our fingers, my girl is playing double agent in the enemy's house, the mole you flushed out of Nonna's house never made it home, and Nonna has me being watched by an old colleague of mine."

Papa leaned forward and rubbed the back of his neck while he thought.

"I agree the waters are murky right now, but everything needs to continue to run as normal. Any change, and they'll suspect something. Behind the scenes, I know we've had to pull back and pivot our original plan in order to help out Sienna with this new one. But, son, it's a good plan, and we haven't had a move this big, ever."

"When should we tell Mama?" He made a face, and I knew she already knew. "And?"

"She isn't happy that Sienna is there, but she has confidence in her. She also knows you wouldn't dream of letting Sienna go after this thing is done."

"Smart woman."

"You have no idea." He chuckled to himself, and I only hoped that someday my marriage would be like theirs. "Let that jealousy curse in from time to time, *figlio*. It will keep you on your toes and won't let you take her for granted."

Francesco wormed his way into my thoughts, and

I asked a question that had been on my mind for some time now.

"Do we know what Elenora and Francesco's plan was after she gave him Sienna to hide?" Papa slid his finger over the spine of her journal. I knew he had been reading it.

"I don't think they really had a plan other than to get Sienna out of there. Francesco alluded to some growing problems within the Coppola house and how Theo was getting more physical. I think it was only a matter of time before something would have happened."

"Hmm, okay." I thought about how frightening it must have been living under that roof and what it must be like now.

"However, I don't think Francesco had any idea Elenora was going to be basically absent from Sienna's life. He did mention that she wasn't very maternal and would even go silent for years on him."

"Begs you to wonder just what she was up to."

"I wondered the same thing." He leaned back. "She was running from something, but Francesco never knew exactly what. He tried to help, but she'd never share any more than just a simple 'I can't tell you.' Apparently, when she returned here and located Sienna, she was more than a little angry. Francesco assumed it was because of who we were. The Capris. And I do think he's right in that, but my gut tells me there's more."

"Mine does, too."

"I guess time will bring the truth."

I nodded and tried to relax, and then eyed the journal

again.

"Find anything?"

"Just a young girl looking for answers at a time when she really needed them."

He went behind the bar to wash out his glass while I stared at the notebook with an idea. Papa left, and I stretched out on the couch, needing to rest my head for a bit.

I hadn't meant to sleep through the night, and morning came way too quickly. I stretched my sore neck and hurried to get ready for the day.

I parked in my reserved spot right next to a shade tree and opened the door to my office building. Niccola and Vinni had met me at the dockyard early that morning so we could go over the tapes from the last two weeks. It had been quiet, and our guess was that Stefano and his rats had a certain guest at their house who was now monopolizing their concentration. I had to quickly push away the thought of Sienna living there.

"Mr. Capri." My receptionist, Sofia, struggled to get her heels back on as she hobbled over to greet me. "Your ten o'clock cancelled, I'm afraid, sir, but your meeting with Smith and Lodge is still a go this afternoon. Also, ah…"

She struggled to keep up with me, but I didn't break stride, as I needed to get behind closed doors to settle my head. I was concerned that the Coppolas might try another distraction while they dealt with Sienna. I opened the door and stopped short when I saw who sat like royalty on my very expensive lambskin couch.

"Mrs. Violetta is here," she said, and I shot Elenora and Oscar an annoyed look. "I'm sorry. They didn't want to wait in the conference room."

"It's fine," I grunted over my shoulder and waited for her to leave before I approached my desk. "I'd say this is a lovely surprise, but we both know I'd be lying," I said in a dismissive tone.

"We need to have a chat." She didn't get up to greet me. That was one of the problems with Elenora. She lacked respect for me but demanded it for herself.

"Given that you're in my office, without an appointment, I guessed that's why you're here." I shook my mouse and woke my computer up.

"I knew your family was trouble from the start." I didn't react, which pissed her off. "You say you love her, but yet you let her leave."

"And yet you can walk into her life, dump all her truths into a hat, and pluck them out randomly to share with her whenever it suited you."

Out of the corner of my eye, I saw her shake her head. Clearly unhappy with my behavior.

"You sank your claws into her when she was young and vulnerable."

I tossed a file I was holding on the desk, growing quickly annoyed with her allegation. "And where was her mother? Oh, wait, you weren't there. I found a lonely girl by the side of a pond who needed a friend as much as I did."

"How do I know you and Francesco didn't manipulate my daughter?"

"Elenora, please, don't insult me."

"Can you blame me? Francesco knew the truth. He could have set the entire thing up."

I exhaled as anger heated my neck. "How can you think so little of the man who still loves you?"

"He betrayed my one request."

"No, he did exactly what he needed to do to protect your daughter."

"How could you send her to that house?" She blurted what was really on her mind then jumped to her feet like she might burst.

"You think this was my idea?"

"She's there, isn't she?"

"In case you didn't notice, your daughter doesn't listen very well, Elenora. You think I didn't try to stop her?"

"You didn't try hard enough."

I swung around my desk, annoyed she was even here.

"The last time I tried to protect her, we spent a decade apart!" I shouted. "Maybe if you had actually shared some history about living in that house, she wouldn't be there right now!"

"I'm trying!"

"Try harder."

"It's not that easy." She shot a glance over at Oscar, and he shook his head as if to stop her from sharing something.

"What was that?" I swung my gaze between the two of them. When they stayed quiet, I shook my head and pointed to the door. "We're done here."

"Your Aunt Noemi," she held up her hands as if to stop me from physically kicking her out the door, "I think she might have been behind the bombing in the city."

"What?" I blinked, trying to follow the sudden change in topic. "First you point fingers at my *consigliere*, and now you have the nerve to point them at my aunt?"

"I know you saw me with her at the party. You must wonder how she knew me."

"Yeah, I did wonder." I felt a headache come on. "But I also know you well enough now not to hold my breath for the answer."

A knock at the door had my head spinning.

"Pardon me, Mr. Capri," Sofia approached and spoke quietly with her back to my guests, "there's someone else here that wants to see you."

"Who?"

"He'd rather not say, given your present company." She motioned that he was in the room next to my office.

The fact that the man knew who was here told me who it was.

"It's fine." I nodded at Sofia. "We're finished here, anyway."

"Elio," Elenora clutched my arm as I went to leave, and I glared down at her hand and then at her, "don't believe me, fine. Francesco doesn't know the truth, but Sienna does." She paused while I waited for more. "She knows enough that she might be able to see what I see."

"Do you ever wonder why no one believes you? Because though you might be telling some form of the truth, you never just say it all at once." I pushed her hand away and reached back to grab Sienna's journal, holding in front of her face. "You want to make things right with your daughter, here's how."

"What's this?" She slid the journal out of my hand and flipped through the pages.

"It's from several years after we met at the pond. She had so many questions and no mother to answer them. Maybe you could stop racing from your past long enough to be a mother."

"You want me to answer questions from back in her youth?" She looked at me like I was crazy, and I cursed under my breath as I pressed the intercom.

"Please escort these people out, Sofia." As they left my office, Elenora dropped the book on the table with a head shake. The woman didn't deserve to be a mother.

I opened the door on the side of my office to see The Finder staring out the window with something in his hand.

"Sorry to come without a call." He turned to look at me. "I came in the back way with Vinni's help."

"Do you have something for me?"

"I do." He let out a long breath as I came closer. "Elio, you know where my loyalty lies, correct?"

"Yes." Once again, doubt filled my head.

"Good. Remember that when you listen to this." He pressed play on the little recorder, and I heard Nonna's voice.

"Where's the girl?"

"She's living under the Coppola roof," The Finder answered her.

"That's not possible."

"It is if she carries the family ring. She also showed proof of a DNA test."

There was a slight pause and a small gasp.

"Do we know where she got the ring?"

"Her mother, apparently."

"Good Lord, I told that little witch to leave and never return!" Nonna puffed in frustration. "And she was actually welcomed in?"

"Yes."

"Damn…all that time she was living under my roof learning our ways! I tried to get rid of her years ago because my gut told me something wasn't right." Nonna spoke as though she was thinking out loud. "And now she's run off and will share everything she knows with the enemy."

"I truly don't think she knew who she was." Hearing those words, I glanced at The Finder and gave him a slight nod, pleased he'd defended her.

"And Stefano," Nonna's voice continued, "showed up where Elio was making the exchange in Fiano Romano?"

"I'm not sure if Stefano was there, because he wasn't actually spotted, but some of the Coppola soldiers were there."

"Has Elio made any contact with the woman?"

"No. I have both being followed, and no contact's been reported."

"So, for all this time, that little witch lived dormant under my protection while she brainwashed my grandson, for what? For her to report back to that snake den?" Her voice was cold and chilly. "She wasn't good enough for him then and still isn't now. Here's what you're going to do to earn your money."

The Finder looked up from the recorder, and I knew the dark truth about my grandmother was about to be revealed.

"She knows too much. I need you to kill her, and if he gets in the way, you better have two bullets."

Elio

I felt like I was under water. My ears hummed, and my mind idled. I simply couldn't think. I knew Vinni was talking about something, but I couldn't follow. Everything and everyone just seemed to flow around me as though I was in a vacuum. Since the conversation with The Finder, I seemed to be stuck in time, not moving forward or backward, just nothing. My phone buzzed next to me, and I glanced at the screen.

Tieri: It's been a while. I know you have a lot going on, but how about drinks Friday night?

I blinked and was tossed into a memory.

"I've known you for, what, six months now?" Tieri, the name he insisted on going by, grabbed the bottle of

rum from the table and helped himself to a glass. "Every time I leave you alone and return, you have that same face on."

"Your point?"

"Have you gotten any help for that?" He tapped his temple.

"I don't need a shrink, Tullio." I shot him a warning in hopes he'd drop the topic. He was the last person I would discuss Sienna with right now. I wanted to be alone with my pain. I missed her so much it hurt to take a simple breath.

"First, I only told you my real name as a gesture of good faith, but if we're going to do this, it's Tieri."

"Do what, exactly?" I rubbed my head.

"My version of therapy." He beamed and slid a map across the table with the southeastern part of Italy circled. "Do you know who lives there?"

"The Rosario Syndicate owns that land. Why is it circled?"

"Because you've been reading the papers. You've seen what they are doing. The whole place is a slaughter shop. Men, women, and even kids' blood stains the streets. Everyone there lives in fear. The Rosarios are holding on to what little power they have left at everyone else's expense."

"My family is aware of this, and we do plan to deal with it."

"Before or after the Coppolas make their move?" He handed me an email he'd printed off.

"Where did you get this?" I scanned the words. He

was right. The Coppolas did plan to make a move to absorb more land.

"I have someone on the inside." He smiled knowingly but grudgingly moved on when I didn't ask him to reveal who. "It doesn't matter. What does matter is us getting there before them." He tipped the bottle of rum to coat the bottom of my glass.

"Why do I feel you have an idea?"

"We can tell your family's chain of command what's happening, or we, the two of us, can be the Santoro brothers to give you some much needed dark therapy to help with whatever the hell is bothering you."

"Santoro brothers?" I smirked at the name.

"Yes, we'll need to get ahead of the media narrative, so we can be anyone we want."

"Why Santoro?"

"He was from an old movie in the fifties." He shrugged.

"And you want to be like the Il Mostro di Firenze but down south?" I was referring to the group that went on a killing spree in Italy back in 1968.

"I have no clue who they are, but I just know we can't be Tullio and Elio. So, choose a name if you don't like my suggestion, and suit up because we leave tonight." He stood and tucked the map inside his jacket pocket.

"Tonight?"

"Sometimes the best therapy is the kind you don't think too much about."

I spun the cap of the bottle between my fingers while I mulled over his proposal. I had planned on a trip to

Southern California to visit an old friend, just to get away and dive deep into another life for a while, but the idea of beating the Coppola family to more land might be just what I needed.

"If we're going to do this, we'd need supplies."

"I've taken care of everything." He smiled wide. "Just meet here tonight at eight and be ready."

I lost count at how many lives we took that trip; it took weeks to get the smell of blood off my skin. After the first few kills with my bare hands, I started to feel alive again. I tapped into a part of me that I refused to acknowledge when Sienna was near. We were young, but I knew there was a part of me that was different. She made my life seem so much better, lighter, when she was with me. But now, she was gone and Tieri was right. Beating the Coppolas out of that land, then tipping off my father so he made his move and claimed the land as ours was a sweet victory.

There were a few times when I'd lose myself in a kill. I wasn't blind to everything, and I did notice that Tieri would slip away occasionally, and once I caught him looking at me with a strange expression almost as though he wondered if I'd noticed his absence. Maybe I should have questioned what he was up to then, but I really didn't care. I was happy getting my next fix feeding lives to the reaper.

Papa never asked questions when we returned, although he did mention some articles he'd read in the local paper about the Santoro Brothers. I thought a part of him knew, but he also would have understood I needed something to slap me out of the state I was in. He knew I needed to live in the dark now.

"There's that look again," Vinni muttered as he loudly sucked the last part of his drink through the straw, bringing me back to the present. "The one that says you're here but you're really not."

"How can you put that shit in your body?" I ignored his comment as I dropped the rest of my sandwich in the trash bin and brushed my fingers clean. Vinni shrugged as he finished off his second burger from McDonald's then homed in on the fries. My stomach rolled at the thought of that disgusting fast-food inside me, and I spun the rest of my water in the bottom of the bottle.

"I have to fuel up for tonight." He grinned as he used his teeth to bite a hole in the ketchup pouch and spread it in a line across a fry. "Mona is coming in from town, and she's hungry."

"Birthday Mona?" I asked, referring to the girl Niccola had gotten him for his birthday.

"Yup."

"Mona? The one Niccola test drove?"

"I've gotten past that on account of she's so bendy and is willing to try just about anything."

"I see." My water bottle joined my sandwich in the waste bin, and I rested my arms on my thighs, feeling the stress. I'd hatched a plan with The Finder after his visit to my office. We'd decided it was time to throw off Nonna so she'd focus on me and not Sienna.

"Has Ugo checked in?" He lowered his voice when Sofia waved at us from the parking lot. We often ate lunch outside of the office, needing a break from the phones and chaos of inside.

"Yeah." I nodded.

"And?"

"She settled in well and is starting to dig around."

"Figures. She adapts well to change." He licked his fingers and paused for a moment while he thought. "Does she want kids?" I shot him a strange look. "Have you guys ever talked about that?"

"I don't know." I looked away, feeling uncomfortable. "I guess we're just trying to get us right before that conversation can happen."

"Mm." He nodded, and I stood, not wanting to talk about this with him anymore.

"I have a meeting in ten and a date tonight, so…" I wanted to worm right out of my skin at what I'd just said. "I'll see you later."

"Are we still doing to the plan at Non—"

"Yeah."

"I planted the—"

"Good." I cut him off again.

"Okay, then. I'll see you later."

I dressed in my Keton suit, the same one I wore at the murder of Bria and Roberto. If I was going to do this, I needed to make it look legit. Nonna knew fashion, and she would be expecting me to dress my best to impress my date. Opening my top drawer, I pulled out my gold cufflinks and inserted them through the little holes in my cuffs.

The whole time I dressed, I kept watch on my

other cell phone. Tieri and I had made quite a name for ourselves in the media after the massacres of the Rosario family. Not to mention the odd job we'd done for those who helped us along the way. They never saw our faces; they only knew our voices. Some jobs were bigger than others, but the worst thing was when *Sienna* had called. I should have recognized the gasp on the other end, but I didn't. I'd never forget her hurt and confusion when she approached me on it in the hotel room in New York. I'd also never forget how I downplayed what I did. I was a soulless monster then, and yet she had gotten past it. Along with so many other things, and still I doubted her.

The fact that Tieri had set me up for her to call when she met with him still sat wrong with me. I should have had him killed for that, but The Finder told me to wait. He told me he was looking into something and needed Tieri alive for the time being. I glanced in the mirror and remembered one of my first Rosario family kills. Blood had soaked into my mask, so I'd torn it off, needing air. My knife sliced through his organs like butter. He screamed and cried, but I felt nothing but excitement, happy to be ridding the Earth of one more villain. Tieri was standing across the room from me with a look of satisfaction on his face…or at least that was how I read it at the time.

The sound of a car door opening had my mind shift back to Sienna. I opened the drawer and fingered the cool fabric of her silky teddy. I wasn't sure how much longer I wanted to do this. I slammed the drawer shut, leaned my arms on the dresser, and bowed my head, mentally preparing myself for what was going to happen tonight.

"Elio?" Mama was in the doorway of my bedroom. I didn't even know she was here. She looked concerned as her hands tapped the doorframe. This was going to be a big play within our family, and we all knew what it might mean if it didn't work.

"She's here."

"All right." I looked away and concentrated on gathering a few more items. I checked the clip in my handgun and tucked it in my waistband.

"How is—"

"She's fine." I cut her off, not needing Sienna in my head any more than she already was.

"Good, good." She nodded. "What's this?" She pulled the journal Elenora had dismissed off my nightstand. She cracked open the spine and let out a little hum as she read the start of it. "You really meant a lot to her, even back then."

"We all did." I ran my hand through my hair but stopped, annoyed. "I offered it to Elenora. I thought she might like to answer some of the questions that Sienna had asked in there."

"That's a lovely thing to do." She smiled warmly at me.

"Too bad she wasn't interested." I grimaced. "How can someone like Sienna come from someone like her?"

"Well," she slowly sat on the corner of my bed, returning the journal to its place, "I get the impression that Elenora likes to dwell on the negatives, while Sienna chooses to see the positives. I also think Sienna learned very quickly that life is what you choose to make it."

"Maybe," I muttered, looking at her. "Regardless, she doesn't deserve to have her as a daughter."

"Perhaps not, but Elenora did bring her into this world, and if she hadn't done what she did, you wouldn't have met her and fallen in love."

"Yes, that's true. I only wish now I didn't have to go fake it with someone else."

"It isn't the first time you've faked it." She lifted an eyebrow with a smile. "Now, come on. Go save your date from Niccola."

Oh, Lord.

Carina looked nice in her lavender dress with her hair pinned up in a low bun. I held open the car door for her, and she slipped in. I looked back and saw Niccola wrap an arm around my mother and pretend to wipe a tear away. I shook my head at him and gave him a polite finger before I joined Carina in the car.

We barely spoke a word as we made our way over to my uncle's villa. We both had a lot on our minds, so making small talk wasn't necessary.

"Nice." She looked up at the vines that hung over the stone wall as she walked beside me. "It's very pretty here."

I didn't respond; I didn't think much of this place.

The door swung open, and to my surprise, there was Aunt Noemi dressed in her riding gear. Her boots were dusty, and it was obvious she'd just come back from a ride.

"Elio?" She looked over my shoulder at Carina.

"What are you doing here?"

"He's here for this." Vinni handed me a cell phone right on cue. He made a quick face when he gave it to me. "It's all charged, and no calls came in."

"Thanks." I held it up and turned to leave when my aunt spoke up.

"I'm still in just as much shock as you must be." Her voice was sad, but my fingers curled as I slowly turned. "I wanted to call or visit, but," she looked visibly shaken, "she just seemed so sweet."

"You had no idea?" I could barely get my words out because this conversation wasn't supposed to happen now. Nonna was the one I wanted to see us. Vinni was supposed to have her in the living room.

"No." Her face scrunched at me. "How could I have known? I've never met her before."

"No?" I saw Vinni come into view, his face confused over my sudden change in plan. "But you knew her mother, didn't you?" Her face fell and the color drained away. "I saw the two of you at Vinni's party. There was an exchange between you two."

"Elio, you must be confused."

"Am I?" I spoke a little louder, hoping to draw some attention to us.

"I thought she was someone else." She folded her arms to put some space between us. "It took me a little while to realize she wasn't who I thought she was."

"Right." I gave her a dark smile as I heard the familiar beads clicking together.

"Hi," Vinni leaned around me, "I'm Vinni, Elio's

cousin, and this is my mother, Noemi.”

“Carina.” She smiled at Aunt Noemi and held out a hand to Vinni.

“How did the two of you meet?” Vinni asked.

“My parents are friends of Elio’s.” She put her arm through mine, and I tried not to react as Nonna came to the doorway and peered over Noemi’s shoulder.

“What’s going on? I heard shouting.”

“Nothing.” Noemi held up a hand. “We were just discussing where Elio should take his date tonight.” She refused to make eye contact with me, which told me I needed to dig harder into my aunt.

“Who are you?” Nonna pushed Noemi out of the way to get a better look at my date.

“My date,” I gritted through my teeth. “Carina, meet my nonna, Greta Capri.”

“Lovely to meet you.”

“Are you any relation to the Coppola family?”

“The Coppolas?” Carina’s hand flew to her chest, appalled at the question.

“As always, Nonna,” I turned Carina around and pressed my hand against her lower back to urge her to my car, “it’s been a delight to see you again.”

Once on the road heading into town for dinner, Carina turned to look at me.

“Your nonna is positively terrifying.”

“Hmm,” I thought out loud, “she’s certainly been showing her true colors lately.”

“I do think you should have let me have a little more time with her. I can act, you know.” She chuckled to herself. "Yup, I played the best tree my elementary ever had."

"Good to know." I pulled out the back-up phone Vinni had given me and tucked it into the pocket between the seats. There was no way I would have ever left my phone in that house.

My heart dropped as I pulled into the driveway of the restaurant I had once taken Sienna to. This was our spot, and I never wanted to take anyone else here, but I knew that several headlights back, parked on the side of the street, was Abramo. He knew what this place meant to me, thanks to Niccola and Vinni's loud conversation the night before.

"Wow," Carina covered her mouth as she took in the scenery from the balcony, "this place is spectacular."

I took a seat and looked in the opposite direction. If I was going to do this, I needed Sienna out of my head. Gusto, the owner, came out with a huge smile, but when he caught sight of Carina, it slipped a little.

"Mr. Capri, welcome." Both his hands were in the air as he hobbled over. "I was hoping you'd come back to visit."

"My apologies, Gusto. A lot has been going on."

"I see, I see." He motioned for the waiter to pour us my favorite wine.

"Please meet my date for the evening, Carina."

"Lovely to meet you," he greeted her, and his gaze swept back to me. "I'll let you get settled, and I'll be back with an appetizer."

I watched him leave, knowing where his mind was

because mine was there, too. Carina and I had zero spark, and anyone with a pair of eyes could spot it.

How was I going to pull this off?

"Elio?" Carina pulled my attention back to her as she moved her gaze to the building across the way. For a split second, I saw a dark figure move. "Dance with me?" She smiled. "You really need to smile, by the way. Your expression is rather sour for someone on a date." She had a point. I stood and pushed back my chair.

Chapter
SIXTEEN

Elenora

"Elenora," Oscar shadowed me as I moved rapidly through the hotel room, "I wish you would just stop and hear me for a moment."

"What's the point?" I bent down to check for any shoes that might have fallen between the bed and the wall. "Everyone is moving on, doing what they want. Where does that leave me?"

"Right here, right where you're supposed to be."

"I can't stay here." I brushed my hair out of my face when the door opened. Francesco stopped short when he saw my suitcase and the heap of clothes thrown inside. "Really?" I glared at Oscar, who now was standing in the corner, refusing to make eye contact with me.

"Where are you going?"

"I'm leaving."

"Why?"

"Why not?" I quickly eyed the table but looked back at him, straightening my shoulders. "My daughter obviously has her own plans and won't listen to me, anyway. She's chosen them over me."

"That's not true, and you know it."

"She made it very clear it's what she wants to do. Even when I told her not to."

"Elenora," Francesco covered his mouth with an exhausted laugh, "she's doing this because she wants to know who her family is, but you and I both know she also wants to help bring down their syndicate."

"She's only doing it for Piero's spawn of a son."

"Don't." He stuck a finger in my face and backed me up a few steps. "I refuse to hear you talk that way about him. You know I consider him my blood. I'll say this one last time, and I feel farther and farther from you each time I say it. One of these days, I'll leave and won't look back."

I held my tongue. Another secret surfaced, one that would help him see why I hated the world so much.

"Maybe you wouldn't leave if you knew—"

"Elio's a good man, Elenora." He cut me off. I didn't even think he heard me because he was fuming mad. "He's loved your daughter since the day he met her. Yes, I pushed them together, but only because they both needed someone. I couldn't be that for her. Your anger toward my family is getting old. When will you wake up

209

and move past it? Angelo is gone," he caught my hand as I went to slap him, "and I'm sorry for that, but the hate you cast onto everyone around you has to stop. If you want to run away, fine, go. I've wasted a lifetime waiting around for you already."

I started to speak, but he cut me off again.

"But, if you leave, that's it. I will not let you be a part of Sienna's life anymore."

"She's my daughter. You have no right—"

"I was the one who did my best to raise that girl while you hid in the shadows. I know why you said you were doing it, because you wanted her away from the Capris. But I'm really not sure if that was your only reason. I know I didn't give a damn about that. She needed someone to look out for her, and I gave her that. I gave her me, someone who'd take a bullet for her." He flipped the lid of my suitcase over. "You want to leave, there's the door, but do it, and we're done." He moved toward the door.

"Francesco, wait." Oscar suddenly spoke up, and I glared at him as he headed for the table.

"Don't," I warned, not wanting him to share it. I wanted to deal with it myself.

"Elenora, I'm sorry, but he's right. He loves Sienna just as much as we do. He needs to know."

"Know what?" Francesco was nearly vibrating.

"This was delivered today, and it's written just like the last one that was tucked in the magazine."

"Last one?" He took the paper from Oscar and started to read it. "When did this arrive?"

"This morning." Oscar glanced at me. "Mail carrier brought it. We have some people looking into it but, I'm sure just like last time, nothing will come of it." He handed him the letter that had come along with the magazine that contained Sienna's article. "About two weeks before we came to see Sienna, it was dropped off at our hotel room just like this time."

"You couldn't hide her forever?" He read the old note then looked at me like I was crazy. "Don't you think you should have told me about this?"

"Sienna knows," I shot back. "She could have told you or Elio, but obviously she didn't." I pressed my lips together as he gave me a nasty look. "Look, whoever it is could know things about me, things I would rather not have come out, so at least for now, I'm going to listen to the warning and leave."

"And what'll you tell Sienna?" As I didn't have an answer for him, he looked at Oscar. "Where's the other note?"

Oscar handed him the envelope. "It's all in there."

He peeked inside and shook his head. "This a real threat, Elenora."

"I didn't say it wasn't."

"Tell him everything or I will," Oscar threatened me but blinked when he caught my glare. "I mean everything about *this*."

Francesco held up the new note. "What else haven't you told me?"

"Please, just stop trying to play hero."

"Just," Francesco grunted, "do me a favor and give

me a few days. I'll put some soldiers at your door, or you can come to the house."

"I'd rather sleep in a barn."

Francesco looked like he wanted to say more, but he simply shook his head and stormed out the door, letting it bang loudly as it shut.

Oscar shrugged. "I'm sorry, but he needed to know."

"That's where we disagree."

"Don't you ever get lonely?" He sighed, and his gaze dropped to the floor. I knew he wanted more from me, but I couldn't, just like I couldn't let Francesco in. I'd been locked up so tight for so long that I wasn't even sure how to feel about anything anymore. One thing I knew for sure was that the Capris needed to pay for their sins, not the least being the fact they now had my own daughter brainwashed. I had to put an end to all of it.

"Lonely is for the weak, Oscar, and I'm not weak." I stepped out onto the balcony and slipped into a memory.

"Look, I get loving someone you can't have," I took my brother's hand, "but you need to see that Noemi is only after one thing—money."

"I can make more money," he sobbed, and I knew he was at his breaking point. Theo had made sure Angelo knew he was worthless, at least in the eyes of those in this hateful house. "I'm willing to change. I even sold my car and got the one she wanted. I sold my coin collection too, and I'm looking to get a loan to travel to America with her. And I have this…" He trailed off like it was all a bit too much for him.

I wanted to break down and cry with him. My poor

brother had been living here for the past three months, knowing that his love, Noemi, came to see my husband. Never once had anyone in the house welcomed him. He was just as much an outcast as I was. I wished I could whisk him away to live in a different country where we could start fresh and mend the hurt that had been thrown at us.

"No woman who really loved you would ever ask you to sell your things or put you through so much pain just to be with her." I hated how much this horrible woman had destroyed my once happy-go-lucky brother.

"Why am I not good enough?"

"Hey," I moved closer, and he rested his head on my shoulder, "you are enough. You are more than enough. She is the one who should be lucky to have you." We sat in silence for a long time, both mulling over our lives and the terrible situations we'd gotten ourselves into. I cleared my head and thought it was time to share something with him.

I dropped to the floor, balancing on my knees so I could see he was paying attention. "You really need to hear me when I tell you this. It's complicated, so try to follow me."

"All right," he said and sat a little straighter.

"Noemi is a parasite." I held up my hand to stop his protest. "Angelo, she really is. Hell, the smell of her has barely left your skin, and she's already wormed her way into two different powerful families since she left you. She's pregnant with Bosco Capri's child and yet spends most of her time here in this house acting as though she's

Theo's lover. Don't you see it? I don't understand why Nonna Rosa allows it, but I know they hide a lot of it from the uncles. I'm sure they'd never approve of it while I'm here and pregnant with his child. That's where my fear really lies." He looked at me oddly. *"Angelo, you see what's happening here, right?"*

"No, what?"

"They need a son, so if my baby," I pointed to my belly, *"is a girl, they'll expect us to try again."* My face dropped. I knew I couldn't do this again, and I knew Theo got that. *"So, here's what I think might really happen. If my baby is a girl, they'll keep it quiet, maybe hide her away for a while, and God knows where that will leave me. Francesco told me that Piero had a son before I left, which means the pressure's really on for Theo to have a son, too. So, I think Theo is keeping close tabs on Noemi right now because if we have a girl and she has a boy, he might order a hit on Bosco and raise the boy as his own. If it's not a boy, Noemi will be stuck with a girl who will be no use to Theo. She might love him, but she'll jump ship and stay with Bosco Capri if that happens."*

"That's all a bit farfetched, isn't it?"

"That's the thing, it's not." I felt my heart rate race.

"Come on, Elenora, like Piero would ever allow Noemi's baby to be raised in the Coppolas' house if his brother is killed."

"Piero is in Sicily, and from what I heard the other night, Noemi requested they keep the pregnancy quiet, her excuse being her pregnancy has been rocky so far. She's supposedly living with her mother on bedrest. They

don't know she spends a lot of time with Theo."

"You make it sound like a suspense novel. Besides, Bosco is dating that Amara girl."

"I get how this sounds, but I've heard and seen things that lead me to believe this could happen. Noemi doesn't love Bosco. She loves Theo, and I bet this entire thing was planned! Theo never wanted me, but that wasn't his call."

He stood and covered his face while he digested my words. I knew I sounded crazy, and maybe I was, but there was something inside of me that told me I wasn't.

"Okay," he spun around, "let's just pretend that all of what you said is true. What are you going to do?"

"I don't know." I sat on the bed to relieve my achy legs. "Theo belittles and threatens me, and I'm sure he'll get more physical once I'm not pregnant. I can't go home, and I can't leave. They make sure I have no money."

"Maybe we should come up with our own plan in case that happens?" he whispered, and I wanted to cry out of sheer happiness that someone understood the hellish position I was in. "I wasn't going to tell you until after the baby was born, but Grandfather left me some money." He smiled, and I looked at him in surprise, wondering why I'd never heard this before. "It's not actual cash, it's tied up in a secondary business, but nonetheless, the net worth is growing every year. I wanted to sign it over to you for the baby, you know, so it has some money of its own. Because, well..." He raised his arms as if to say this place sucked. "Maybe I should sign it over to you now, and that can be your ticket out of

here. *You could sit on it and use it when you need it?"* I flew into his arms and hugged him so tight my belly hurt.

"Thank you, little brother!" I started to cry, but he pulled back when we heard voices outside the door. I felt him flinch at the sound of Noemi's god-awful voice.

"Angelo, remember." I found myself nervous that he'd slip right back into old habits now that he'd found a solution to my problem of getting the hell out of there if I needed to. *"Remember the webs they've woven to make sure they both come out on top."*

"I know." He looked away, and I knew he was still caught up in her spell. *"Can you promise me something?"* He sighed as he ran his hand over my large belly. *"No matter whether it's a boy or girl, promise you'll protect it from them?"* When I didn't respond, he looked down at me with a question. *"What?"*

"I don't know." I pushed back from him, feeling like I wanted to crawl right out of my skin. *"Shouldn't I feel more loving toward it?"* I begged him to understand. *"I mean, you see mothers cradling their bellies, talking and singing to their unborn child, but I feel detached. It's just a foreign thing inside me."*

"Hey," he shook off his own hurt and became strong for me once again, *"no one can blame you. You hoped for years you'd have a child with Francesco, and now you've had to have one with someone you don't even like. I get it that you can't feel the same way about it. I'm sure once you hold that baby, you'll feel the love."*

"Yeah." I reached down and rubbed my stomach, hoping he was right, but I knew I certainly lacked that

glow other mothers had.

"Okay," he suddenly stood and wiped his cheeks with the backs of his hands, "I'm going to talk to her—"

"No, Angelo, you're going to make things worse."

"One last time. She needs to hear me out. I think if she can just see all that I gave up, she'll know how deep my love runs. I just need her to know."

I wanted to shake him. Did he not retain a single word of what I said? These people were dangerous!

"Please Angelo, don't. Theo is already so angry."

"The big bad wolf doesn't scare me." He checked himself in the mirror then puffed up his chest. He stopped at the doorway and looked back at me. "I'll bring the papers over tomorrow so we can get the two of you squared away. I know Grandfather would want the money to go to the little one."

"Okay. "My heart sank when I thought of my dear sweet grandfather who'd passed away almost a year ago. "Angelo?" I waited for him to look back at me from the doorway. "Please be careful."

"Of course." He smiled the way he used to when we were carefree kids. "I can't wait to be an uncle." He blew me a kiss and left.

"What do you want to do?" Oscar yanked me from my memory.

"I want to be left alone," I snapped, and when his footsteps trailed off, I allowed my mind to slip back and travel to the painful part of my heart that held those old those memories.

As soon as I signed the paperwork, Angelo made

sure everything was filed immediately. It was such a huge relief to know I had the money to leave if I needed it. My brother had given me exactly what I needed, and I felt a power shift within me. He hadn't dropped by my room or joined me for drinks over the past day or so. I hadn't seen Noemi around either. I wondered if she was upset. Perhaps he'd tried to talk to her again. When he didn't come to dinner again that night, I made a conscious decision to seek him out the next day.

I woke the next morning with a bad feeling. I couldn't shake it or describe what it was, but there seemed to be a tenseness in the air. I quickly got dressed and started to look for Angelo. I knew most of the places in the house you could disappear to, but I couldn't find him anywhere.

"Pippo?" I called to the oldest of Theo's uncles. He was a mean thing, but he was nicer than the rest of them. "Pippo, please." I stopped as I felt a sharp pain in my belly. Lord, this baby was determined to split me in two.

"Are you all right?" He came over and took my arm, making sure I didn't fall.

"Have you seen my brother? I need to speak to him."

"Maybe you should sit down?" Something in his tone sent a shiver through me. I straightened my back and pushed through the pain to give him a warning look not to lie to me. He simply stood there and matched my demeanor. Pippo was an elder, not someone you ever questioned or challenged, but in that moment, I didn't care. My gut told me something was wrong.

"Theo," he called over my shoulder, "you need to attend to your wife."

"Don't," I held up a hand, "treat me like a child." I fought the urge to lose it as I knew something dark was coming. "Where's my brother?"

"Elenora," Theo's attempt at kindness brushed over my skin like fire, "come with me."

"Why?" I tried to raise a hand again, to stop him from touching me, but I doubled over in pain. "Don't touch me! Just tell me."

"Always so stubborn." He leaned down and picked me up, cradling me in his arms like he cared about me. It was a lie, all of it was lies. It was a sick illusion until the baby was born. Once inside our bedroom, he rested me on the bed and let out a deep breath.

"I'm not sure how to tell you this—"

"Then just say it."

"Fine," he grunted. "Apparently, there was a hit put out on your brother."

"What?" I immediately grew cold.

"Someone put a hit on your brother, Elenora, and the Capris followed through with it tonight."

"Wait." I shook my head, trying to follow his words. "Someone wanted my brother dead?"

"Yes, and one of my soldiers who I had following Piero reported that he and some of his men were just outside of Rome. They were seen there, Elenora, and so was the body of Angelo. Your brother is dead."

"No!" I tried to stand, but all went dark as the sound was sucked from the room.

"Whoa!" Theo shot forward and grabbed me before I hit the floor.

The next thing I remembered was Theo's voice telling me to breathe. I was on the floor with my head on his thigh. I curled into a ball in shock. My childhood with Angelo flashed in front of me, his grin as he splashed in puddles in his gray rain boots, his dark blue eyes, his crooked smile, his shaggy hair, his laugh. It was all too much, and a horrible sob ripped through my soul, and I broke. I broke like I never had before. The one person who was a part of me, who really loved me, was gone, and I was alone... All I could picture was how he must have felt right before he was killed.

Oh, my God, I can't do this without him. *I closed my eyes to shut out the pain.*

I wasn't sure what time it was, but it was dark, and my hips were sore from the hard floor. My eyes hurt to open, and it took me a moment to realize Theo was still with me.

"Hey," he said softly, and I tried to speak, but my heart wouldn't allow it. "I'm not going to pretend to understand what you're feeling right now, but I got a call from one of my men, and there was an eyewitness who said it was one of Piero's soldiers who did the hit. I guess if anything, it's good to know who did it."

"Right." I felt my body turn to stone as his words burned my insides. "Good."

"Look, I need to go, but are you okay? I mean, this type of shock could affect the baby. Do you think you need to see a doctor?"

"I'm fine," I said, but I really had no control over anything that I was thinking.

He shimmied out from under my head, flipped on the light in the closet, and changed into a business suit. I knew where he was going—to see Noemi.

Once he left, I rolled onto my side and gave in to the sorrow that sucked me down into a terrifying darkness.

A few days later, I still hadn't left my room. I managed to move to the patio chair from my bed, and, though the baby was active, I paid it no attention. I was numb. No one bothered me, which was nice, but I'd become a wallflower. I felt nothing, cared about nothing. I was merely a vessel.

"You can't stay out here again today." Nonna Rosa was suddenly next to me. She sat easily without the use of her cane like the fit old lady she was. She hung the cane on the edge of the table, and I stared at it.

She placed a little white box next to me. When I didn't bite, she nudged it closer. "Please open it. It's a tradition to give the baby's mama something for the little one. It's meant to represent our family. If it's a girl, they wear the teddy pendant, and if it's a boy, they wear the lapel pin. I know you're going through a lot right now, so I thought I'd give them both to you early. To show that no matter what, we'll love this baby."

With a great effort, I snatched the box off the table and flicked the lid open. There, nestled in white cotton, was a little silver teddy bear pendant on a thin chain, and a lapel teddy pin.

"The child gets one or the other depending on which sex they are. They're usually given to the mother just before the birth and then to the child when they're old enough to wear it. Their family ring is engraved when they're born, and the father holds on to that. But, as with all the men in this household, they must earn their ring as well as their seat when they're old enough to understand what it really means. It all might seem odd to you, but it's a tradition I hope will continue for years to come."

"So," I licked my dry mouth, not buying her kindness for a minute, "you're telling me if this baby is a girl, you're all going to love her unconditionally?" I challenged.

"All things considered, we'll cross that bridge if we have to." She dismissed me, and I shot her a nasty look to let her know I saw right through her lies.

"No, I want to know. What if it's a girl? What happens then?"

"You will try again."

"And the baby girl?"

"We will deal." She was curt in her answer.

Deal…that word hit me hard.

"Hello in there." Oscar put a hand on my shoulder, and I jumped. "Sorry, I didn't mean to scare you, but I've been calling you." I dabbed the tears that were racing down my cheeks. "The car is here."

"Why?"

"Because," he offered me a hand, "we need to get out of here and get something to eat."

"I'm not hungry."

"Well, I am." His manner had changed, and I found myself standing and following him outside.

Once in the car, he turned to look at me.

"Elenora?"

"Mm?" My heart was heavy, and no matter how hard I tried to push away the feeling, it wouldn't leave.

"I know things aren't the way you want them to be, and I know better than anyone what you've been through, but if I may…" He looked nervous. "Life is short, and your brother would want you to be happy. Whether that's with Francesco or someone else, don't you think it's time to let someone in?"

I looked away and fought against my usual answer of *no*, I knew he was only trying to help, but no one could understand the storm inside me.

"Honestly, Oscar—" I stopped as the car lit up in bright blue flashing light and the driver hit the brakes. "Were you speeding?" I shouted at the driver.

"No, ma'am."

"Did you miss a traffic sign?"

"No, ma'am. I know these roads very well." He pulled the paperwork from the dash box and rolled his window down as the police officer approached.

"License and registration." The officer shone his flashlight over Oscar then me, letting it linger there for a moment.

"What's the problem, officer?" Oscar leaned forward to shield me from his view.

"Your taillight is out." He reached for the handle and opened the driver door. "I'd like all three of you to step out."

"Why?" I suddenly felt nervous.

"Nothing to worry about, ma'am, I just need to make sure you're all right."

"I can assure you I am."

"Just doing my job."

I rolled my eyes and motioned for Oscar to get out of the car. I followed, scowling at the light rain that had started.

"See, Officer," I squinted to read his name tag, "Hector, I'm just fine."

He motioned for his partner to search the car, and after a few minutes the officer seemed satisfied.

"Ma'am, a word, please?" Officer Hector waved at me to step away from Oscar. "I understand the frustration you're feeling, I really do. I just have to be sure you're not being held against your will."

What?

"I'm confused. Where would you get that idea?"

He nodded as though agreeing with something. "You'd be surprised at the things I've come across. Sometimes a simple pull-over can uncover people in very dangerous situations. Sometimes the ones in danger are totally blind to it, if you know what I mean."

"Well, I'm good, really, so if you don't mind, I'd just like to get to our dinner. We've a reservation."

"Of course." He leaned forward and opened the door and motioned for me to climb in. "You have a good evening, and please get that taillight taken care of."

"Will do, officer." The driver rolled up his window

and got back on the road, all the while muttering about how these young officers were on a power trip.

I used the towel Oscar had pulled from the trunk and dried my wet hair. We'd been pulled over before, but this time it definitely felt odd. It had to be more than just the broken taillight. Maybe they were looking for someone, and they were just pulling over random people. Either way, I wasn't impressed that I was now dripping wet on my way to dinner.

SEVENTEEN

Sienna

"At the end of the day, gentlemen," I looked up at their serious expressions, "the Coppolas and the Capris are after the same three things. Money, land, and oil. Label me what you want, but I am the best move you've got right now."

"We're impressed." Pippo, the oldest of the three, nodded at his two brothers with satisfaction. They all sat in chairs on a little platform in front of me. Apparently, this room was where they conducted most of their business. "You're a quick study, Alessia." I bit my tongue as I wanted to correct him on my name, but I knew better.

"Thank you."

"I have one last question." Lotto, the youngest,

waved a hand to get my attention. "Why, after all these years, would you want to be in the seat of power after you've expressed your disgust with the Capri family?"

I took a moment to answer him. "The Capri family rules with compassion and reserve, and while that seems to work for them, I don't think it gets the best results. I believe fear is the best way to rule an empire. If you show weakness, it can be used against you. The Capris' weakness was right at the core of their foundation. Proof of that would be letting me live right in their midst." I paused, letting the drama of what I'd said linger in the air. "Without even knowing who I was, I was able to come into their home, their very lives. I was able to learn their ways, how they think, even overhear what moves they plan to make. I've seen their books, I know how much money they have, and who plays what roles. Like it or not, I was partly raised as a Capri since I was child. Well, perhaps I didn't actually live there, but I spent a lot of time there."

The men all were nodding, but no one attempted to speak, so I continued.

"I had my own protector, you see, and he just so happened to be their own *consigliere*. I'm still trying to understand how or why I was taken from this life, from my own family, but I'm back, and I come bearing the gift of knowledge of your enemy."

I leaned back and straightened my shoulders. Still, not one of them spoke, so I tried another tactic. "I understand why you'd hesitate to trust me, but I'm willing to do whatever it takes to show my loyalty to my father." I looked up at the ceiling when, in reality, I should be looking down at hell. "If you give me a chance, I want to prove my loyalty to the family, to the people, and most of all to you."

That was the longest monologue I'd ever had to remember.

"Willing to do whatever it takes?" Betto, who had remained silent until this point, lifted a skeptical eyebrow at me.

"I understand that having a female Donna isn't something you're ready for, and I respect that." I wanted to roll my eyes at the three sexist old men in front of me. "All I ask is that you let me marry someone of my own choosing and let us run the seat as equals. But I'd need a little time to get to know them first. I mean, I think we can all agree arranged marriages haven't boded well for this family." I watched their faces and decided to add, "I will not have my son taken away from me the way I was taken from my father."

A blanket of silence fell over the room, then they huddled their gray heads together and began to whisper in hoarse voices. I was sure they were thinking 'just get her to marry, and we can push her into the background and let the man rule.' Normally, that would have made me fight harder, but since I knew this was one big lie anyway, I pushed that thought away. After a bit, I wasn't sure what to do as their whispered conversation continued, so I entwined my fingers in front of me and waited patiently. I wouldn't back down on this, and they needed to see that.

"I think that's a fair offer." Pippo nodded his approval. "Brothers?" Betto and Lotto both nodded their agreement, and I fought the urge to smile with pride. I knew I needed to win these three over, and with Nonna Rosa out dealing with Stefano, this was my time to make my move with them. It was the reason I had stayed holed up in my room all the previous day while Ugo taught me everything he could about the Coppola way so I could have this meeting.

"So, do I have your support to work with Stefano?"

"Yes." Pippo nodded.

"Then in that case," I took a step forward, "I hope by my standing here today and agreeing to do everything you ask, I have gained a little of your respect?" I looked at the three of them, one by one, starting with the youngest brother, Lotto.

"What are you getting at?" Betto seemed the most curious.

Here we go...

"I know Stefano stepped in when my uncle passed, and I'm sorry I never had the pleasure to know him either. But I'd like to think the Coppolas would never make a deal trafficking Libyan girls while keeping the Qawi family in the dark. I understand we've had a rather rocky relationship with them after what happened last year. Isn't it a bit soon to be playing with fire?"

"Explain where this is coming from." Pippo's bark nearly made me jump out of my skin, but I didn't react.

"You asked me to educate myself on the family's connections, and when I did, this stood out the most.

Qawi is one of our biggest allies in the southeast. I can't imagine they'd be okay with hearing that Stefano has our men grabbing girls off their streets, then planting them in Capri's export containers to frame *them* for trafficking."

"What the Qawi's don't know won't hurt them." Lotto waved me off. I got the feeling he didn't believe me.

"This is the first I've heard of this." Pippo held up a hand to Lotto. "Little brother, we can't risk another falling out with them. They already threatened to cut us out last year and deal directly with our American connections." He then looked at me. "Stefano made this move?"

"Yes, sir." I spoke clear and crisp. "They may not find out what happened, but from what I understand, a girl they kidnapped has gone missing. It would only take her making one deal with the police, and Qawi will look to *us* for answers."

"They'd be too scared to flip."

"Are you sure about that?" I held Pippo's piercing gaze as he tried to call my bluff.

"Here's the thing, my uncles. I want to learn the family business from the inside out, so when I marry, my husband and I will work together to protect and grow the family name, income, and land. If we have any chance of taking down the Capris, then I need to have the best teacher there is. Is Stefano the best person to teach me, or is there someone else?"

The seed had been planted.

Pippo leaned back in his chair with a heavy sigh and

then shot a glance over at his brothers.

"Give us some time to discuss this."

"Of course. Thank you for giving me this chance." I turned on my heel and walked out of the meeting room with my head held high.

Once back in my room, I sagged against the wall and sucked in a deep breath.

That was intense!

"Hey." Ugo emerged from my bathroom. No doubt he'd been waiting for me for quite some time. He placed his hands on my shoulders and looked me over. "Where have you been?"

"Playing one hell of a role with the uncles." I started to laugh on my crazy high. "I did everything you said to do."

"Even the part about the trafficking?"

"Yes."

"And?"

"And I think I put the first wedge in place."

His face sagged with relief and his hands moved to his mouth as he digested it.

"I nearly had a stroke up here."

"Yeah, you and me both."

I wanted to celebrate, pop champagne, and jump around to music, anything to rid myself of the anxiety of what I had just done, but I also knew this was only the beginning.

"How are you feeling?" He eyed me carefully.

"Honestly?" My grin spread across my face. "Fantastic."

I had won the uncles over and planted the seed of doubt within them about Stefano. Now it was in their hands. It was the first chip I'd taken at the Coppola foundation, and I knew it wouldn't be my last.

The house was quiet and calm for the next few days. I knew a big part of that was because Nonna Rosa and Stefano were off on a short trip. As much as I was curious about what that was about, I decided to just sit around and let the staff get used to me being here. They had no reason to suspect me and were relaxed around me. Donte had taught me a lot about how the staff worked in a house this size. I knew the head cook carried a lot of weight and to always get in good with the *consigliere*. Both would know everything that was happening inside and outside the house. At that particular moment, it was the reason I was tucked in a comfy chair under the planter box that sat below the kitchen window. To anyone else, I was enjoying the sunny day, but I was also getting an earful from one of the staff members about someone who was coming back tonight. I was very curious to know just who *she* was.

My mind drifted off, and I wondered what the Capris were up to. My stomach twisted when I thought of Francesco and how he'd worked so hard to make sure I never ended up here. I wished I could see Elio. I missed him the most, but I knew he was the last person I could see.

I hated how wound-up he'd been the last time I saw him. I knew he needed me physically, but right now, I wasn't able to give him that. I closed my eyes and remembered how his kisses felt. I could almost feel the way his hands would grasp at me, so desperate for a connection. The smell of his suit came to me, no doubt fresh from the cleaners. I leaned farther back in the lounge chair and let my head go deeper into my thoughts. The way his eyes were so hungry for me and how he risked everything the other night at the party just to see me because that was what I did for Elio. I grounded him.

"Good dream?" Salvo's shadow blocked the warmth the sunlight had provided me. "Because you looked really happy."

"The best." I played along, not wanting to show any disappointment that he'd interrupted my moment. "Then you came along," I joked.

"Oh, please, I'll wait." He took the seat next to me and waited like the sarcastic ass he was.

So, I continued to play along. I closed my eyes and took a deep breath then counted to twenty before I let one eye open to look over at him. "Now, I'm done."

"I'm so glad." He chuckled as he held up his phone. "I was hoping you could help me with something."

"Sure." I sat up and removed my sunglasses to see his screen better. "What am I looking at?"

"Well, you know the Capris," I nodded as my curiosity took over, "and you know Elio better than anyone, so can you tell me who this is?" He pressed play on the video, and it took me a moment to realize it was

Elio dancing with another woman. I inched closer and squinted, realizing they were at the same restaurant he first took me to. It was as if a sledgehammer had just come down and swung into my stomach. The blow was hard to absorb, so I pretended I was thinking. I knew the heat from my hurt was spreading up my neck, and it would be only a few seconds before my cheeks would give my feelings away.

"I know the place, but I don't think I know who she is." At least my voice didn't betray me.

"They seem quite close." He swiped to another video, and it was all I could do not to toss his phone in the little fountain next to me. "See, right here." He pointed to when she rested her head on his shoulder and he stroked her back tenderly.

"Maybe a friend of Aurora's?" I pulled my sunglasses back down and blinked at the prickly feeling that assaulted my eyes. "There were always a lot of women trying to get their claws into Elio and his cousins, so to see that doesn't really shock me."

"Was he faithful to you?"

"Does it matter?" I loathed his question.

"Yes," he cleared his throat, "because any man who would be so lucky to have you should hold you on a pedestal, not take you for granted."

"Well, it's a good thing we aren't together anymore, then."

"Yes, I think it is." He tucked his phone away but showed no sign of leaving.

I looked away, not wanting his attention. I just

wanted to be left alone to mull over what I'd just seen, but that wasn't going to happen. As much as seeing that video burned me to the core, I knew it was Elio's part of the plan. I knew this moment was coming and what it meant when it did, that Elio needed to make a move because something big happened at home. Still, it hurt.

"You never heard of him seeing anyone all the time you were together?"

"Not to my knowledge," I whispered, hating to say anything remotely bad about Elio. He might be a lot of things, but when he was created, they had me in mind.

"He never hurt you?"

"I never said that." The words popped out, and I instantly wanted to take it back. Those were my thoughts, my wounds to deal with.

"It explains a lot."

"Pardon?"

"Sometimes you can't see me, but I want you to know that I know. I can see you've been hurt." He shrugged.

"What did I miss?"

"You miss the fact that I'm often nearby, that I smile whenever you talk, and that I find any excuse to touch you." He brushed his fingers over mine.

"It's not intentional," I lied. Though I did think Salvo liked me, I certainly didn't realize it had reached this point. I had been so caught up in my role that I'd almost missed an opportunity to gain information from a great source, and he was sitting right here in front of me. Should I risk it? I did need to find someone and hold off the marriage for as long as I could before we made our final play.

"And now that you know how I feel?"

Oh, I didn't like this feeling at all. I felt like I was cheating not only on Elio but his entire family.

"You have my attention," I swallowed around the sandpaper that lined my throat, "but you need to know that this," I waved around the property, "is a lot for me right now, so if something was ever to happen between us, it would have to be at a painfully slow pace."

"I understand." He smiled warmly. "Did anyone else catch your attention at the party?"

Yes, the man who kissed me.

"Yes, the man who checked in on me twice." I matched his smile, which took a lot of effort.

"Did the uncles explain about the party?"

"Yes, and I've already run my plan past them, and they've agreed that things will go at my pace, with the understanding that I will marry someone of my choosing, but I'm to understand there is a deadline."

"Look at you." He nodded, impressed, then his voice went serious. "Stefano is going to have a real problem with this."

"I know, but—"

"But you're Theo's daughter, so he will have to step down."

"Yes, he will." A sudden flurry of movement made us both jump.

"You two-timing slut!" Anna flew at me, but Salvo grabbed her by the shoulders, hauling her away from me.

"What the hell is she doing here?" Anna spat.

"She…" he barked and pushed her back hard, causing her to stumble. His tone suddenly went dark. "Is Theodore's daughter."

"Bullshit!"

"It's true."

"So help me God," she stuck a finger in my face, "if I have to live under the same roof as you again, I will lose it."

"Maybe you shouldn't have switched sides so quickly." I stepped toward her, tired of Anna already. *Please don't tell me she was the mystery guest the staff was referring to.*

"What did you say?"

"Don't act dumb, Anna. It's unbecoming."

She lunged at me, but Salvo was ready for it and again pushed her backward.

"Anna, enough. No more."

"Wait." She looked between the two of us and closed her eyes with a curse. "Of course." She laughed then said in a high-pitched voice, "Let me guess. You two are dating."

"Anna, you and I tried to date, and it didn't work." He shrugged. "Then you moved on to Stefano. I'm not hanging around anymore." His phone rang, and he gave her a warning to stay away from me. "Hello? Yeah, what's up?"

"Wow!" I chuckled, wanting to fuel her up even more. If I could make her freak out and the uncles were near, they'd see their grandson's girlfriend was just as much of a loose cannon as Stefano was.

"You've something more to say?" She stepped closer as I gathered my belongings and moved, hoping to draw her toward the patio door.

"No."

"No?" Her pointy cheekbones flushed, and I fought a smile as I stepped inside. "You don't get to play the little innocent act here, Sienna. You don't have them wrapped around your finger like you did the Capris." One of the soldiers who often hovered around me looked Anna up and down, and she flashed him a smile even as she was spewing her hate toward me.

"You just spread your legs for anyone with a pulse," I whispered and saw her hand pull back to slap me. *Whack.* It stung and made my eyes water, but I just stood there holding her gaze. "You were nothing at the Capris' and you're nothing here." I heard the click of the cane and Pippo's voice.

"Once again, Anna, your only skill is jumping from one bed to the next," I quickly threw at her.

"Ahh!" She lunged at me, and we tumbled to the floor. As hard as it was not to punch or kick her, I just covered my head while she attacked me like the savage she was.

"What on Earth!" Nonna yelled, and Pippo grabbed Anna and tossed her into a chair.

"Are you mad, woman?" he yelled at her. "Do you know who you were just assaulting?"

"She's a liar and slept with your enemy!" she cried to anyone who would listen. "I don't care if she's the

Pope, she can't be here!"

"That's not your choice," he snapped at her, "and you can very easily be replaced yourself."

I sat up as footsteps approached and pulled my hair away from my face, then accepted the hand Salvo offered.

"What's going on?" Ugo took a step toward me but stopped himself at the last second.

"She's a Capri!" Anna snarled.

"I can promise you that she's very much a Coppola," he said darkly. "I know because I hand-delivered her here myself, right from her mother."

Salvo rubbed my back, and I caught Ugo's motion for me to go upstairs. His face looked ticked off, though I knew he was just acting the part.

"Excuse me," I muttered, holding my sore jaw. It had taken two solid blows from Anna's wild swings.

Salvo started to follow me, but I guessed Ugo stopped him.

Once inside my room, I headed to the bathroom and ran a cold face cloth under the tap then dabbed at my face. A moment later, the bedroom door opened, and Ugo looked in.

"What's going on?" His body filled the doorway.

"Anna came out of nowhere, and I pushed her buttons to attack me in front of the uncles." I stopped to look at him over my shoulder. "Wait, you knew that was the plan. Why're you questioning me?"

"I'm not talking about Anna. I'm talking about Salvo."

"Oh, that." I waved him off. "He told me he liked me, and I figured since I'm supposed to be *looking* for a husband, I might as well pick the lesser of all the evils."

"Lesser?" He scoffed. "Sienna, no. You have no idea who you're playing with."

"He's been nothing but nice to me."

"Right," he stepped farther into the room, "he's playing you. He's been putting up with Stefano for years, and now he sees a way in. He'll seize the opportunity, and he'll stop at nothing to get it. Don't let him fool you. He's more dangerous than Stefano ever was."

"But this is all an act. I'm not really going to marry him. I just want to use him as a buffer to keep the other men away so I can focus more time on how to take the family down."

"What would Elio think of this?"

That got my back up quickly. "Elio is too busy on his date to care what I'm up to."

"You know that's not true."

"I know," I admitted and gritted my teeth to try to keep my head on straight. "I know."

"He's the darkest side of evil, Sienna," he warned harshly. "He and Elio go way back, and I know that once Salvo got word of who you were and that you once dated Elio, he saw an opportunity, and he isn't going to let it go by. Ask Elio about him sometime. He'll tell you some stories that'll make your hair stand on end."

"Okay, I hear you."

"Oh, damn, if Elio finds out that Salvo is your pawn in this game—"

"Then don't tell him."

"Thanks for the advice, but I like my head where it is."

"Look," I winced as I touched my lip with the cloth, "Elio is doing his part his way, and so am I. If Salvo thinks he can get to Elio by dating me, then make sure Elio doesn't bite. Elio isn't supposed to care anymore, so make him prove it. I can't be the only one taking hits here." I rolled my eyes at my pun.

"I don't like this one bit."

"I know." I squeezed his arm to let him know I'd heard him, and I'd take what he said to heart. I most definitely would be more aware.

That night, I tossed and turned in bed until I couldn't take it anymore. I slipped on a robe and headed to the kitchen for some water. Soldiers lined the perimeter of the yard and cast creepy shadows wherever there were huge windows. I was just glad they were outside and not inside. Just as I rounded a corner, I heard voices and came to a stop, tucking myself into the corner of the room as they drew closer.

Oh, no…

Chapter

EIGHTEEN

Sienna

"Look I get you're not happy with me, but the silent treatment is a little juvenile, isn't it?" Ugo muttered as he fiddled with his tie in the reflection of the driver's mirror.

"I'm not mad at you," I murmured from a million miles away.

"You're something." He let out a long breath and settled back down into his seat. "Because two nights ago you had your hands up ready to fight whoever, and now you're here but not really."

"I'm just processing."

"Are you purposely trying to act aloof?"

He shook his head at me as I went back to staring out the window and watched as the raindrops hit then stretched out thin against the glass.

We were heading to dinner with the uncles at a very posh club in town. They'd asked me to join them so I could be introduced to their American clients. I knew they also wanted to show off my skill at speaking English. I agreed, of course, curious to learn about their clients so Ugo could fill Elio in on what their next move might be. At least I got to wear my new dress. I knew Elio would love the dress, and I felt bothered that he wasn't going to see it. It was strapless and had gold gems of all different sizes that formed a unique pattern starting from the center outward. It matched my diamond upside down triangle necklace and matching diamond cuff.

A sudden feeling of uneasiness came over me as her face popped up in front of me, and I gave in to the memory of who I'd seen the other night.

"This can't get out. My family can never know. And what if Elio now knows the truth? What if she told him?" Her voice chilled me to the bone. *What was she doing here? What on Earth was her involvement with the Coppolas, other than dating Theo a lifetime ago? The questions circled around and around in my brain.*

"That's not my problem." Nonna Rosa cleared her *throat as though uneasy around Elio's Aunt Noemi. "You moved on from my son and got pregnant by a Capri."*

"I moved on because I wasn't good enough in your eyes. At least I loved Theo."

"Loved?" Nonna Rosa questioned her. "Or did you just see power and money to live a comfortable life?"

"Look," she glared, clearly annoyed with the

conversation taking a turn, "I need to know if that girl knows things. If my life is about to come crashing down, I need to do damage control." *She leaned forward.* "I never breathed a word about anything to anyone in the Capri family when I left. My loyalty was always with you."

"And we left you alone as promised."

"Until you needed something, and I did try to deliver."

"No, you didn't, but your mother did and failed."

"You should never have gone to my mother. Look," *Noemi closed her eyes,* "just give me a chance to talk to Sienna, and if she knows something, I'll deal with her myself. Make sure she keeps quiet."

"And what do you have in mind?"

Wait. What might I know? That she dated Theo? That was the past and none of my business. From knowing Noemi in the short time I had, she seemed kind and quiet, and I had no clue what she was referring to.

My ears caught her words again. "I know something that will crush their lives with one simple name."

"Beware what card you remove from the stack. You're close to crumbling what power you have left."

"You have no idea how I've stacked my deck against you." *Nonna's cane scraped into the floor, but she remained silent.* "Don't forget, Rosa, you're not the only one who knows the good doctor's name."

"No." *Nonna stood, completely unaffected by Noemi's statement.* "That'll only pull her focus from where it needs to be. That's done and over with now."

"It's still something that will—"

I stepped back and hit a picture frame. It fell to the floor with a clatter, and I froze for a split second until I heard the click of a cane and then bolted. I came face to face with that scary Coppola neck-tattooed soldier. I didn't know what it was about that line of crosses that freaked me out, but it took everything for me not to scream. Instead, I ran up the stairs, into my room, and dove under the covers. I boiled with anger. What could Aunt Noemi possibly know that could destroy me and the ones I love? Did she know something about Elio, something that could hurt me if I knew? Hadn't I suffered enough in my relationship with that family?

Ugo touched my arm, and I jumped, blinking back to the present. "What's wrong with you?"

"Nothing," I insisted and tried to push the questions from my mind.

"You'd better pull yourself together. We're here."

"Yes, okay." I fumbled out of the car, my heels wobbling on the gravel. I walked toward the big gray door then turned back to look at Ugo, who was typing something into his phone. I waited for him to join me, then the soldier opened the door for us.

I made an effort to do as Ugo had directed and gathered my thoughts as I walked toward the table. Around it sat several men and one woman. They all eyed me from my Gianvito Rossi shoes to my long, wavy, still-damp hair as I approached. A side door opened, and the beat of music could be heard from the club a floor below us. I dismissed the distraction and looked back to the people in front of me.

"Ah, you must be the ghost from the past." A rather tall man chuckled as he took my hand and kissed the top of it, making sure to pay homage to my ring. His English had a slight accent, but I couldn't place it. He introduced me to everyone in turn, and I made a point to look each one in the eye and repeat their names.

My chair was pulled out for me, and I sat down and crossed my legs. Then I turned to look over my shoulder as everyone's eyes slid off to someone else. I did a double take as Salvo sat down next to me and draped an arm around the back of my chair.

Pippo gave me a slight nod and leaned in, turning his face away from the others. "Salvo shared with me that you two are dating. He would be a solid pick and one my brothers and I approve of."

Seriously? I wanted to glare at Salvo. He sure hadn't wasted any time letting the uncles know about our conversation the other day.

"I hear your English is quite good." The woman in the group pulled my attention over to her, and I could tell by the way her gaze kept raking over me then going back to the men that she and her colleagues were skeptical.

"It is."

"Where did you learn?"

"My best friend is from New York." I focused on my pronunciation to sound even better. "He didn't like it when I would visit and not be able to understand the conversations that went on around me. So, little by little, he taught me." I paused, wanting to address the elephant in the room before the uncles could bring it up. I needed to gain some power, so I decided to be blunt, let them know I had nothing to hide. "Of course, it also helped that my ex spoke perfect English and so did his family."

"Is that so?" She was digging, so I hit her with it.

"Yes, but something tells me you would already know the Capri family is fluent in many languages."

It was as though all the air in the room was sucked out with their collective gasp. I was ready for it, so I casually picked up the wine menu and started to read.

"I hear Summas is really good." I pointed to the name and looked over at Salvo, who was smiling. Clearly, I had impressed him, and I only hoped I had impressed the others too. I gave a quick glance at Pippo, who sported a smug grin. The only one who looked uneasy was Ugo. He tugged at his tie and kept looking at his phone.

"You dated Elio Capri?" The woman shifted in her seat, and something in the way she said it told me that she might have had some interest in Elio herself.

"Yes, for quite some time, actually."

"I was under the impression Elio didn't have girlfriends." The tip of her finger traced circles on the table surface, a tell that she was threatened by me.

"Well, I'm not sure I'd have given myself that title. He had many women, and they all wanted his attention. I think I just put up with his bullshit more than the others, plus I make a fine *lampredotto*. We all know the way to a man's heart is through his stomach." I laughed, drawing the others into the conversation. If there was one thing I knew about men and business meetings, it was that they needed to be included to feel important. "So," I addressed the tall man, "why don't you tell me what we can help you with tonight."

And just like that, Pippo jumped in, and we started to discuss various contracts. He led me through several of them.

"What do you think?" Pippo asked me as he pushed his plate away and leaned back, making room for his stomach to puff out.

"Well…" I paused to choose my words carefully. Elio had asked me to mention a company in front of the elders, as Piero couldn't understand why the Coppolas weren't trying to go after one of the biggest contracts out there right now in the United States. "I remember hearing about this company from Elio, Cooper Industries. Do you know them?"

"Yes, we've done business with them in the past, but they haven't offered us anything over the past few years." The man seemed lost in thought.

"What have you heard about them?" Pippo cut in. "Perhaps we could approach them again."

Shit. I didn't need to them going after Cooper Industries. I just wanted to know why they weren't fighting for a deal.

"Well, it's important to understand how much the company is still worth, since they had to make that big settlement a few years back. I'm sure you heard about it, as it went public. There was a deal that fell through with a third party, and they took the hit." It was true something big happened, and Cooper Industries had kept it very quiet.

"Good to know." Pippo flashed me a smile as the tall man nodded and pulled out his phone.

"Can I ask something?" I addressed the tall man. He put his phone down on the table and gave me a wave to go on. "Why do you think Cooper Industries isn't offering you anything?"

Silence fell over them, and I wondered what door I'd just opened.

Pippo cleared his throat, visibly uncomfortable. "I'm not sure. They haven't answered my emails for a while now."

"Mmm." I let it go, but something didn't sit right with me. "If I were you," I pointed to the company folder I had in front of me, "I'd sign with Dry Docks. That's the company Elio wants the most."

"Good to know." Pippo nodded at the tall man, and I smiled back but for a very different reason.

The chatter started up again, and I eased back in my seat, feeling pretty good that I'd sold a dead bird to these people. Elio wanted nothing to do with Dry Docks. They were run by a hot-headed Texan who would question the Coppolas motives every step of the way.

"I think I just fell in love with you." Salvo leaned in, and his lips brushed my ear softly. Painful goosebumps broke out over my body as I willed myself to stay still. "Gorgeous and brains, you're a deadly combo."

"You've no idea." I grinned, slipping a mask over my emotion. I wanted to wring his neck for speaking to Pippo before I could.

"It's taking everything in me not—"

"Excuse me." I had no interest in letting him finish his sentence. "I need to use the ladies' room." I placed my napkin on the table as Ugo got to his feet.

"I've got her." Salvo stood, ushering me ahead of him. I gave a quick glance at Ugo to let him know that I wasn't comfortable being alone with him. "It's right there in the back." He pointed, and as I started to walk, I felt his hand slide down my spine to rest low on my back.

Just as we turned down the short hallway, his fingers moved around to my hip, bringing me to a stop. I purposely kept a distance from the wall, wanting the extra space to escape if he tried anything. I hoped to God Ugo was on our heels.

"I know you have other prospects to weed through, but I'm hoping this will help convince you that I'm the best choice." He leaned in, and before I could react, something whipped over my head, and I stumbled sideways into someone's hard hands.

"Sienna!" Salvo's voice came from a distance, and I cried out as I took a swing at whoever was holding me. I connected somewhere on their body, but I was being hauled off somewhere, nonetheless.

"Salvo!" I yelped as cool air whooshed over my hyper-aware skin. I felt myself being pressed into a car. Once I was seated, the car took off, and I scrambled to rip off whatever was over my head, hardly registering that my arms and feet were free.

"What the hell?" I snapped as I focused on the faces that grinned at me. "Are you all insane?"

"She's got a good right hook." Niccola rubbed his chin and looked at Vinni.

"You sure you took care of Salvo?" Vinni asked him as he glanced uneasily out the back window

"Yeah, Gain is tying him up right now." Vinni glanced at me. "Don't be pissed—"

"The hell, I am pissed!" I shouted, trying to settle my nerves. "What the hell's going on?"

"Elio needs to see you."

"So, jumping me at the restaurant like I'm gonna be sold on the black market was your idea of getting me out of there?"

"We needed to make it look like a snatch and grab." Niccola tried to calm me down.

"Couldn't you have told me?"

"No," he shook his head, "your reaction needed to look legit."

"Let's try it again, and I'll give you legit," I snarled, and he fought his grin.

"Oh, I really missed you." He chuckled, further pissing me off. "The house is just not the same."

"Well, at least you have something to remember me by." I pointed at his chin, and Vinni laughed as he texted someone.

We took a hard corner and pulled into a driveway, then through a still-rolling-up garage door. We disappeared into the dark, leaving no trace we were even there.

Vinni reached for the door handle then turned back to offer me a hand.

"Oh, now he's a gentleman." I snickered, but at the

same time, I was beyond relieved at who was behind my kidnapping. "Are you going to bind and gag me too?"

"No," Elio stepped into the light, looking dark and sexy as ever, "that's my job."

"She's pretty feisty." Niccola popped out of the car, holding his jaw dramatically. "If you were at all concerned she didn't have any fight left in her, you were wrong."

"Right, so don't do it again." I laughed at him.

"Come here." Elio slid his hand around my neck and tugged me to his mouth.

I didn't have time to think as he kissed my open mouth and commanded control over me. Giving in to Elio was exactly what I needed, but the only problem was once I let my mind go, it brought back all the unwanted thoughts I had forced aside this evening.

He must have sensed my hesitation and pulled away. He looked down at my dress and made a primal noise of approval. "Follow me."

He opened the door to a room that had a hazy look like someone had just finished a box of cigars, but there was no smell. Black leather benches and oversized chairs created a horseshoe around a roaring fireplace. It was classy and dark all at the same time.

"Are we in a warehouse or something?" I made my way over to the desk and took a seat. I crossed my legs and admired a bottle of whiskey then scooped up his drink and smelled the contents. Yikes, it was strong. I set it aside and watched him.

"It's a meeting place." He locked the door behind

us. "A friend of mine owns the place."

"What are you doing here?" I asked, suddenly worried our entire plan was going to crash down around us. "You have to stop showing up like this."

"Hey," he cupped my face and stared into my eyes, trying to read me, "I have more soldiers here than I do at home."

"Isn't it risky?"

"I pay them a lot."

I pushed him away, slipped off the desk, and covered my face. I felt a strange shift within myself.

"What's wrong?" His tone was low and different.

"I don't know!" I wanted to shake right out of my own skin. "I sure as hell didn't think I was being kidnaped by you, for starters." I glared at him, and he glared right back.

"And?"

"Don't *and* me." I tossed a hand in the air. "That was terrifying."

"It was for a reason."

"I'm sure it was." I put more distance between us, and I could tell he didn't like it. "But right now, it's like part of me is connected but the other half isn't."

"What's bothering you?"

"Where to begin."

"Name something, and we'll start there."

All right, he asked for it. Here it comes.

"There's a part of me that is terrified of the person who looks back at me in the mirror. There's a bigger part of me that likes it." I stared at him and slowly walked backward to sink onto the leather bench. I crossed my legs and drew his gaze to my thighs. "I like that I'm manipulating those people, worming my way in, like certain others have done to you. I kind of feel like a cancer feeding on their blind spots and vulnerabilities." I lowered my voice and laced it with a dark and seedy undertone. He loosened his tie and tossed it on a chair as he undid a few buttons. "I like that I have this secret that will eventually tear them down, stone by stone, leaving nothing but me on top." I breathed, heavily turned on by my own words. I strained my neck to look up at him as he moved close to me. "But most of all, I'm excited to see Nonna Rosa's face when she learns the truth that her dear little abandoned granddaughter is actually the mastermind behind their downfall."

Elio's eyes flared with excitement, and something strong passed through us.

"Don't deny who you are, Sienna." He traced his fingers down my jawbone. "You say you don't belong in my world, but I think you just proved yourself wrong."

I snagged his hand and slid his middle finger into my mouth, sucking lightly. He smirked, and his other hand brushed along my collarbone and dipped low across my breasts.

The fireplace flickered behind him, darkening the grooves in his face and showing me a darker side of Elio. In this very moment, it was exactly what I needed. To feel normal with this new me. I gently pulled his finger out from between my lips and slowly stood, dragging the length of my body up his.

"I killed someone the other day," I whispered. "It was a test, and I didn't think twice about it." I licked his neck, wondering when he was going to take me. "Shot him right in the chest and carried on a conversation with Nonna Rosa while the life slowly drained from him."

His fingers drew circles on my bare thighs, and I grew impatient. I wanted him to take this wound-up, claw-me-from-the-inside-out feeling out of me.

So, when he didn't react, I played dirty, walking backward toward the wall.

"Salvo tried to kiss me."

He chuckled and painfully, slowly drew his hands up under my dress circling my needy nub.

"Aww, *bella*," he said quietly, almost eerie, "are you trying to get me angry?"

"He told me he liked me." *Come on, Elio, give in.* "Told me he wanted to marry me."

"And?" His lips hovered over mine in his dirty game of power. I ground my hips, seeking more from his hand.

"And I said I'd think about it." I felt and heard my lace thong ripping. His fingers moved to break the seal and slowly teased my entrance. His other arm came up and leaned on the wall by my head. Our shadows, cast on the wall next to us, moved in unison.

Elio was broad and tall and had a way of carrying himself that oozed confidence and danger. It was something I'd felt when I was younger and clung to for safety. Now, as an adult, I felt it awaken every tiny part of me, and it made me feel alive and sexy.

"Good." He licked my bottom lip.

"Good?" I tried to focus, but his skilled fingers were doing all the right things. He hummed as his teeth nicked my lip again. "All right. I'll give in to him, then."

"Don't mistake my silence for permission." He kissed up my jawbone to my ear, swirling his tongue around the lobe. "When this is over, you will be my wife, Sienna." He pushed his fingers into me and let out a hiss. "We will have children." I started to see the wonderful end of the tunnel. "We will rule all of Italy together." I vaguely heard the sound of his belt buckle. His pants lowered, and he lifted me off my feet.

Then he lowered me back onto the leather bench and grabbed my ankles and slid me down to the edge where he was standing. He bent my legs and leaned forward, running his hands down my legs and over my belly.

"Boomerang effect." He moaned and lifted one ankle, so my leg was flat against his stomach and chest. He smiled at my high heel, kissing just above the ankle bone. "Nothing sexier than you naked in heels."

"Almost naked." I pointed to my bra and snapped the clasp in the front, letting my strained breasts burst free. I wiggled it free and grinned up at him.

He grabbed my other leg and flatted it to him beside the other. He moved to get better footing then freed himself and slid deep inside me. Then he went still.

"Yes!" I closed my eyes, realizing just how badly I needed Elio. Capri or Coppola, it didn't matter. We were one when we were together. A name couldn't take that from us, and no matter how terrified I was to let my guard down with him for the third time, when Elio was inside me, nothing could break us.

He pulled out and nudged the tip against my swollen bud. It was greedy for more attention.

"I missed this," he grunted. "I need you. Without you, I can't settle, or focus, I'm just…" He stopped himself when he realized what he was saying.

"Just what?" He looked away, but I pushed up to my elbows to show him I wanted to hear him out. We did our best when he was in me. "Tell me."

"Lost." His gaze shifted to mine.

"Me too." I confessed.

He leaned forward and pushed in as he covered my heart with his hand. I covered his and shimmied closer as he started to pump into me. Not fast and not hard, just a good pace that built us up to a slow, delicious feeling. Every so often, he would circle his hips, hitting all the right places, and moaned as he started to build to his climax. I was right there with him, lost in my own little world of lust and need.

When he needed to, he let go of his control a little and lifted my hips, tilted the angle, and dove back in. His neck strained, and his abs were tight. He looked glorious as his muscled arms held me up and his fingers dug into my bottom like he was fighting the urge to feast on me. My breasts bounced around as I tossed my arms over my head, too exhausted to hold on anymore.

He swiped the pad of his thumb over my nub, sending little sparks of lust all over my body.

I let out a silent scream as my orgasm tore through me. I shook and quivered, then warm liquid filled my veins as he watched me with hooded eyes. He bent forward and hooked my legs over his shoulders and licked my nipples as he kept his pace inside me. His hand lifted my breasts, and he squeezed them together, kissing and nipping some more. I tangled my fingers in his hair and tugged at the roots with a groan.

"I needed this," he moved to my neck drawing my hot skin between his lips, "so much."

He flicked his hips hard, and I gasped at the delicious feeling that ricocheted through me. I was happy I was flexible, because Elio was determined to get as deep inside me as possible.

"I'm going to come so hard you're going to feel me for weeks." He chuckled as he reached over my head and lifted himself a little higher. His chest hovered over my face, and I pressed against the bench to help drive him in even deeper.

"Elio!" I groaned between pain and pleasure.

"You can fake being someone else's." He thrust again. "You might be able to sell it." Another deep delicious thrust. "But no man will have you," thrust, thrust, "like I do." His body suddenly curled around mine, cocooning me in his strong arms, as he released a primal growl that made my toes curl and my stomach coil for more.

NINETEEN

Sienna

After a few moments, when Elio's ragged breathing settled, he very slowly peeled his body from mine, lowering my legs as he went. His erection was semi-hard, and I wanted to go again, but something told me we didn't have enough time. I quickly cleaned up and got dressed, and he did the same.

"What?" I asked when he shot me a strange glance.

"I don't like this." He shimmied into his jacket then fixed his shirt underneath. "You should be home in our bed where I can spend the night inside you."

"Elio, we have the most amazing sex." I sat back down on the chair to fix my shoe. "No one can ever deny that, but we've still got a lot of things to work out between us, let alone everyone else."

He chuckled darkly as he rolled his wrist to glance at the time. He moved to stand in front of me and hooked my chin with his hand.

"*Bella*, you can work out whatever shit you have going on with me, but you'll do so while living with me, at our home."

"Is that so?"

"Yes," he gently kissed my lips, claiming them, "it's true."

"And you think just because you say it, that makes it true?"

He stared deep into my eyes and let all his walls down. "When will you learn, Sienna? I'm never letting you go." His lips touched mine again. "Ever."

The hitch in my breathing let him know I was incredibly turned on again, and he gave me a knowing, sexy smile.

"Just accept it."

"Maybe that's true, but you're going to have to earn it when you pull crap like you have in the past."

He smirked, clearly intrigued with my newfound sass. "That's only fair. Now, we've some things to discuss." He pulled away and sat in the chair across from me.

The crackling fire and the low hum of people outside settled my lust enough to think straight. "Cooper Industries never offered the Coppolas a contract." I started right in, wanting to show him I could do both sex and business. "I did steer them clear with the possible money issue, but you should make your move fast in case Pippo changes his mind and starts knocking on Cooper Industries' door for answers. I got the impression there was some bad blood there."

"How so?"

"I don't know, exactly. Pippo just shut the conversation down pretty quickly. He basically said they refuse to work with us."

"The Coppolas, you mean," he corrected me, and I smiled.

"Of course." I squeezed his arm, reassuring him I hadn't forgotten who I really was.

"I'll look into it, and I'll let the pilot know we are heading to Las Vegas this week." He pulled out his phone.

"Elio," I lowered my voice, "there's something else." He looked over and put his phone on the arm of the chair, giving me his full attention. "You should know that your aunt Noemi used to date my father." He did a double take, then his expression went blank, and he sat very still as he listened. "Mama told me about it once before, about how Noemi used to date her brother, and how she dumped him and had a relationship with my father after that. Once my father was killed, she must have jumped families because she ended up with your Uncle Bosco." The only way I could tell Elio was even hearing all I said was because he blinked a few times.

"Elenora told you this?" His voice was haunting as I nodded. "When?"

"A little while ago?"

"When?" He repeated.

"Remember our fight, and you wanted to know what the spike was in the polygraph test? That's what I didn't tell you."

"Why?" He looked pissed.

"Because it wasn't my story to tell."

"And now it is?" He stood. "What changed?"

"Elio, you were looking at me as someone you couldn't trust. Would you've really have heard me if I shared it then?"

He tried to keep his cool. One hand went to his hip while the other covered his mouth. I watched him as he tried hard to fight his urge to let loose, and I really needed him not to lose it right now. "What changed for you to suddenly tell me this?"

I stood and faced him as I tried to decide if I was making the right choice to explain further.

"You have to promise you won't get mad, because if you do and she finds out, they'll both know I overheard them talking."

"Who," he stepped closer, closing the gap between us, "and what did you overhear?" He sent a chill up my spine.

"Noemi and Nonna Rosa were in the kitchen of the Coppola house, and—"

"Noemi was at the Coppola's house?"

I stopped him with my hand. "Yes, and Noemi was saying how she wanted to talk to me, to see how much I knew about her past." He opened his mouth to speak again, but I held my finger to my lips and shook my head to let him know there was more. "She was upset and said it would ruin her entire family if they ever found out, and that…" I stumbled to find the right words.

"What? Tell me," he demanded as I hesitated.

"That she had something on me, and when I found out, it would destroy me."

He turned away from me, grabbed a ceramic figurine, and threw it into the wall. I jumped but stood tall, not wanting to back down from him.

"Elio, say something."

"This is going to kill Niccola and Vinni!" he roared, and I felt terrible knowing it was true. They both loved their mother, and though they might get past that she'd once dated the enemy, they might not once they heard she was still talking to Rosa Coppola. The past was the past. You couldn't judge that, but the fact that she was still in contact with them was just wrong.

"I know, and I'm sorry." I tried to get him to calm down. "That's why I'm telling you this now."

"Where was this before?" he shot back.

"I only just found out the last part." I used the same harsh tone he used on me. "This puzzle that you and I are piecing together is way beyond what we thought. Haven't you noticed that yet? Everyone has a piece of the story." I paused for a few beats to let him think. "Elio, you have to admit, it's pretty ironic that our story was woven together even before we were born. Maybe we were meant to be together, or maybe we weren't, but regardless, we have a hell of a lot more to get through before we can stand back and see this storm for what it is!" I took a moment to catch my breath. "So, get mad and throw things, but don't point your anger at me anymore. That's pushed me away enough times already, and it stops now." I headed for the door and yanked on the handle. "I need to get back. Who knows what—"

Slam. The door shut.

I turned to find him vibrating with anger and his eyes cast on the floor.

"I may have a temper," he ground through his teeth, "but it only comes out when it comes to you. I just can't believe all this, this stuff that's happening. I want you home, by my side, where I know you're safe, not chasing leads, living in a house full of snakes, and acting like you're looking for a husband." He closed his eyes for a moment and took a deep breath. "However," he looked straight in my eyes, "I know that's not something that can happen right now. I'm trying. I really am, and I want to tread carefully not to lose you again."

"Okay." I shifted, happy for that, at least, and knowing he'd heard me.

"God, my own aunt. I'll put a tail on her." He shook his head then cleared his throat. "Has there been any talk of where Mariano is?"

"No."

"Okay." He nodded and took a deep breath. "I've something to tell you, too. We killed Bria and Roberto."

"What?"

He ignored that and continued his story. "It was time. We had to clean house, and every day that went by only made it harder. Now we need to make some moves here. Anything at all you think is worth me knowing, big or small, tell Ugo, and he'll contact me."

"I understand." I shrugged. "Kind of wish I was there for it, though."

He smiled, and his eyes lit up. It must have been glorious. I had a few fun ideas of my own that I needed to work up to.

"Look, you need to tell the Coppolas that Mariano's the one who took you tonight. I can't have *them* protecting him if he shows up. We need to flush him out, not give him a place to hide. Stefano's already tired of him, and the uncles are nervous of him since he's been with us for so long. Besides, they all know he's using. He's too unpredictable."

He went on to tell me what I needed to say, and I listened carefully to all of it. I secretly wondered what would happen once we parted ways. I only hoped he wouldn't go after Noemi. As scared as I was about what information she had to tell me, I was also painfully curious to know what it was.

"Is there anything you're not clear on?"

"No, I think I got it all." I checked the time on his watch and knew I needed to get my head in the game.

"One more thing." He reached in his pocket and pulled out something. "I know why you gave it back to me, and it worked that her soldiers saw it, too, but I miss seeing it on you." He held up the necklace I'd left in the envelope. The crow looked up at me as it rested against his palm. "I also understand you might not be seeing clearly right now, but you're a Capri before anything else. For now," he opened the clasp and slid the crow off the chain, "I'll hold on to this for you, until you return home." He slipped the chain over my head and pulled my hair through the rest. I'd missed my necklace terribly, but I didn't feel it was mine to take when I left. I held up the little teddy, thinking how lonely it looked without the crow.

"Thank you." I felt a sense of sadness wash over me. There was a part of me that still wasn't sure if I'd ever see it again. What if our plan didn't go as hoped and his family decided they were better off without me, or if Nonna Rosa just shot me then and there right on the street?

He cupped my face and kissed me roughly. I knew he didn't want to say goodbye. "You need to go."

He walked me outside the room. Vinni and Niccola were playing a card game on the hood of the car. When they spotted us, they both jumped quickly back into work mode, and the cards disappeared.

"Ready?" Vinni grinned as he picked a bit of fluff off my sleeve, clearly showing they'd both known full well what we'd been doing.

"Yeah," I answered as I felt a tug on my arm. I looked up at Elio.

"I love you."

"I…" I paused as my words froze in my throat. My heart held them back, defending what little control it had left over me. I did love Elio, but the scars inside were still raw, and that part of me needed a little more time to heal. Elio was explosive, and after his temper reared its head back there, I'd felt uneasy. "I love you, too." I gave him a little smile then disappeared into the car.

I'd seen the frustrated expression on his face as he stepped back. Yes, I'd hesitated, but I did say the words because it was true, I did love him. I was just still a little wounded.

"You good?" Niccola asked as he joined me in the back.

"Yes," I replied and reached down and ripped the side of my dress. Then I flipped forward and ran wild fingers through my hair, letting my own anger soar. "Hand me that, please." I pointed to the water bottle, and he watched, fascinated as I wet my fingers and smudged my mascara. Then I sat upright and tightened my jaw. "Now, let's see just how well I can sell this."

"You frighten me a little." Niccola grinned, impressed. "You'll make one hell of a Don wife. Oh, here."

He handed me the bag to put over my head, and I hesitated but put in on then peeked out to see him pull down a mask to hide his own face.

"Okay, be ready," he warned. The tires squealed as we came to a screeching halt at the curb. Niccola opened the door, slid out, and roughly pulled me out onto the pavement. I fell to my knees—that was my idea—and I waited for the car to speed off. With shaky hands, I yanked the bag off and blinked around and saw a man drop his bag of groceries as he rushed to my aid.

"Are you all right, miss?" He helped me to my feet. "Should I call for help?"

"No." I started to cry, and then, in a panicked voice, "Please, can you call someone else for me?"

Ten minutes later, Salvo and Pippo hopped out of a car near where I sat on a bench by the side of the road, looking like I'd been through the wringer.

"Are you hurt?" Salvo touched my arm, but I pulled it back as though nervous of his touch. "Sienna, come, let's get you to the car."

"Tell me everything you saw, and whatever she told you," Pippo barked at the man who had helped me.

"She was tossed out of a car by a man in a mask." The man was visibly shaken. I felt bad that he was involved, but his part was crucial to the story. "He dumped her on the street with a bag over her head. Wh-when she saw me, she refused help but used my phone to call you."

Yes, that's right, tell them everything you remember.

"Make, model of the car?" Pippo urged the man for more details.

"Black, tinted, town car, the man was taller than her, black jacket and jeans." He rubbed his face. "I'm sorry. I don't know any more than that."

"Salvo?" I squeezed out some tears. "Can you take me home now?" The word *home* scorched my tongue, but Elio would have been proud of my performance.

"Of course." Salvo scooped me up in his arms and carried me to the car. I watched over his shoulder as Pippo handed the man a wad of cash, and I knew he'd make sure the poor fellow kept his mouth shut. I smiled to myself as Salvo helped me into the car, and Pippo followed, looking furious.

The ride home was quiet, and it worked in my favor as I carefully planned my words for when we got back to the house.

To my surprise, when we arrived, Nonna Rosa stood at the door, balanced on her creepy cane. After a quick once-over, she ordered Salvo to take me to the sitting room where she took a chair across from me.

"Are you hurt?" I could tell by her voice and the way she fixed her jacket that it wasn't the first question she wanted to ask, but she had other ears in the room, so she started there.

"Nothing a hot shower and a good night's sleep won't fix." I allowed my voice to become strong.

"Good." She switched hands on the cane, and it made me think she used as more as a shield so no one could get close. "Do you have any idea who took you?"

"Yes, I know exactly who it was." I cleared my throat, "Mariano DeSimone."

"As in Stefano's contact at the Capri house?" Salvo cut in.

"That'd be him." I gently touched my jaw like it was sore. "Apparently, the Capris killed his parents, and since I used to date Elio, he came after me."

"What did he say?" Pippo moved farther into the room.

"I guess Elio's been laying low for the past few days, and Mariano thought by coming after me he'd flush Elio out." I chuckled darkly. "He was wrong. He never came."

"How did you get away?" Nonna's cold eyes pierced

through me, so instead of saying it, I held up my hand to show my ring.

"He finally listened to me and when he called Stefano, he confirmed it."

"Stefano knew about this?" Salvo's voice boomed through the room.

"I don't know if he actually did," I winced as I reached for a glass of water one of the maids had brought me, "and I'd really like to think he didn't." My voice was sincere as I talked of Stefano's possible involvement. "Regardless, Elio didn't come, Mariano didn't get what he wanted, and I came out all right. It's a win in my book."

"I thought you forbid Stefano from seeing that train wreck," Pippo snapped at Nonna Rosa, and she turned her wicked look on him, but he didn't back down.

"Come on." Salvo helped me to my feet. "You've had enough tonight, and you don't need to hear these two go at it."

He walked me to my room and pulled back the covers, making sure the bed was just so. If my heart wasn't already taken, I would have been intrigued by Salvo. I didn't know him all that well, but he was at the very least a gentleman, at least on the surface. Opening my jewelry bag, I retrieved the bear pendant and slipped it back onto the chain. I had missed the weight of it but missed the crow more.

"Are you warm enough?" he asked with his back to me as he closed the window.

"I'll be fine, thank you." I sat down on the chair next

to the side table.

"Well, I'll let you be."

"Salvo?" I stopped him before he could leave. "I'm not…never mind." I waited for him to take my hook.

"What is it?"

"Do you think you could stay just for a few more minutes?"

His face softened, and he joined me in the little sitting area.

"My nerves are a little shot." I rubbed my hands together as if rattled.

"That's understandable." Then he seemed to get an idea and held up a finger and whisked out of the room. He returned moments later with a bottle of rum and two glasses. "This always helps me." He poured us both about a half a glass and winked as he handed it to me. "Sometimes you need a little more than the recommended dose," he said and chuckled.

He picked up his glass and threw back a big gulp. He grew silent then as he thought about something. Just as I opened my mouth to speak, he beat me to the punch.

"Do you miss your old life? I mean before all of this with the Capris?" He swept his arm around.

"Parts of it, yes." I pressed my lips to the glass then pretended to swallow. "I miss feeling comfortable and knowing who people are." I looked toward the window. "There are so many people I don't know walking the grounds here that I feel like a stranger instead of family."

"Well, as far as the soldiers go, don't even bother getting to know them. Ms. Rosa is very particular about who works here. One wrong move, no matter how small, and they're gone. I see new people here all the time." He shrugged.

"Seems like a lot of vetting."

"It's the lifestyle."

"And we're not supposed to even talk to the staff? Why?" I pretended to take another drink and noticed he followed, making a good dent in his.

"Why would we?" He shrugged again. "They're the staff. They're here to serve us."

There was the word *us* again...I really wondered how much time Salvo spent here.

He eyed my necklace over the lip of his glass. "Were you wearing that tonight?"

I sniffed and placed a hand to my chest to feel the chain, I was so happy to have it back. "Mariano took it, but now it's back." I kept the story confusing like my head was just as rattled as my nerves. "It's the only gift my mother ever gave me." I pulled the pendant up and watched him eye the teddy.

"Is that *the* teddy bear?"

"Why would you say *the* teddy bear, not *a* teddy bear."

"Oh, you don't know?" He looked at me oddly as he went on. "All the children in the family get them in some form or other when they're born. Girls get pendants, and boys get pins. Usually, the dad gives it to the mother once the baby comes. It's a family tradition."

"I didn't know that." I studied the tiny teddy bear, trying to picture my father gifting it to my mother. "I can't believe I'd been wearing a part of who I was all along, and I had no idea." I laughed lightly, hating how much of my life was controlled by others. "Regardless, I've had it since my childhood, and I just can't part with it."

"Why did Mariano return it now?"

"Mind games." I shrugged matter-of-factly. "They're the only moves Mariano has left."

"He's a mess." Salvo leaned back with a pissed-off expression as he downed what was left in his glass then poured himself another. I failed to point out that he drank like Mariano. "I hate that Stefano ever got mixed up with him. His day will come."

"I hope I get to see it." I truly meant that. "You're very comfortable here, and respected, maybe even more so than Stefano."

"Yeah, well," he shrugged, "I know when to push and when not to."

"Meaning?"

"I've been friends with Stefano for as long as I can remember, way before his father passed." He swirled the liquid around his glass before taking another big sip. "He was always a hotheaded, egotistical womanizer who carried a mighty big chip on his shoulder. Everything increased when he became Don."

"I hate that it was him who took over," I blurted and shook my head. "Sorry, that was rude."

"No, I understand what you're saying. He certainly doesn't fit the mold, but he was next in line, and Nonna Rosa had been grooming him since he was small. And since, well, you know…you weren't here and—"

"And I'm a female."

"Yeah." He shrugged, and his face went pink. The liquor was taking its effect. "From what I know, Oscar could have taken the seat, but he had no interest, and he left when you all did. I don't know if it was a fluke or even if the man is still alive, but I always wondered about him." He chuckled softly.

"Wondered what?"

"I've always heard that Oscar loved your mother, and that when you and your mother disappeared, he followed."

"I wouldn't know." I decided to keep myself out of that lie. I didn't trust my mother not to show up here and blow this entire plan. I let my mind wander for a moment and remembered that Oscar was always only an arm's reach away from mama. If he did love her, did they ever date? I hoped not, for Francesco's sake.

"So, yeah, Stefano took over after his father passed, much to the uncles' disapproval, and now you're back, and Stefano is losing his mind."

"I didn't mean to cause the family any problems."

"I actually think it's for the best if Stefano steps down. He's drunk on power and, well, other things, but he's petrified of Mikey, so maybe now she'll focus more on you and less on him."

"Mikey?" That jolted me alert. "Is he here in the house?"

He closed his eyes and shook his head like he just screwed up.

"Please, never let anyone know you know that name." When I stared at him, hoping he'd give me more information, he cursed. "I'm saying too much, and that's not good." He stood and took a moment like he was lightheaded, then took my hand and kissed the top of it gently. "I should go and let you get some rest. I'll see you in the morning."

"Hey, Salvo." He turned back around when he opened the door, and I stopped my urge to bombarded him with questions. "Thanks for staying."

"Goodnight, Sienna."

Just as he went to close the door, I saw Stefano with a suitcase.

Good. Leave.

TWENTY

Elenora

I walked slowly beside my parents as we followed my brother's casket down the aisle of the church. The service had been short and the gathering small. As I walked, it felt as though all eyes were on me, and I hugged Alessia to my chest, thankful she was blissfully asleep.

I was numb inside and out. I shivered as I felt the air from the open door. I knew Nonna Rosa thought I was suffering from postpartum since the baby's birth, but I knew it was a broken heart.

As the graveside service came to an end, I found it hard to pull myself away. "It's time to leave." Mama's harsh tone jolted me from my thoughts. "You've had your time, and Ms. Rosa is looking to leave."

"She can wait."

"Elenora," she hissed, turning sideways to hide her words from those around us, "watch your tone with me or I'll—"

"What? What will you do, Mama? Sell me off to someone else?" I turned away, not wanting to see her face.

"How dare you?" she cried.

"How dare I?" I shook my head. "I did what you asked. I left everything I knew, gave up my own dreams, all to pay off your and Papa's mistakes. Look what it's cost me!"

"Cost you!" She yanked on my arm to turn me toward her. She glanced down at Alessia and lowered her own voice in case she woke her. "You were the one who brought him to that house. You were the one who exposed him again to that wicked woman who broke his heart, and then to find out she's dating Piero's brother! She probably made a call to him, and that's who took away my sweet boy." She started to cry, and I wanted to scream.

"Are you saying this was my fault?"

"No!" She sobbed, but her words had cut deep. "I'm just saying look at who you used to date. Francesco is one of them. Your actions have consequences, Elenora. The Capris are evil people." She dabbed her swollen eyes and clutched her purse. "You let the Capris get close, and...and I just wished you could have seen that they are monsters before it was too late."

"It's time to go." Papa looked drained as he took

Mama by the shoulders and turned her away from me. "Please, Elenora, I need to get your mother home."

I turned away, hating that somehow my brother's death landed on me. Once they left, I looked toward the parking lot and caught sight of Theo, and my heart skipped a beat.

Theo had an arm wrapped around Noemi and was looking down at her with such love that it made my blood boil. I couldn't even have this one damn day without my husband fondling this woman. I watched as his other hand slid over her belly. I had to laugh at the absurdity of it all because her husband, Bosco Capri, would murder both of them for me if he could see her like this with Theo right now. Her being present at my brother's funeral was just so wrong in so many ways.

"Elenora," Nonna Rosa's voice was so loud Alessia jumped in my arms, "it's time to go."

I tuned her out and stood at the end of the fresh grave and looked down at my brother's coffin. I said a silent goodbye and tossed him the flower I'd taken from the church and allowed myself a few minutes to remember him, then just like that, my beloved brother was gone, and I was left with a baby, a hateful husband, and two families who had turned their backs on me.

"I can stay a bit longer," the minister said gently behind me. "It's really no trouble."

I wondered if he was only being kind because of who we were, but then shook myself and took comfort that he would do that for me.

"No," Theo said harshly as he appeared at my side,

"we're finished here. Come, Elenora."

"I'm not a pet, Theo. I'm a sister grieving the loss of her little brother. "Why don't you take your girlfriend home before her baby daddy sees what's really happening here."

"Need I remind you of the arrangement?" Theo hissed down at me, and it took everything inside me not to kick him square between the legs. He was a cruel bastard, and the longer I lived as his so-called wife, the more I saw him for who he really was.

"I really don't care. The only person I care about is now ashes below my feet."

I turned away, but he grabbed my arm and jerked me backward so hard it caused Alessia's head to bump my shoulder. Her lip went out, and she started to cry. The Minister's face pinched and turned white, but he wisely turned and walked away.

"Feel free to join him." His grip tightened, and his expression told me not to push any further. "Now, shut that baby up or I will." He let go, sending me back a couple of steps.

As I watched him head up the walk toward Noemi, I knew he'd meant every word of what he'd just threatened.

"Are you all right?" Oscar reached out for Alessia and rubbed her back affectionately as he held her to his shoulder.

"No," I sniffed as we walked together toward the car. "Do you think you could help me with something?"

"Of course."

"It's not a small request." I shot him a look.

Chapter
TWENTY-ONE

Elio

"Are you sure you can do this, Vinni?" I admired my suit in the mirrored walls of the elevator and adjusted my tie to sit just right.

We had arrived in Vegas late the night before and had spent the day going over the plan for the day. It would be risky, but when was it not when it came to our business? My two trusted soldiers, Harris and Gain, accompanied Vinni, Niccola, and me, while three more waited with the car. The last time I was in Vegas, we'd had a ru-in with a few of Jacob Raine's men, and I hoped, now that he was dead, we wouldn't have any problems.

"I think I left my stomach down there." Vinni turned his back to the window wall behind us.

None of us had a problem with heights, but a few years back, Vinni had been trapped in an elevator just like this one for hours. Since then, he got a little squirrelly when the shiny doors closed for more than a few minutes.

"Finally," he growled as the box stopped at our floor.

The doors opened, and Vinni pushed his way out first, followed by the soldiers. We moved in sync down the long gray hallway. I nodded at Vinni to branch off while the rest of us kept pace.

"Mr. Capri," Bronson Cooper, the son of Justin Cooper, stepped out and greeted us at the door to his office, "how was your trip?"

"Smooth, thank you," I said in English and waved off my soldiers. I knew they would find a strategic place to wait until we finished our meeting.

"Gentlemen." He directed us toward a conference room. Niccola joined me as we stepped through the doors. I immediately took a seat near the head of the long, oval table with my back to the wall, facing the door. Niccola always liked to be closer to the door and sat on the opposite side.

"Niccola," Bronson addressed him and nodded a greeting as he entered behind us. "Can I get you two anything?" He motioned to his assistant, but I raised a hand to indicate we didn't need anything.

"No need." I pulled out a pen and flipped open my folder, showing him I was ready for business.

"I admire you, Elio. You don't waste people's time and get straight to the point." I nodded my thank you for the compliment. "When you said you were interested in the offer we sent, I was pleasantly surprised. I know our grandfathers have done business in the past, and I'm hoping today we can do the same."

"Well, we're certainly open to negotiation. Let's see, shall we?" I smiled and clicked my pen.

We spent nearly two hours working on the ins and outs of a contract. Bronson was smart and quick, which was refreshing. Niccola added a point here and there, making sure nothing was forgotten as he kept a close eye on his phone.

"Well, that's it, then." Bronson pushed the freshly signed paperwork away from him and leaned back with a smile. "Let's have a drink to seal our new business deal, shall we? What's your poison, gentlemen?"

"What do you have?" I didn't want to waste any more time here, but we hadn't heard anything from Vinni yet, so I needed to buy more time.

Bronson pushed the intercom, and moments later his assistant came in pushing a cart. "Twenty-five-year Dalmore," he said with a satisfied lip smack as he opened the top, and after we both nodded, he poured out three healthy glasses. "I'll be honest. I don't know a lot about single malts, but I've tried this one, and it's exceptional."

"It is." I took a small, appreciative sip and thought for a moment as I admired the grooves in the glass. "Do you mind if I ask you something?"

"Sure."

"Though I'm happy we could make this work, I have to ask, why not the Coppolas? They've worked with your father before. Why make the jump back to us?"

"Ah," he chuckled darkly and twirled the glass between his fingers, "I was brought up to do business face to face." He cleared his throat and shrugged. I sensed he was making an effort not to say much more. He seemed to make a decision and leaned in slightly as he spoke. "Let's just say I've been burned by Mikey Coppola more times than I'm proud of. Fool me once…" He gave me a look, not finishing the famous saying.

I froze as I felt that name burn through my brain. Mikey Coppola was the M in Stefano's notebook, the very man he was terrified of, and who was now apparently making bad deals. Niccola shot me a knowing glance when Bronson looked away.

"Fair enough." I glanced at Niccola again when he tapped the table once, letting me know Vinni was finished. "Well, I'm pleased we did this." I closed my folder and slipped my pen back into my breast pocket then stood and offered my hand. "If you ever plan a trip over my way, please let me know. I'd be glad to show you around."

"I will." He walked us out, and my soldiers materialized around us as we heard the ping of the elevator. Vinni smoothly stepped in without drawing any attention to himself. We didn't speak a word to each other until we were behind the protection of the bulletproof SUV.

"All right, Vin." I nodded for the driver to ease into traffic. "What did you find out?"

"I like this company, not just because they seem

pretty legit, but their staff are chatty." He pulled out his phone and checked his notes; his job had been to gather information. "Cooper Industries goes way back, and the old man likes to do things the old-fashioned way, face to face. His son, Bronson, seems to respect that, and it works for them. Apparently, a Mikey Coppola was the one they were dealing with, and he refused to even talk on the phone, just strictly used email."

"That's odd," Niccola thought out loud. "What else?"

"They had three contracts in the last while. All of them were signed off for at least five years, yet one ended after only two. Another deal went a bit longer, but the last one was dropped after only three weeks."

"Interesting." I rubbed my chin as I continued to strain to watch a red sports car in the side mirror. I had noticed it when we left, and it had just made the same two turns we'd made.

"Yes, and all three were terminated by Cooper Industries. Apparently, the Coppola half of the buy-in vanished, and the profits never materialized."

"So, they faked their accounts, moving money in and out while the contracts were being signed," I muttered as I caught the eye of our driver, and he nodded. I knew he'd also been watching the red car that tailed us.

"Yeah," Vinni opened his jacket and stretched his neck, "they've been blackballed and have been spreading the word ever since."

"Then why would Cooper go to the Coppolas with an offer?" I said, even as I realized the obvious.

"I don't think they had any intention of signing with them. I think they were hoping to flush out this Mikey guy."

"Yeah, I would have done the same," I replied as I put a finger to my lips, and both Vinni and Niccola stopped talking and looked at me. "I'll be right back. Nothing to worry about." I stepped out of the car and spoke quietly to the lead soldier, Gain. "Let me deal with this." I smiled knowingly at him. I knew who it was.

"Sir?"

"Just give me a moment. It's all right." He spoke to the men, and they stepped back but didn't stray too far from the car. They knew as well as Vinni and Niccola not to question me.

I whirled around just as the red car squealed to a stop at the curb. I grinned as I approached knowing, it would be Eli. He was the stepson of the owner of the Wynn hotel chain and happened to be a good friend. He was rich, reckless, and drove that exact souped-up car. When Eli heard I was in town a year or so ago, he'd made a point of pulling me over to ask me to go for a drink. He was crazy but had a heart of gold and was a great man to know in Vegas.

The window rolled down, and he grinned at me like a sixteen-year-old who'd just gotten his first new car.

"When they told me you reserved a room, I made sure to let our friend know you'd be in town. He wanted me to give you these." The woman in the passenger seat had been eyeing me up and down, and she smiled with lips that were as red as the car. She showed me she liked what she saw as she held out a gold-colored envelope.

"You're lucky I called off my soldiers." I took the envelope from her manicured nails and checked the contents. "Is he?" I raised my eyebrows at Eli.

"No, not him, but it's supposed to be the biggest night of the year, and he'd sure like it if you came. It's going to be Cavendish and Giro." He gave me a knowing smile. Yeah, that would be a big night.

"Sounds like my night just got a whole lot more interesting."

"Yeah, and he says he has a treat for you too."

"Is that so?"

"Yep, so don't let those go to waste."

"Thanks, I won't." I held them up as I walked back toward my men.

Vinni looked over my shoulder as I opened the door. "Who was that?"

"Eli. Change of plans. Tell the pilot we're spending the night here."

"Wait," Vinni's eyes went wide, "we are having a night off in Vegas?"

I couldn't help but grin at my excited cousins when we arrived at the hotel, and they piled on the elevator.

This should be fun.

"Hey." Vinni looked out the window as we arrived at the back door to one of Vegas's biggest strip joints. *Dirty Deeds* was written in small neon lights above the door. "Have I ever been here before?"

"Nope, it's new." Niccola opened the door after Gain, one of our soldiers, scouted the area and had deemed it safe for us to get out.

"You smell that?" Vinni breathed in deeply as he ran a hand through his hair. "Sex, top shelf booze, and a promise of a great time."

The bouncer, who looked like my trainer's very bored brother, took the tickets and immediately snapped his fingers when he saw that I was on the top of the list to get in this evening.

"Welcome, sir. Your seats are up at the front, and he's waiting for you."

"He who?" Vinni asked as he followed me.

I ignored him. We stepped through some curtains, down a hallway, and into an elevator. Before we even started our descent, the roar of the crowd found its way to us.

I closed my eyes and breathed in the old familiar rush these underground fights always brought me. The smell of the cold cement, the taste of cheap beer, and sound of the crowd growing more and more excited as the time ticked down to start the first fight.

I reached up and brushed my hand along the skinny pipes that ran the lighting throughout the arena, something I used to do on my way to the ring. I used to imagine I was pulling the energy from it, fueling my warmed muscles with its power. It made my head wild.

We followed the usher out through the crowd to where I spotted my friend and his entourage.

"Fuck," Vinni cursed behind me, and I laughed out loud as he took in Trigger and some of his MC members. They made for a pretty scary sight with all their tattoos and leather.

"Glad you made it." Trigger stood and offered me a handshake. It was something I admired about him. I knew he hated to be touched and knew the reasoning behind it, so the fact that he'd made an effort to show that kind of respect to me said it all. I gripped his hand firmly and grinned.

"I think he senses my fear," Vinni whispered to Niccola, who muttered a curse to shut up.

"You're lucky my men didn't take Eli out with the way he brought me the tickets."

"You know he likes to play chicken." He snickered.

"Indeed." I laughed, and we took our seats front row and center. "This brings back some memories."

"Good and bad, I bet." Trigger chuckled. "And of course you remember Brick." When I nodded, he continued. "Well, my wife, Tess, bought the strip joint for Brick's girl Minnie, and it was her idea to use the bunker below it as a fighting ring. Brings in good money and gives us control of who fights where in Vegas."

"Smart."

"Mm," he grunted, "took some blood to make it happen, but in the end, it was worth it."

"Good."

A blonde woman, dressed in the shortest shorts I'd ever seen and a tiny top that struggled to fight the good fight to contain her ample breasts, came over and stood in front of Trigger.

"They're short a girl for the rounds." She flipped her hair back. "I'm stepping in."

Trigger laughed and leaned back, looking amused. "Elio, this is Tess, my wife. She's suddenly got a death wish."

"Lovely to meet you." I stood and offered a hand.

"Oh, I've heard a lot about you!" She was very pretty and full of confidence, and something told me they'd be very amusing to watch together.

"How can someone so small move so quick?" Rail, one of Trigger's club members, leaned over with his hands on his knees, all the while sucking in smoke from a cigarette. "I tried to tell her no, Trig, but she threatened the stage again."

"I won't let Minnie's biggest night be ruined because Monica drank too much last night and is stuck with her head in the toilet," Tess argued with her hands firmly on her hips. "Be pissed, Trigger, but she's my girl, and I'm doing it." She turned and stomped off toward the ring, and Trigger shot out of his chair after her. Rail sat down with a huff and shook his head at me.

"That girl's got she-balls," he laughed, "and we've got about twenty minutes before the three F's happen."

"Three Fs?" I wasn't sure if I wanted to know.

"Fight, fuck, fail." He shrugged. "Well, most likely Trigger will fail because Tess, for the most part, wins."

"Lovely." I glanced at Niccola, who laughed in amusement at my reaction.

"Kind of sounds like you, boss." Vinni ducked

when I threw a punch at him. Brick thumbed Rail out of Trigger's seat and acknowledged me with a nod.

"Hey, let Tess know I think I just saw Lexi upstairs."

"As in Keith's Lexi?" Rail looked confused, and I wondered who they were referring to.

"Yeah," Brick shifted to get comfortable, "looks just like her, but you know Keith would have given us a heads up if she was in town. But whatever, just get Tess to call Minnie and figure it out."

"Yeah." Rail hurried away, disappearing into the crowd.

"Fuckin' great crowd tonight," he said as he tossed me a beer from a tray one of the waiters held. Then he motioned for the waiter to hand my men a beer, too. I didn't drink beer often. I preferred sipping on the finer things, generally things that were stored and marinated in oak barrels, but I appreciated the gesture and certainly wouldn't turn it down.

"Thanks." I took a sip. "May I say you seem disturbed by something?" Life experience had heightened my senses when something was off with a person.

He studied my face for a moment. "Just been dealing with a lot of personal shit. Not sure if it's even worth my time anymore."

"I see."

"Did Trigger tell you about this place?" He changed the topic.

"He did say your Minnie owns it and that it allows him to control the underground fighting in Vegas."

"No, I meant…" He trailed off when he saw Trigger

coming our way. "Enjoy the fight."

"You as well." I wasn't sure what he'd been getting at, but I let it drop as I focused on the lights dimming and the announcer coming into the ring. "Everything good?" I asked Trigger as he sat in the chair Brick had vacated.

"If I go missing, ask my wife." He chuckled darkly and downed the beer Rail handed him. I rather enjoyed this side of Trigger.

The bell rang, and we sat forward for the fight. I felt like I was eighteen again.

Trigger almost lost his last nerve when Tess came out wearing nothing but a string bikini. She held up a number and glared in his direction. I could only imagine what would happen later when they were alone. I shifted my own desire back into place as I thought of Sienna and all the times we'd fought and had great make-up sex. Shit, I loved a good fight with her. It always ended well.

By the third round, I was so engulfed that I barely noticed when one of the security guys leaned over to tell Trigger something.

"Seems we have company." Trigger rubbed his head. "Blue section, standing by the post." I followed his directions and spotted him.

Stefano.

He must have followed me here. I imagined he probably had heard about Cooper Industry's offer and wouldn't have trusted what Sienna had told the elders. We certainly hadn't hidden our travel plans, so it would have been easy for him to locate us. He probably had people reporting our whereabouts the whole time. How he'd gotten in, I had no idea, but money talked. Knowing he had worked with Jacob Raine in the past meant he still had people in the United States to keep him in the know.

There were ten minutes left of the fight, so I took the time to hatch a plan and shared it with Trigger.

Elio

The fight ended, and Cavendish won, which meant Trigger won, as he called it, a shit ton of money. We rode that high as we slipped through the back door and down the hallway usually reserved for the fighters.

"What I wouldn't do for one of my blowtorches right now!" Vinni called to me with a delighted laugh. Vinni had a unique hobby and one that was well polished while he worked with the Mexican Cartel a few years back. He and Niccola joined Brick and Rail and another of their members and headed in one direction. Trigger and I headed in the opposite direction. There was only one job to do—grab Stefano. Trigger knew I was to be the one to have the pleasure of killing him. Trigger's men were going to handle the Coppolas' soldiers so we would have Stefano to ourselves.

We whipped around a corner, only to be met with a spray of bullets. The sound echoed off the walls and sent the paying guests, who were trying to leave, into a frenzy. We pivoted around the corner, and I took a breath as we fired some rounds down the hall. Again, more bullets flew our way. Trigger gave a hand signal for some of the men to circle around. I stayed close to Trigger as we made our way through a maze of halls. I lost track of where we were going and was glad he seemed to know where we were headed.

"Hold back," Trigger whispered as he caught sight of something. "I'll be right back."

He slipped away, and a round of shots suddenly broke out. I saw a guy slip inside a room ahead of me, then with his back to me, he stepped out and started firing down the hall. I stayed close to the wall and waited until I heard the click of the empty magazine, then in the hair of a second as he reloaded, I drove a single bullet into his neck and then another into the man who appeared ahead of him. I was always taught "Reserve your bullets and aim for the main artery. No kill is pretty."

I hurried farther down the hall as I heard more shots and a scream of panic. A door behind me opened, and a girl's face appeared. She had bright red hair and big eyes.

"Shh." I motioned with my finger and attempted to urge her back inside the room, but she stood her ground and pulled out a gun as she pushed my hand away.

"I'm not scared of a few bullets. Name's Minnie."

"Brick's girl?"

"When he's not being an asshole, yes." I couldn't help but flash her a quick grin as I started moving down the hall with her following.

"By your accent and the fact that you got that fancy suit on, I'm guessin' you're Trig's friend, Elio Capri," she said a million miles an hour behind me.

"Yes."

"Who we hunting?"

"Coppolas."

"Who? Oh, well, fuck, whatever. I'm game!" I glanced back and found myself entertained by her whole attitude in this generally dangerous situation.

We followed the sounds of gunshots and whisked through a room that led us to another series of hallways.

"This place is a maze," I murmured.

"Let's get a bird's eye view, mafia boy." She grinned and motioned for me to follow her up some stairs then to a skinny metal ladder where she scooted up like a little circus performer. I tried not to appreciate the view above as I followed. We ended up at a very narrow walkway that circled the whole way around the stadium.

"Look, over there." She pointed to the far corner where Rail and Brick were cornered by two Coppola soldiers. Careful where I stepped, I hurried over and fired straight down, hitting one of them between the shoulders while Vinni took out the other. They both looked up.

"Hey, baby." Minnie leaned over the railing and waved her gun. "You're welcome."

"What the hell are you doing?" he yelled and looked

around. "Get down from there."

"A thank you goes a long¬—"

Bang!

She flew backward, and I caught her before she fell.

"Minnie! Minnie!" Brick shouted like a wild person. I laid her down on the grate and inspected her wound.

"He just clipped my shoulder," she grunted. "I'm fine." She was right; it wasn't too bad. The force of the bullet had sent her spinning backward but hadn't done any real damage. "Go and shoot that fucker in the balls for me."

"You sure?" I hated to leave her, but I knew Brick would appear at any moment. I could hear what sounded like a bull moose coming up the ladder. I needed to get to Stefano before he slipped away again. She pushed my arm to go, and I left as Brick's head appeared at the top of the ladder.

"She's okay," I called as he ran toward us.

I looked down to get my bearings and spotted Trigger making his way along the other side of the arena. I figured he had his sights on Stefano, so I headed in their direction, trying like hell not to lose my footing. When I got to the ladder, I clung to the sides and dropped straight down, hitting the floor without a sound. I wanted to head them off. I'd pretty much made it down when a door flew open below me and Stefano ran out with a few of his soldiers on his heels. They looked to have been stripped of their weapons. Vinni stepped out from behind a wall across the other side and saw me. I motioned for him to stay put. Neither of us had been spotted yet.

"Where is he?" Stefano shouted to one of his men, while the others put their hands in the air, looking annoyed. "He can't just vanish!"

"I can't get hold of any of the other guys," the soldier huffed.

"Well, we can't fucking stay here!" Stefano headed for the door. "Get me to the car!"

I could have ended it all right there—point, aim, shoot—but where was the fun in that?

I retraced my steps to the elevator and found the stairs and opted for those instead. My excitement was getting the best of me, and the smell of the promised blood was already in my nostrils. I took the stairs three at a time and ripped open the door. I came face to face with one of Stefano's men and reached forward before he could react and wrapped my hands around his neck then drilled my knee into his face. His body gave out and dropped to the floor just as the door to the strip club opened. The music pounded and paired its vibration with my heart. A bartender looked at me then at the man at my feet and back to me again.

"The douche bag in the white sports coat went that way," he grated and pointed with his head.

I nodded my thanks and brushed by him. I wound my way through the lap dances and desperate moans, then outside to the pouring rain.

There he was, standing in the middle of the parking lot with two of his soldiers. They looked lost as they just stood there. It didn't click with me why.

I pulled out my gun, flipped my coin into the air,

and called it. Tails. It landed, and I grinned and took off toward them.

Bang! I took out the man to his left. Bang! I took out the other.

"Whoa! Elio!" Stefano shouted as he backed away. I tucked my weapon away and swung, and my fist plowed into his stomach. When he doubled up, I headbutted him, sending him backward with a yelp.

"The Reaper waits for no one," Trigger grunted from somewhere behind me. Rail and another guy started cheering and making catcalls at Stefano. I realized they'd been waiting for me to arrive. I blocked out all sound and gave in to Zazzero. He'd been waiting for this moment to come forward.

My wet hair fell and sent raindrops into my eyes as I leaned back. I cleared my vision and aimed my foot and high-kicked him in the stomach with my other. He fell to the ground with a thud, but I wasn't finished. I grabbed his jacket and pulled him to his feet.

"You threatened what's mine." I saw Sienna's face when I drilled my fist into his chin. "You touched what's mine." I repeated the action to the other side of his jaw. "You hurt what's mine." I grabbed him by the hair and dragged him to the side of the brick wall. "I'll return the treatment you've shown me and my family."

"Just wait," he muttered, barely coherent, "just wait."

"I'll be sure to send Mikey your regards." His swollen eyes widened, and I saw his terror just as his life slipped away.

Taking his head, I held his mouth open, rested his teeth on the brick, and with all my force drilled my elbow into his head, hearing his jaw break and his neck snap.

I let his body slump as I fought to catch my breath, feeling Zazzero slowly fizzle into the background. Leaning over, I removed his family ring and tucked it in my pocket.

Running a hand through my hair to slick it back, I joined Trigger and his crew. Vinni and Niccola stood quietly. Rail and some other men I'd yet to meet were nodding with approval.

"Hi. I'm Morgan." He held out a hand. "We've met before, but a long ass time ago." He spat, and it landed close to Stefano's bloody head. "I take it you're done here?" He grinned.

"So, this is your friend?" Tess joked with sarcasm, and Trigger, to my surprise, laughed loudly.

I looked over at the body then at Vinni and tossed him the ring. "Hang on to this for Sienna."

"Yes, boss."

"Whiskey?" Trigger slapped my shoulder.

"That would be perfect."

***

Tess was a great hostess and made sure we got the grand tour of the house. I had to admit the place was impressive and was in full swing, even for this late at night. I knew Vegas never slept but was still amazed at how many people were partying. Niccola and Vinni were enjoying lap dances while Morgan and Rail hooted their encouragement. Brick was off attending to Minnie. He'd messaged Trigger she was going to be just fine.

"Is that a man dressed as a woman?" I eyed what looked like a woman sitting on Vinni's lap, but the jawbone was way too strong not to be a man.

"That's Shantee." Tess smiled in amusement. "Niccola asked if she'd hit on Vinni, and as you can see, she's got no problem with that. She loves to fuck with the straights."

"I see." I nodded and grinned. This place must be entertaining at times.

"At the risk of me overstepping," Tess eyed Trigger, "how did the two of you meet?"

"We were both young and were good at fighting." I let Trigger take the lead on the conversation. I knew he was a very private man and wasn't sure what he'd say.

"Yes, but you were living in Italy. What brought you all the way here?" she asked. Trigger nodded at me to talk, letting me know he was all right with it.

"I liked to fight, and Sicily is a small island, not much opportunity to find opponents. My father was working with a client in California, and as a young boy who would take over the family business one day, my father wanted me to attend as many meetings as I could."

"They were fine with a young boy at those kinds of meetings?"

"They didn't have a choice." Trigger chuckled. "They're the mafia, babe."

"Okay, understood. Keep going."

"I'd heard about the fights here in Vegas from one of my father's clients. I was happy to come to any meetings

I could. It gave me the chance to check out the ring. Long story short, I'd fight there from time to time."

"And you met Trigger there?" She was trying to move the story along.

"Yes, we'd been paired to fight. We were both the same weight and, I liked to think, about same caliber of skill."

"Who won?" Her eyes told me she was enjoying the story.

"The first fight he got lucky." I chuckled, but we knew the truth. "Trigger won that fight fair and square. But I learned from that fight I had a couple of weak spots to work on, and I spent the next three weeks correcting the problem so when we fought the second time about a month later, I won." I paused. "Although I really wished I hadn't."

"It's fine, man," Trigger muttered.

"What do you mean?" Tess looked at the two of us.

"He saw what happened when I didn't win." He glanced at her, and she reached over and slid onto his lap.

"We come from different worlds," I added. "From that day on, I knew I couldn't fight him. I wouldn't be the reason a father'd beat his child."

"Now I get it." She placed her hand on some papers on the table, and Trigger handed them to me.

I flipped over the stack of papers and read the name of the fight club at the top. I realized they were ownership papers. Trigger had signed them, and under that was my name.

"You're looking to expand into different companies

in the US." He paused. "Fight clubs are big moneymakers. I can't think of anyone else's name I'd rather have on there."

"But…" I wasn't sure what to say.

"Call it even." He looked away, and I knew he was thanking me for seeing him for who he was all those years ago.

I took the pen Tess handed me and scribbled my name next to his.

Sienna

"Oh, come on!" I tossed the book aside and flopped down on my back, staring up at the gray clouds. I was suddenly chilly. Though I appreciated any library, the Coppolas didn't share the love for the same kind of books as I did. I wanted action, adventure, love, angst, happily ever afters. Good Lord, give me some kind of smutty fairytale. All I could find was a dry story about losing hope. The girl finally gets out of her hated boarding school, only to get smacked with her parents getting killed. Seriously? I invested three days into this, only to have my heart dropkicked into the garbage. I knew I really needed to make a trip down to the bookstore to feed my literary addiction, but first…I eyed the stone hot tub and thought I should warm up first.

"Miss?" A voice jolted me from my thoughts, and I scrambled back in my lounge chair. I looked up and found I was not alone on the rooftop. "Here, I've bought you a few minutes."

I eyed the phone he held, even as I begged my eyes to avoid looking at the crosses that ran along his neck. I watched one of them stretch as he swallowed.

"Who..." I cleared my throat, hearing my nerves get the best of me. "Who is it?"

"Answer it and find out." He smiled.

Careful not to make contact with his skin, I took the phone and held it up to my ear. "Hello?"

"*Bella*," Elio's voice was like velvet, "we don't have much time, but I have something to show you."

"Show me? Elio, where—?" I hopped up and looked around, hoping he was here.

"Miss." The soldier moved closer and handed me a crumpled-up piece of fabric. Inside was a Coppola family ring.

"Whose is this?" I studied the birthdates and read the newest one and felt a shot of adrenaline race through me.

"Does this mean Stefano is dead? What happened?" Confusion mingled with excitement about what this could mean and filled me with even more questions.

"He followed me to Vegas, and I finally had my day. It's one I've been waiting a long time for."

"Oh, my God, this is mind-blowing!" It felt like a knight had just been knocked off the chess board, and we were one step closer to taking down Nonna Rosa. "Are you okay? You're not hurt, are you?"

"No." He chuckled, and I felt myself warm with desire for this man. I missed him, and I didn't think I realized just how much until right now. "I did find out something, though, and I need your help."

"Of course. What is it?"

Elio spent the next few minutes filling me in on how someone was using the Mikey name to make dirty deals. Once I got the plan, I handed the phone back to the tattooed guy, and for the first time I looked him in the eye with a little smile. He smiled back and seemed a lot less formidable than before.

"He asked me to watch you. I apologize if I scared you, but I had orders not to approach you until told otherwise." I let out a poof of air and found myself smiling widely. "What?" He tilted his head and raised an eyebrow.

"Sorry." I started to pick up my belongings off the chair. "It's not you. I guess I am happy he would risk bringing you in to watch over me. You know, *here*."

He smiled as he began to slowly back away. "Glad we finally had a chance to clear the air. I'd better go now, though."

"Me too. Well, it was nice to meet you, ahh…" I waited for him to say his name, but he didn't. It was probably better that way. I stared down at Stefano's ring for a moment, then tucked it in my pocket and raced inside to change into my swimsuit. I wanted to plant yet another seed of doubt among the den of snakes.

Since the house was quiet, and the staff seemed to be going about their day, I felt now was as good a time as any to say something.

"Excuse me," I called to one of the house staff as she whisked by with an arm full of linen, "have you seen Pippo?"

"He's in a meeting."

"Where?"

She looked over her shoulder and studied me for a moment. "They are in the office, down past the garden."

"Thanks." I'd met with them there before, so I knew where they were. I slowly headed that way and shook my head at the weeds that had completely taken over the garden. I couldn't get over how much the place lacked anything even remotely pretty or healthy. I bent down and helped a poor little yellow flower that was being choked out by the enemy weeds.

"There you go, little fella." I cleared the soil around it, then stopped when I heard voices coming from a window. It was Pippo, and he was giving Betto shit about something, I could hear both their raised, angry voices. No wonder the weeds had taken over here; nothing good could manage to grow near these people. I stood and brushed the dirt from my hands then headed toward the door. I gave a firm knock.

"Enter," Pippo's husky voice called, and I prepared myself to play the role I had ready as I stepped inside.

"A thousand apologies for interrupting, but I heard something today, and I felt it was only right to share it with you three right away." I looked each one of them in the eyes, making sure they all felt equally important.

"Out with it, Alessia. We don't have time," Lotto, the youngest, harped at me.

"Please, Lotto, it's Sienna," I couldn't help but comment, and I saw Pippo's puffy eyebrow raise at my correction, but I didn't care. "I felt it was my duty to dig a little into why the Coppolas weren't working with Cooper Industries anymore, and I found something very interesting."

"Well?" Pippo seemed extra impatient this afternoon, which I would use to my advantage.

"Who is Mikey Coppola?" I watched their faces drop and continued. "Because according to Branson Cooper, who apparently just signed a ten-year contract with the Capris, a Mikey Coppola made some dirty deals that have now tarnished our name. They are spreading lies that we can't be trusted and that we are low on funds. Though you might not think this should be any of my business yet, it will be. I think it's important, and considering my position, it's important that you know I'm aware of this."

I could feel the confusion as they spun their wheels and tried to comprehend what I'd just brought them. It would be safe to say the uncles were totally taken off guard.

"Aless—" Pippo stopped himself. "Sienna, please give us a few moments to talk in private."

"Of course." I knew they would need time to process, and I tried not to smile. "I was just about to go for a soak, anyway." I headed out the door, closing it firmly. When

I reached the partially opened window beside the flower bed, I bent down to listen.

"She must have heard wrong." Lotto dismissed my news. "Our brother is long dead."

"So, how would she have come up with the name Mikey, then, if she's never heard it used before?" Betto, the middle brother, challenged Lotto. "There are only four people in this family who know about that name, and one is not here in this room."

"We all know that Micco," Pippo interrupted, "used the name Mikey to handle certain business transactions. The only person who would be so deceitful and underhanded to use it would be Rosa." There was a long stretch of silence, and I tried not to move as I stayed hunkered down under the window. "Lotto, bring up the books. We need to check any dealings Rosa and Stefano have handled in the last two years."

"Hang on," I heard Betto say as he tapped away on the keyboard, and a few moments later, I heard a gasp. "Pippo, look at this account. Look at these withdraws. I haven't touched this account in over thirteen months."

"That wicked old woman!" Pippo shouted, and I took the opportunity to make my way back the way I'd come. I knew I'd just cracked open the whole messed-up game she was playing.

Nonna Rosa's photo stared at me as I entered the kitchen to grab a bottle of Prosecco and a wine glass. For someone so old, she sure wasn't losing her mind in the slightest. She was sharp and quick and, I reminded myself, that made her very dangerous.

With newfound confidence, I poured myself a generous glass of wine then stepped into the hot tub, sinking carefully into the water. Steam swirled around me as the jets beat at my sore muscles. I leaned back against the pressure and closed my eyes as I sipped. I took a moment to enjoy my win.

"I knew you were still working with them." Anna's nasty voice broke my moment. My lips curled into a dark smile. "Once again, you have everyone around you fooled but me."

Anna was like an unwanted hair in your food. You might remove it, but just knowing it was once there was enough for you to want to toss the rest of it out.

"Oh, Anna," I chuckled, taking a long sip from the tasty Prosecco, "you really don't have much of a life if you have to follow me around like an obsessed lover who can't seem to move on. As flattered as I am, crazy is not my type."

Her face flushed. Apparently, I'd hit a nerve. *Interesting.*

"You think I'm obsessed with you?"

"Well, you seem to go after the same men I do, you stalk me, and I've seen you naked more than anyone should."

"Screw you!" she spat. I laughed, amused, and it pissed her off further. "I'm calling Stefano!"

"Sorry, sweetie," I dripped, "Stefano can't come to

the phone right now." Her brows drew up tight, and her neck contracted in confusion. I pulled my necklace up from below the bubbly water and dangled his family ring for her to see. "You understand, it's nothing personal."

I could see the truth dawn on her face. "You crazy bitch!" She broke out in a sob. "He was my future!"

"You honestly think he was keeping you for the long haul, Anna?" I made a *tisk* sound with my tongue. "He was using you. Just like you were using Mariano, and Mariano was using me to distract Elio from seeing them make their moves. And you were all good, but not good enough." I watched as each of my words ate away at her acid core. I hoped I could tear her down the way she tried to do to me. There was a time when I thought the whole eye-for-eye thing was wrong, but now with all I'd been through in my time with these very people, I hoped she hurt as much as I had.

She looked away for a moment, then her bony shoulders straightened like her mental pep talk had worked, and she turned her icy eyes back in my direction. She started to walk toward me, and with every step she took, her skin seemed to grow more red. Her hands fisted, and I knew I'd finally gotten through to her. *Well, guess what. This orphan now has a family with a hell of a lot more power than yours.*

She stood close and leaned down to whisper, "If my father was still alive, he'd have regretted ever saving Piero Capri, but he taught me well, and guess what, Sienna?" She let out a bitchy laugh. "I saw you eavesdropping on the uncles, so your day of having any kind of position here is over once I tell them what I saw."

I didn't give it a thought as I reached up, wrapped my hands around her neck and pulled her down hard, holding her head below the waterline. She bucked and flung her arms around, trying to pull herself up, but I just held on tight as she fought me. Soon, the water filled her lungs, and she slowed in her struggles. Once the convulsions stopped and her arms went limp, I pulled her forward and let her slip under the hot water.

"There you are," I said as my fingers found my dropped glass. I tipped it upside down then refilled it with more Prosecco. "Ah, yes." I took a moment to savor the taste and let out a happy sigh. "I wish I'd thought to bring some strawberries," I said to the body that was now bobbing around in the jets. "Perhaps next time."

A shadow flickered at the corner of my eye, but I ignored it. Instead, I admired my family ring that caught the sun's rays as it peeked through the clouds.

"I can do this job." I raised my glass to Anna and went back to my soak. "Hey," I called to a soldier who appeared on the patio and pushed Anna away from me with my foot. "Deal with this." I flicked my wrist at Anna then leaned back enjoying my newfound high.

I used the side of my hand to clear the mist off the mirror and brushed my wet hair, thinking how much I enjoyed getting rid of the people who bothered me in my new life. For years, I'd put up with so much, but not anymore. Mama's face popped up in my head and got me thinking. I'd wasted a lifetime wondering who she was and if I was even the slightest bit like her, and now...I didn't understand why I even cared. It wasn't about who I was, anyway. It was about who I was now and who I would be in the future that mattered.

"Sienna," Ugo came rushing into the bedroom just as I exited the bathroom, "what on Earth did you say to the uncles?"

"Why?" I slipped a sweater over my bare shoulders and admired the new cotton dress I'd picked up a few weeks ago.

"I overheard Lotto mentioning that you told them something, and whatever it was, it's got them riled up."

I held up a finger to stop him saying anything else, then went back to admiring my outfit. It looked good. I took a deep breath and turned to him.

"Remember that notebook I told you about a while back?"

"The one Val found? It was Stefano's, right?"

"Yes, that's the one. Well, he had the letter M written through it with these little tally marks. When Val was kidnapped, she overheard something about this person named Mikey who Stefano was terrified of. We couldn't figure out who it was. Well, when Elio was in the United States for a meeting with Cooper Industries, the owner had mentioned he won't do business with the Coppolas anymore because their contact, *Mikey*, had burned them one too many times. Vinni asked around, and sure enough, Mikey was making dirty deals and funneling money elsewhere. Elio asked me to bring it to the uncles then to wait and see what happened. After I left their office, I eavesdropped, and guess who Mikey really is?"

"Who?"

"Nonna Rosa."

"What?" He covered his mouth.

"Yeah, you see, Mikey was your nonno's name, one he used when he did business, anyway. His actual name was Michelangelo Coppola, right?"

"Micco, for short, but yes." He looked at me oddly then seemed to make the connection.

"Makes sense that she'd use her husband's nickname. She's a woman living in a man's world, after all." I shrugged. "Oh, and one more thing. Anna's dead."

"When? How? Where?" His head was spinning.

"Today, drowned, hot tub." I pulled out my lipstick and started to apply it. "She threatened me, so I killed her."

"You killed her?"

"Yeah." I nodded and went back to slicking the color across my lower lip. "She needed to go."

"You really do fit this lifestyle."

I beamed, as I went to the door. I'd decided a little retail therapy would just cap this day right off.

I grabbed my purse and opened the door to find Nonna Rosa staring back at me.

"Jesus," I half laughed, "you just kind of appear, don't you?"

"I would like you to join me."

Ah, no.

"I have plans to head into town." I wasn't about to waste the rest of my high with her.

"I have something to share with you. It won't take too long."

"Where are we going?"

"To our church."

"Right now?"

"Yes, now. My car is waiting. I promise it will be worth the trip."

I looked back at Ugo, whose face was a picture of confusion, and he shook his head for me not to go, but Nonna stepped forward and said, "It won't take long," and urged me to follow her.

She said nothing, just looked out the window as if enjoying the sights beyond the tinted glass. I caught her driver watching me in the mirror a few times, and I stared back, making him look away first. I wasn't scared of him, or any of them anymore, really.

Finally, after a twenty-minute drive through the busy streets of Rome, we stopped in front of a church.

The driver opened Nonna's door, and the soldier who rode in the front seat opened mine.

"All right, you got me here. What's going on?"

"Come inside with me," was all she offered as her cane clicked on the flagstones that led to the front door. *Oh, sure, now that stupid cane makes a noise.* I swore she had tennis balls to mute that click when she wanted to sneak up on people in the house.

The church was quiet, and thousands of tiny candles flickered in the draft we created. The minister was sitting in the front pew reading his Bible. He smiled and stood as he spotted us.

"Welcome." He waited for us to get closer. "You must be Alessia Coppola."

"My name is Sienna," I corrected, and Nonna clucked her tongue. The minister looked between us then smiled like it didn't matter what my name was.

"Sorry I'm late." I whirled around to find Salvo rushing up the aisle.

What the hell was happening?

"It's all right, Salvo." Nonna pushed him next to me. "It's not like we can start without you."

"Hi." He smiled down at me, and my fight kicked in.

"I'm not sure what you all think is going to happen here, but you can think again."

"Sienna," Nonna used my proper name, "just listen. We are running out of time, and this ceremony needs to happen now."

When it was over and the papers had been signed, the Minister and Salvo stood to one side and discussed the architecture of the building. Nonna Rosa and I sat quietly facing the cross that loomed over us. Churches were never a place I would go to find comfort, which was something I should work on because they were so beautiful and peaceful even when you were sitting next to such an evil human. I wondered if she could feel the angels above judging her for her sins. I bet they were judging me. I guessed being good was a subjective observation. Were you good for helping an old lady across the road? Yes. But were you also good for drowning a conniving little bitch in a hot tub while you sipped Prosecco? Also, yes. It was really all relative.

I smirked, thinking if only the priest could read my thoughts.

I took a deep breath and stared down at the hideous ring that cloaked my finger and figured it was time to make my next move.

"I know," I whispered, letting the words dangle in the air.

"Know what?" Nona Rosa sounded annoyed I'd broken the silence.

"I know that you're Mikey."

Her cane fell from her hand and clattered to the floor as her cold, gray eyes latched on to mine. Slowly, she swooped it up, stood, and as she moved down the aisle, I distinctly heard her say into her phone, "She knows."

Elenora

"Why did you bring me here?" I sipped my drink and looked around at the overly romantic atmosphere of the restaurant. It was like loe threw up in there, and I wanted to leave. Red flowers hung everywhere, a violinist played love songs in the corner, and couples held hands and laughed to show how happy they were.

"I thought it was time we had a talk." Oscar, who had dressed extra snappy for the evening, topped up my glass and flashed me a smile. "You and I have quite the history, don't we?"

"I suppose."

"I know things haven't always been easy, but then when is life easy?"

"Life is a sick game of how many times we can disappoint each other," I muttered, not interested in his topic of conversation. "Have you heard anything from Sienna today?"

"What? No."

"I bet Elio knows exactly what's going on, but not me, her mother, the woman who gave up everything to give her life and—"

"Elenora." He cleared his throat and shifted in his seat. He hardly ever called me by my name, so I looked back over at him. "Please, I'm trying to tell you something."

"Well, out with it, then." *Seriously, cat got your tongue?* When he stuttered as he tried to remember where he was in his head, I reached for his phone on the table and sent a quick text off to Ugo. I demanded an update. I demanded to know everything first, but no, that wasn't going to happen, was it?

"I'm trying to tell you that there's a reason I never left your side." He paused when the phone alerted me there was a text message.

Ugo: Trying to get through to Elio. I'll call when I'm finished.

I slammed the phone down and cursed.

"Second to the Capris again!" I shouted, so beyond finished with being ignored and not respected by own people.

"I'm in love with you," Oscar blurted, and I stood and tossed my napkin on the table.

"I need a walk." I couldn't deal with any of this right

now. Once outside, I took a deep breath and found a little bench out of reach of the streetlight and sat down to try to calm myself. As I sat there, I allowed myself to drift back into a memory.

"Oh, you're here." Theo shot me a dirty look as he came into the kitchen. He reached for a glass of water. "I thought maybe you were so full of sorrow you'd disappear for good."

I pulled my heavy eyes away from Alessia in her bouncy chair. She'd cried all night, and was still at it. I was exhausted. I glared at the man I'd love to bury deep underground. He didn't care how mentally finished I was, and his daughter certainly wasn't helping my sanity.

"Shut her up. She's going to wake the entire house." Noemi came in behind him, looking tired and uncomfortable as she rubbed her big belly.

"My God, I'm so tired," she complained, and I snapped.

I grabbed a knife from the counter and with my free hand snagged some of her long brown hair and yanked her toward me. I rested the tip of the blade on her belly and blinked back the rage that stormed inside of me.

"You think you're tired?" I spat. "One more word, and I'll carve that demon right out of you."

She screamed, and Theo shoved me backward into the table where Alessia screamed even louder.

"She tried to kill me!" She sobbed in his arms as I held my throbbing elbow.

"Are you insane?" Theo roared above all the noise. "You could have killed the baby!"

I just lost it. I was his damn wife, but all he saw was her. I hated this life. I hated it here. A person could only take so much. I was finished!

"Maybe Bosco needs to know where his knocked-up girlfriend is spending all of her time, because she sure isn't at her mother's place with her feet up. Unless you count the times her feet are up here." I outed to the room what I wasn't supposed to know.

"What did you say to me?"

"I'm taking my daughter and leaving this compound behind!" I shouted an inch away from his face.

His eyes formed into slits, and his chest puffed out like the cocky man he liked to play. His hands snapped around my neck and squeezed.

"You think you can threaten me in my own home and get away with it?" He shook me hard, and I lost my footing. He was much stronger than I, and was able to hold my weight with little effort. "You're nothing but a cheap market wife with a big mouth. If you even think of separating me from my daughter, I'll snap your neck in front of her and leave your body to rot in the sun." He dropped me to the floor, and as I managed to stay on my feet, he backed me up until I hit the wall.

He might have been terrifying, but I was mentally gone and apparently had a death wish.

He pulled back, I thought to leave, then jerked back and slammed his fist into the wall next to my head.

"Next time I won't miss your face."

"Francesco," I could barely get my words out into the phone, the shakes were so bad, "I-I can't do this."

"Whoa, what happened? What's going on?" I heard laughter in the background, and I wanted to lash out at him for being happy while I wasn't.

"I'm leaving. I can't live here anymore. He's going to kill me." Silence. I checked the phone to see if it was still connected.

"Do you have a pen?" his voice commanded.

"What?" I tried to follow him.

"Get a pen," he ordered.

"Okay, I've got one." It took me three tries to get the address right.

"Be ready at eight tonight. There will be a car at the south entrance. It's now or never, Elenora."

"Yes, yes okay." I nodded into the phone.

"Don't leave the house, just wait for my call."

That evening, I had what we absolutely needed packed in two bags. I took all the jewelry and the spare gun he kept in the nightside table. Then I remembered something important. I rushed around to Theo's closet and quickly spun the dial on the safe and snagged the family ring that had Alessia's birthdate on it along with the teddy bear necklace. They were her birthright, after all, and I had every right to take them.

Oscar helped me and Alessia into the car then went back for our things. When he returned, he had Ugo, Theo's teenage nephew, with him. I knew he'd had his fair share of problems in that house, so I didn't blame him for coming. His mother was merely a shell of a person.

"I can't stay here either," he sighed, "and you could use me."

"Very well." I handed him the baby while I pressed a hand to my racing chest.

Oscar drove for miles to the house Francesco had found for us. Before he left, he gave us strict instructions not to go out, to keep the front lights off, and not to make any calls no matter what. Little did I know that wasn't to be the scariest night of my life...that night would come a week later.

"Elenora." Oscar's voice drew me out of my thoughts. He stood several feet away as he spoke. "Ugo called. He said Sienna is in the city with Rosa. He was vague on the details, but she's fine."

"Was that so hard for him to do?" I sneered at him.

"No, ma'am. I suppose it shouldn't be that hard for people to tell you the truth, but yet it is."

I dug around in my purse. "You've got the valet ticket, not me."

"Right," he patted his pocket, "I'll go get the car, drop you off. I've some things to do."

"Did Ugo get hold of Elio?"

"Not immediately. He didn't answer. But he called back right after."

My blood boiled, and I knew I had hit my limit with that family. "How nice I was second in line for a call."

Chapter
TWENTY-FIVE

Sienna

Nonna's cane squeaked on the polished floor as she hurried down the aisle.

"Where are you going?" I called out behind her. "Don't walk away from me. We're not finished here."

"Oh, dear, we are far from finished here." She picked up speed and soon reached the big wooden door and pulled on the handle. I was on her heels as we both stepped out onto the top step. The rest was a blur, it all happened so fast.

"You have crossed this family!" Pippo yelled from a car window as it screeched to a stop in front of the church.

One by one, the uncles piled out, looking fit to kill.

It was clear they were coming to stop Nonna Rosa, but they were too late.

Nonna put her hand on my arm to delay me. "Stop."

Pippo's face was red as he began to take the steps. "Rosa, how could you—"

I couldn't hear the rest over the scream of tires rounding the corner. When the motor geared down and the window descended, I felt my stomach bottom out. Salvo appeared from nowhere and pulled us both back into the church.

Every bullet that hit the building vibrated through my chest. The stained-glass window next to us exploded like a ball of glitter tossed into the air by a child. I felt Salvo's body as it bowed above me to protect me from the glass.

Then it was over, and everything went quiet.

I wiggled out of Salvo's hold, scrambled to my feet, then slipped on some of the glass. I felt a few pieces nip at my skin and was almost happy I could feel.

"Stay down!" Salvo ordered, but I needed to see what happened.

"Oh, my God." My hands flew to my mouth as I took in the bloodbath at the bottom of the stairs. Pippo was slumped over Lotto, their bodies shredded by bullets. Betto lay a little farther away and was recognizable only by his clothing.

Salvo dragged me down the steps and pushed me into the car as he yelled at the driver to get me out of there and take me to the house.

I strained my neck to look back at Nonna, who still

stood at the top of the stairs, both hands resting on the top of her cane. She gave me a strange look as the door slammed shut and the car took off.

What the hell was happening?

"Are you okay?" the driver asked. This spoke to just how crazy and awful the whole situation was. The driver had never spoken to me before unless he absolutely had to. He had angled the mirror to see me better, so I figured I'd make the effort to reply.

"I'm fine." I was annoyed that things had happened so fast, and I'd allowed myself to be sent back to the house. I should have stayed to find out what happened. I understood now why the uncles had been angry; they had every right to be there. They were the head of the family, after all. I couldn't believe Nonna Rosa had set it all up without their knowledge. "Jesus," I huffed into my hand as I let it all process. What would happen now? What did all this mean? Who could have been behind it? Losing the elders was huge, and I couldn't imagine where we went from there. I certainly wasn't prepared for this yet, so I needed to get my head in the game to be ready for the next shoe to drop.

When I arrived back at the house and stood in the entryway, something strange came over me. I realized I was alone in the house for the first time. No uncles, Nonna, Salvo, Mariano, Stefano, or Anna. All were either dead, missing, or out dealing with the aftermath of what had happened. I'd hoped for a moment like this since I arrived.

I rushed toward Nonna's office, ignoring the house

staff as I passed through the rooms. I stopped at her office door and found it locked. I remembered seeing her coming out a few times, and she always turned toward the window. I never thought much of it until now. I ran my hand along the top of the windowsill but felt nothing. Humm. I searched the curtains, and just when I'd thought my theory was wrong, I looked down into the track and saw the key. It was completely unnoticeable unless you knew what you're looking for.

"There you are." I fished it out and disappeared inside.

The office was bland and simple, much like Nonna was. I shook her mouse on her computer, and it flickered on, and her password bar popped up. I started typing in different words, but then it hit me, and I typed it in.

Mikey.

Her desktop was full of files. I didn't care what was important and what wasn't. I wanted it all. Opening the transfer link the way Ugo showed me, I highlighted everything and started to transfer the Coppola data from her computer to Elio's.

I spotted her old filing cabinet and shimmied it open with the letter opener from her desk. I chuckled at how outdated her office was. Quickly, I flipped the tabs on the files, speed reading the names. I had no idea what I was looking for, but I felt I'd know it when I saw it.

When my birth name popped up in the M section, I pulled it out and fingered through what was inside. There was a copy of my birth certificate, a photo of my father holding me as a baby with my mother in the background looking uneasy. Then…a baby photo with a date on it. It was two years after I was born. Who was this? And why was it in my file? There were indentations along the side of the photo like someone had written something on a piece of paper over the photograph. Moving it in the light I made out the words.

You should.

I shook my head, not wanting yet another mystery to solve, and tossed the paperwork into my bag along with a few other photos. I was about to close the cabinet when I spotted both Ugo's and my mother's files. Curiosity got the best of me, and I shoved those in my bag too.

I jumped when I heard something crash. I looked up at the ceiling, as I was quite sure my own room was above this office. I checked to see where the progression of the file transfer was.

Damn, it was only at forty percent.

I heard another noise above and couldn't ignore it anymore. I turned off the monitor, returned the mail opener, and locked the door behind me as I left. I would just have to go back later and hope Nonna stayed away for the rest of the night. I decided to skip returning the key. That way, I could ensure I was the only one who could get into the room. I raced up the stairs, down the hall and flew into my room.

What the hell?

A girl lay on my bed. Her stomach was bleeding, and she was struggling to breathe.

"Oh, my God!" I rushed forward and climbed on all fours toward her across the mattress. "Anja?" I recognized her as the girl Stefano had planted at Noemi's house. "Oh, Anja. What's happened? What are you doing here?" A strong smell assaulted my nose, and I fought to clear it away.

"Leave," she struggled to speak, "you need to leave."

"Who did this?" I grabbed a pillow to press against her stomach wound, but I knew I was too late. The poor young woman who'd been caught up in a power tug-of-war would never go home again. I had hoped she was long gone and back with her family. I realized that was naïve of me.

"She thinks I know," she grunted.

"Know what?" I grabbed her hand. I wanted her to get it out so I could repay whoever had done this to her.

"Her secret."

"What secret?" It was frustrating that her mind was working in spurts. It felt like talking to my mother. Her eyes widened, and she looked above me, a tear rolled through her eyelashes.

"Behind you," she whispered urgently. Fear filled me as I turned to look.

Noemi was holding a gun in one hand and a lit candle in the other. When she moved, the flame shook and flickered.

"There's no one who can hear you scream," she said as she closed the door, and I felt my blood run cold. "The kingdom is falling."

"What are you doing?" I felt Anja's hand go limp in mine, and I glanced at her lifeless eyes and let out a sob. I felt so bad for her.

"She knew!" Noemi's shifty eyes moved to Anja. "She embedded herself in my home and figured it out."

"What did she find out?"

"I can't…" She stepped to the window, and I moved off the bed. *Bang!* She shot just over my shoulder. I screamed and froze in place. That was way too close. "Try that again, and I won't miss. Back on the bed."

I slowly climbed back on the mattress and swiped my hair clear of my face. I lifted my smelly hands and looked at them. What the hell was that?

"Your mother killed the one person I loved!" Tears streamed down her cheeks as she became more and more upset. "I can't have loose ends, Sienna, I just can't!"

"My mother never killed my father." She was losing it.

"Did she tell you that?" She laughed. "So many lies. So many powerful people. She shot him straight between the eyes, as he begged for his life, begged to see you one last time." She broke into a sob. "You will never meet the man who gave you life because your mother chose to take his."

I wasn't sure who to believe. My mother always said my father had been killed, but she never actually said by whom. Did it really even matter?

No. I squared my shoulders. I wouldn't let the past rule me.

"Noemi," I said softly, "you may have a gun, but what you do next will determine the rest of your life."

"I've worked too hard to get where I am today. I can't have it all come crashing down around me."

"What about Niccola and Vinni?" I grasped at something that might make her rethink what she was doing.

"All of this," she shouted, "is for them!"

"What do you mean?" I raised my hands to try to calm her, but she was too far gone.

She let the candle slip from her grip. It fell to the floor and ignited instantly in a massive whoosh of flame that took on instant life and jumped in multiple directions.

The smell was kerosene.

In the time it took for my head to realize what it was, my entire room was on fire.

"No loose ends," she yelled over the fire, then she ran out the door, locking it from the outside, leaving me to die.

The flames became unbearable, and I watched helplessly as Anja was consumed by it. My eyes and throat burned, and I grabbed a shirt off a chair and held it over my face. The fire's roar was deafening as I pressed myself against the wall. I was cut off from the door and knew I couldn't get down from the balcony.

It was do or die, and I refused to be taken out now by some crazy woman. I backed myself up as far as I could and leapt right through the flames over the bed toward the door. I felt the flames nip at my skin, but I drove my heel into the old door handle and broke it, then I wiggled my fingers inside and slid the lock open. I raced out of the room, only to find the walls around me were on fire. I could hear screams as others tried desperately to escape. There was fire everywhere. Noemi must have soaked other places of the house as she left. Chaos and confusion were everywhere as I raced down the hallway for the stairs. I wondered desperately where Ugo was. Once I reached the bottom, I stopped a terrified maid I recognized.

"Ugo, have you seen him?" I yelled at her. I watched a man who was ushering people out the side door.

"Yes, he's out," she assured me. *Oh, thank God.* Sounds of things crashing and popping from upstairs told me this house wouldn't be standing much longer.

Smoke alarms were wailing, and I tried to think. I wondered if the computer files had transferred, but it was too late to worry about that now. I knew I needed to get out of there.

"Move, move, move." I tripped over a woman, sending us spiraling into one another. We both fell to the floor. As we scrambled to our feet, I looked at her. I'd never seen her before. She was about my mother's age, with jet-black hair. She held a bag that overflowed with valuable items from the house.

"Alessia?" Her eyes narrowed in on me, and I glared at her as I knew she was stealing. "Oh, my God."

The roof above us cracked and popped, and I glanced up. When I did, she ran, and I lost sight of her in the dense smoke. I knew I had to move, as the flames had now cut off the exit to the side door. I picked up a coat from the floor and wrapped myself in it for protection as I frantically looked around.

"What are you doing?" Elio's soldier with the cross tattoos threw his arm around me and pulled me with him into a room and slammed the door. Ugo was there, and he raced forward and hugged me.

"Oh, thank God, you found her. Are you okay?"

"Barely," I gasped as I coughed up a lung.

"Sienna, we need to get out of here, now!"

"How? The window?" I frantically looked around for a way out.

"No, the tunnels. Thank God they aren't sealed off." He pushed on the side of a long mirror on the wall, and it slid open, revealing a passageway. Cold air flooded us.

"Follow me."

"That's impressive," I managed as I dove into the opening after him.

We reached a set of stone steps, and he went down first. I followed, and the soldier clambered after me.

"I hope you know your way out," the soldier said.

"Me too," Ugo muttered as he surveyed three possible directions to go.

"Which way?" I tried to catch my breath, feeling the effects of the smoke in my lungs. We were all coughing constantly.

"This way." He headed to the right, and we didn't question it. Ugo kept talking to himself. "Your instinct is to take the middle path. It's the easiest decision." He wheezed, and I could tell he was trying to keep his head on straight. "But after spending the night down here, I remember it's a dead end. The left tunnel branches off to others, and that's an entirely new mess you're in. I made a map once. I wish I still had it."

"Wait." I stopped short to listen, and the soldier

bumped into my back with a thud.

"We have to keep moving." Ugo tugged on my arm.

"Do you hear that?"

"Hear what?" He grew impatient.

"That." I rushed in front of him, following the sound of voices.

My feet pounded on the uneven stones, and I tripped a few times. The lights flickered, and I was horrified at the thought that we might all be plunged into darkness soon.

"What the hell?" I raced toward what looked like a cell. A few men were locked inside.

"Please," a man came running up to the steel bars and stuck his hand out, "I did what was asked. Please let me out!" More voices and banging came from farther down. What was this place?

I raced around, trying to find something to break the locks with. I spotted a pipe and hit the lock with all my might, but it didn't have any effect.

Ugo and the soldier came running up.

"There's no time for this." The soldier looked back the way we came. "We have to leave."

"Then leave," I yelled at him as I slammed the lock again. This time it seemed to give a little. I wasn't stupid. I bet Elio had men stashed places, too, but this wasn't Elio's doing, so I couldn't leave them.

Ugo grabbed the pipe from me and gave it a sharp crack, and it broke away.

"I don't care what you do, but I can't take a chance that these men might die here."

He cursed and ran his hand over his tattooed neck. He grabbed the pipe and went to the next cell and knocked off the lock with one swipe and released an older man from inside. I wondered how long these men had been locked down here.

"That's it," Ugo called out, taking the lead. I urged the two younger men to follow him while the soldier followed with the older one. I brought up the rear.

"Here it is!" Ugo called as he pushed the massive door open that led to the sweet outdoors.

"Go!" Ugo called to the survivors. "Leave before anyone spots you."

They didn't waste any time running down the road well away from the police, fire trucks, and the massive crowd that had formed.

I dropped to my knees and sucked back the fresh air and was soon dizzy.

"Easy," Ugo coached, "slow breaths."

I sat up and looked at the chaos around us. Ugo dropped down next to me and let out a relieved sigh.

"I didn't think I was going to find you," he huffed. "Thank God Berto did." He pointed with his chin.

"Is that your name?" I glanced at my tattooed rescuer.

"Yeah." He smiled.

"Well, thanks for all that." I waved my hand at the flames. "I'm sure glad we are on this side of it."

"This is the one time I'm glad I was on the outcast side of the family," Ugo shook his head, "otherwise I'd have never known about the tunnels. Who would have guessed I'd really have to use them to escape after all these years?"

In silence, the three of us watched the Coppola house slowly burn to the ground. It was a sweet but sorrowful sight.

"I think we should go," Berto suggested. "It might be better to be thought of as dead right now. If you know what I mean." He gave me a quick smile, and I thanked him again, then he vanished into the chaos.

I was about to stand up when a silver BMW pulled to the curb just up from us. I put a hand on Ugo's arm, and we both stayed down. I was glad I still had the old gray coat to cover my dress and tugged it closer around me. Two men got out of the car and took a few pictures with their phones. They surveyed the crowd as though looking for someone. One looked our way, and I put my hand over my eyes as I tried to get a good look at his face. I felt like I may have seen him before.

I bumped Ugo's arm again. "Do you recognize them?"

"No, I don't think so. Hard to tell from here."

They got back into the car and drove off. Odd. Although I was sure word had already spread about what had happened here, and everyone in town would be wanting to get a glimpse. Still, the one man looked familiar. I was sure I knew him.

"Come on. Berto's right. Let's get out of here." Ugo urged me along, and we slipped into the crowd.

We were soon sitting on a park bench a few streets away to catch our breath. I wished I had a cool drink to sip and was about to suggest we find something when Ugo spoke.

"Nonna Rosa never came back to the house." He looked up, and I could see something was bothering him. He tilted his head and seemed to be trying to find the right words.

"What's wrong?"

"The uncles are dead, aren't they?" I nodded, wondering how he knew that. "I…I think I might have been the reason the uncles were killed."

"What? Why would you think that?"

"Nonna told you in front of me that she wanted you to go to the church. She made sure I stayed home and knew the uncles would come and ask where you went. They didn't like you being alone with her. I can't blame them." He side-eyed me. "The uncles are like clockwork. They always come home from cards at exactly seven p.m. When I told them where you were, they raced out. What the hell happened at the church?"

"I made a big play. I wanted Elio to know first, but…" I leaned forward and whispered in his ear.

"Oh, my God." His eyes widened as my words sank in.

"Not a word, okay?"

"Okay." His eyebrows pinched when he looked down at my ring finger, then back up at me. "I overheard Rosa talking to her *consigliere*. She started to panic when he mentioned a phone call and they needed to get rid of the emails. Whatever it was must have been huge, because later I heard was a comment from one of the maids about how most of Nonna's belongings were gone from her room. Now I really wonder what's going." He swallowed hard.

We stood there in silence for a moment as we absorbed the depth of what he'd said.

"I'm nervous about what this all means," he huffed. "Nonna does nothing without a plan in full swing." He rubbed his face, the events of the day weighing heavily on us both. "I still can't believe they're dead."

"Well, then," I smacked him on the shoulder and grinned, "three down and a few more to go."

His eyes widened, and he let out a snort that turned into a laugh as he let go of his part in all of it. Really, wasn't that why we were there? Nonna had just made a good play.

"We should really get out of here. I'm just not sure exactly where we should go. I can just imagine the wolves that will be circling. I'll call Oscar."

"No, wait." I stopped his arm. I needed time to figure out how to play all this, and I really wasn't sure I wanted anyone to know we were okay yet. "May I use your phone?" I took the phone and pressed the buttons, pleased I remembered his number. I spoke quietly into the phone and was happy to find he wasn't far away from where we were.

"We are being picked up in a few minutes," I assured him and was pleased he didn't question my decision on who I called. "Ugo? Thank you for saving me back there."

"You're family, Sienna."

I hugged him, pleased we had both made it out in one piece. I wanted to tell him about Noemi, but first I needed to decompress. "Did you know Anja was living at the house?"

"Who?" He yawned.

"The mole Stefano planted at Noemi's house."

"She was living there?" His eyes bugged out then fell into a dark expression. "My guess, she was being held down in the tunnels, too. Stefano never let anyone go."

"I'm so glad he's gone. I'm just sad I didn't get front row seats for the viewing."

"Yes, hell just gained another bastard."

He was right, but there were a few more I wanted to send down there, and I was determined now, more than ever, to start knocking them out.

"He's here." I stood and felt my muscles strain. I would be happy to go to bed right now with a long, cool, bubbly spritzer.

"Hey." Ugo stepped in front of me blocking my view of the car. "Are you sure you trust him?"

"I really do."

TWENTY-SIX

Elio

"Oh, my!" Mama clung to Papa with her fingers to her lips as we watched the news reporter share what was happening. The Coppola mansion was totally engulfed in flames. That alone should have been something to celebrate, but not when I couldn't reach anyone to ask if Sienna was all right. My fear fueled the frustration I felt as I jabbed the off button on the cell. I fought the urge to throw it against the wall.

"Let me try again." Francesco excused himself from the room as he tried to call Ugo. I repeatedly tried Berto's phone, and Vinni was contacting as many people as he could.

The front door opened, and I rushed out of the room,

hoping by some miracle it was her. I stopped short when I saw it was Abramo and a large group of soldiers filing into the house. Nonna walked her way among them as she barked orders.

"What are you doing?" I snapped, not wanting to deal with her right now.

"The Coppola mansion is in flames, Elio. This would be the perfect time for them to attack. They will be desperate and think we won't be expecting it. We need to lock this property up tight. I've worked too hard to see any more cracks form in our—"

"We," Papa corrected her. "We've worked hard to make sure this family doesn't fall."

"Yes, well, that's what I meant."

"Was it?" He stepped forward and towered over his mother.

"Piero," she gave him the same look she used to use on me, "I'm merely trying to help here."

"We didn't ask for it." He stood his ground. "We ran this syndicate just fine in Sicily, Mama, and we're doing just fine running it here as well. You coming here, trying to toss your power around, isn't going to work."

"I see." She reached down and straightened her blazer and eyed Abramo before looking at me. "And what about that woman? I trust she's not here, hiding in some room?"

"No, actually," Vinni's voice cut in, and we all turned as he held up his phone with his eyes bulging, "she's dead. A lot of them are. There was a big hit at their church before the fire. A bunch of the Coppola family were killed too, all the uncles, maybe even the Nonna."

His words echoed in my head as everything in my body stilled. I could feel Nonna's eyes burning into me. I knew she was gauging my reaction.

"How do you know, Vinni?" Papa gasped out the question that was stuck on my tongue.

"My guy just talked to the priest of the church." He cleared his throat and refused to make eye contact with me as my world crashed down in silence around me. "He, ah, was there when it happened."

"What?" Nonna butted in. "But I heard Sienna died in the fire."

Church? The word made its way through my swimming head. What in the world was she doing at the church?

"No, she was at the church, and apparently when they were walking out, they were caught in the spray of bullets. I'm sure she didn't suffer." His voice squeaked at the last bit as he looked hard at me.

"Humm," Nonna grunted. She sounded unimpressed. "Well, that takes care of that. Come on, then. We'll have some big moves to plan."

Mama took a step toward me, but I gave a slight head shake. I was still trying to process what was happening.

"Boss, we need to go." Vinni's voice held an urgent tone.

"Where?" Nonna turned to me. "We need you here, Elio. We need to start scooping up their clients."

"That's right, Nonna Greta." Vinni directed himself to her. "That's exactly what this is about, and you're going to make us late."

"Elio?" She swung her gaze over to me.

"Why are you questioning us?" I snapped. "Why don't you go home, and we'll deal with this situation once we know all the details."

"Pardon me?" She drew a breath and brought herself up to her full height. I knew I shouldn't, but I couldn't ignore the elephant in the room anymore.

"Give us a minute." I nodded to Mama and Vinni but motioned at Papa to stay as they left. He needed to hear this. Nonna waved off Abramo, but he shook his head and only sent the soldiers outside, then he closed the door and stood next to it. I ignored him.

"Nonna, I spent my childhood looking up to you, learning from you, but somehow you lost your way." I let my voice slip into a conversational one. I needed her to back off. "We can either move on from what happened, or we can continue to butt heads." I held her gaze and stepped closer to show her I wasn't beneath her thumb anymore. "You must understand, I'm not the little boy you can boss around anymore. I will be the head of this family very soon, and you will respect that, or we'll have a big problem. Do I make myself perfectly clear?" She glared at me without a word then looked away and snapped an order at Abramo.

With an annoyed sigh, I grabbed my coat.

"Where are you going?" Nonna shouted after me.

"To find out who the hell killed Sienna." Vinni followed me outside, and I didn't say anything as I eased into the back seat and tugged at my tie, wanting to be alone. Panic threatened to take over, but I wasn't even sure how to start my unraveling.

I barely felt Vinni start the car and drive down the road. I knew he said my name twice, but everything felt far away, my hands grew cold, and my head prickled. Shit, I might pass out or worse, vomit. I hated this feeling.

"Boss?" Vinni turned around at a stop sign, looking concerned for me. "Please, can you hear me?"

I heard him, and though my body was like stone on the outside, I was my own burning building on the inside. Nothing mattered until I knew exactly what happened to her.

We turned down the driveway, and as the gravel crunched under the tires, I blinked away the madness inside my head and looked around. We were at one of our guest houses. Why were we here?

"I'm really sorry, boss," Vinni said as he put the car in park, looking straight ahead. "You have my word I'll never do anything like this to you again."

"What?" What was I missing?

"It needed to look real."

Something inside me shifted, and I squinted through the darkness at someone running toward the car. I stepped out and saw her.

She raced toward me as I ran toward her with my heart bursting with joy and fear at the same time in case it turned out to be a crazy hoax. When she was close enough, she leapt into my arms and wrapped her body around mine, kissing me like mad. I squeezed her hard and kissed back then buried my head in her neck, deeply taking in her scent.

"I thought you were dead!" I kissed up her neck, then placed her on her feet, holding her face in my hands. "I was told you were dead."

"Almost, in more ways than one." She paused, and I knew there was a story coming. "But nice to know our plan of pretending to be dead worked."

"Our?"

"Humm." She gently pulled back and pointed at Ugo, who was coming up behind her with The Finder.

"Sorry to scare you, boss, but a lot's happened." Vinni's eyes begged forgiveness. I would deal with him later. "A lot of people are missing. Rosa, Salvo—hell, Mariano. You needed to have a real reaction in front of everyone."

The Finder stepped forward. "I brought them here."

"How did you find them?"

"She called me." He indicated Sienna. "I'd heard something was going on and was in the area anyway. I got a call from Sienna needing my help. My apologies for not calling the moment I got there, but she wanted me to wait."

I held Sienna close to my body with one arm and held out the other to shake his hand. "Thank you."

"I told you once, and I'll say it again. I've always been and will always be loyal to you, Elio Capri. In spite of the pretense with Ms. Greta, you know I'd never hurt Sienna. I just knew that if I didn't take on her request to remove your girl from the picture, she'd only hire someone else."

"I know that, and I thank you for it and for your loyalty, my friend." I tossed him my keys. "Take my car. I'm sure Abramo is looking for me. Lead him into the city."

He looked over his shoulder at my '65 Buick Riviera and smiled. "I really did choose the right side to be on." He winked, tossing me his keys in return. "I'll call you later."

"Elio," Sienna reached up and ran a warm hand along my jawbone, "I need you." Her voice whispered close to my ear.

Vinni grinned, and I knew he'd heard her.

"Come on, Ugo, that's our cue to leave." He chuckled. "Come on back to our place. I bet you could use a beer.

"Sienna," Ugo looked unsure, "we really should discuss what this all means."

"We will." She glanced up at me quickly before shook her head at him.

What the hell was that?

As they drove away, we headed inside the guest house.

Savage was the only word to describe our behavior toward each other. We ripped each other's clothes off in desperation, our lips crushed together, our hands were everywhere as we both panted with need. It was intoxicating. Once we finally reached skin, our bodies bonded with heat, and our frantic friction sent us both over the top in an explosion of pure ecstasy.

I hugged her to me and gently put my hand around her neck. I rubbed my thumb against her rapid pulse. I could feel her. *She's here.*

"I thought…" I paused a moment and felt again the terror that had taken me prisoner earlier. "I saw so much bloodshed in my future," I admitted. "You ground me. You stop me from diving into parts of myself that I don't always like."

"It was a terrible day." She snuggled into me. "So many awful things happened. There was a point when I didn't think I was ever going to see you again." A tear fell from her gorgeous navy eyes. "But we're here now, and I need to *know* we're here, together. Make me feel you."

I bent down and lifted her up, her legs wrapped around my waist, as I carried her into the bedroom and lay her on the master bed. I drew my body over hers and wasted no time sliding inside her. We both let out a moan as I moved her hands up over her head then kissed down her neck, across her collarbone, down to her beautiful breasts.

"Home," I breathed as I sucked on her perky nipples and flicked my hips, needing more friction as I grew harder and harder.

Her hands wiggled out of my hold, and she threaded her fingers through my hair, then over my shoulders, then dug her nails into my back.

I hissed and roared, throwing myself upward at the

delicious pain that came with that.

"You like that?" she growled in my ear.

"Mm," I grunted like the primal animal I was with her when we were like this, "you're going to make me lose control."

"Oh, yeah?" She reached down and cupped my balls and rolled them through her fingers. "We wouldn't want that, would we?" I was completely at her mercy, and she knew it.

I grabbed her sides and quickly rolled over, taking her with me. She straddled me as I palmed her breasts and watched her start to rock back and forth.

She moaned, and her hands fell to my chest, clawing at my pecs as her climax grew. Her hooded gaze hooked onto mine, and just as she fell apart, I reached up and pulled her head to mine so I could swallow her moans of joy. She shook and squeezed her legs as it tore through her, and the entire time, I devoured her mouth, wanting more.

I lost track of how many times we both came that night, but when we were too tired to do anything more, I wrapped my body around hers and slipped back inside, and we didn't move until morning.

I woke to the sound of a car door closing. I quickly peeled myself from her and glanced out the window to make sure it was Vinni. I blinked and rubbed my tired eyes and glanced at the clock. It was nine already. I leaned over and kissed her shoulder to whisper it was time to get up, then went out to let him in.

"Unshowered, in jeans and a t-shirt." Vinni scoffed as he came in and put a couple of bags on the table. Then he dropped into a chair and made himself comfortable. "So, is this what vacation-Elio looks like?"

"You had sex," Niccola stated with his normal bluntness as he walked in. "Good."

I laughed and rushed to help Mama as she neared the door loaded down with bags. Papa also followed with his arms full.

"I cried last night, happy tears." She hugged me and sniffed. "Oh, look at me getting all emotional again."

"That was quite the night." Papa dropped his bags on the table with a huff, and I knew this whole situation had taken a great toll on him. "I'm just so glad she's all right."

"It looks like you're going to feed an army." I laughed. "And I'm happy, too," I assured them all. "Did anyone call Wyatt?"

"I did, and he's on his way," Vinni chimed in from the other room.

Mama immediately put herself to work doing what she loved. She began to prepare a meal. We offered to help, but she brushed us off, insisting we'd make a mess of things. We all gathered around and began to talk. We needed to try to figure out how to move forward from here. Papa did a recap on everything they were able to find out.

Rosa Coppola had disappeared. No one had seen her

or Salvo after the shooting of the uncles at the church. The Coppola syndicate was now under Rosa's reign, and Lord knew what that meant. Mariano was still in the wind as well. Lots of scenarios were discussed, but eventually we all agreed to wait for our contacts to come up with something.

"Was Ugo able to get any of the files on the companies they worked with?" Papa asked.

"Ugo was going to, but I haven't asked him yet this morning, and I felt we should let him have the night off since I was a little preoccupied myself."

"He'll be over in a little bit," Vinni chimed in again. Apparently, he had everything under control. "He just needed to check in with Oscar."

"Well, let's hope he did. If we can get ahead of it before everything snowballs, we'll be in great shape." Papa looked over my shoulder and smiled widely. "There's our girl!" He rushed by me and scooped Sienna up in a huge hug. My heart warmed, and all my problems evaporated in that moment as everyone took their turn with her. Hugs and loving words had her face flushed and happy.

We all sat down and enjoyed Mama's breakfast feast.

"Piero," Sienna leaned to the side and removed something from her dress pocket, "I'm not sure how much was loaded to the account, but there's at least fifty percent from Rosa's computer. I used the transfer link Ugo had shown me so all that could be removed should be there." She handed him a small paper. "It's the login and password."

I thought Papa was going to lose it he was so excited.

"You're really something special." He leaned over and kissed her head.

"I just hope there's something on there that's worth reading."

"There will be. I can feel it."

I was beyond impressed with her. Just when I thought she couldn't impress me more, she did that. She really had grown into something amazing.

"That's so strange to see." Niccola pointed to Sienna's ring next to mine as we held hands.

"I know." She admired our hands.

"Interesting that you, Sienna, wear yours on your right hand."

Oh, yeah, she did have it on her left before.

"More jam?" Mama handed me the jar, but I declined, knowing it was now or never.

I stood and offered a hand to Sienna.

"Take a walk with me."

"Now?"

"Yes." She excused herself and took my hand. I walked her away from the guest house, down into the sprawling field. A squirrel ran by with his tail held high. He had a nut in his mouth, and I had to laugh as he sped by us. "He has something he wants to keep, too." I squeezed her hand.

When we were near the creek, I led her under the weeping trees I knew she loved then stopped and turned her to face me.

"We've been through a lifetime of ups and downs, you and I, and we've still managed to come out the other end together."

"We have." She gave me a sexy smile, the same one she'd worn when we finally made it to the bedroom last night.

I laughed. "Hold that thought. We've proven that the boomerang effect is real. We've been bent, stretched to our limit, but we always end up right back here." I covered her heart with one hand and slipped the other in my pocket. "Sienna, we were made for each other, so let's give the stars what they've been asking for." I pulled out the ring and let the five-carat cushion-cut diamond sparkle under the Tuscan sunshine.

"Elio—" She started to speak, but I held up my finger for her to let me finish, because for once in my life, I was scared as hell of her answer.

"Sienna, will you marry—"

Boom! An explosion blew a fireball into the air behind us. I dropped the ring as I threw myself on top of Sienna. Everyone came racing toward us, calling out to see if we were all right.

"Everyone okay?" Papa yelled. He reached for his gun then cursed when he realized he didn't have it. I didn't have mine either. There was no reason I'd need a weapon here. Now I saw I was very wrong.

"Yeah." Sienna clung to me.

"Oh, look, the family's all here." A sarcastic voice had us all whirling to find Elenora behind us, pointing a gun.

"Mama?" Sienna twisted around in my arms, but I wasn't letting go. Something in Elenora's eyes told me she wasn't herself right now.

"Piero," she swung her gun to Papa, "you must be pleased with your handiwork on the uncles." Her gaze shifted over to Vinni, who had taken a step. "One move, and I'll blow your head off. Let's have your gun. Toss it over there."

Vinni pulled out his gun and did as he was asked.

"Elenora," Papa took a step and slowly slid in front of Mama to shield her, "we were not behind your brother's death."

"Don't lie to me!" she screamed. "All you do is lie."

"Mama, it wasn't him," Sienna said. "It was Nonna Rosa."

"And you," she spat. "I didn't spend a lifetime in hiding only to have you brainwashed by these people."

"You want to talk about lies?" Sienna tried again to draw her attention, but all of Elenora's focus was on Papa. "Answer me this, Mama." She gently pushed my hand back, but I wasn't having it and held tight. I'd seen the darkness in Elenora. "Did you kill my father?"

"What?" She looked at Sienna and shook her head but kept the gun on Papa. "See how they fill your head with lies?"

"Noemi told me. She saw you pull the trigger. She told me you shot him while he begged to see me one last time."

"He was a monster!" she screamed. "They're all monsters!"

"You did it, didn't you?" Sienna shook her head slowly as if she couldn't believe it was true. "He might have been a monster, and maybe he did deserve to die, but you lied to my face from the very start. So, who's the monster now, Mama?"

"I gave you life! You ungrateful child."

"And by withholding my truths, you nearly destroyed mine."

"Elenora, please." Mama tried to calm her, but it did the opposite.

"You're trying to take my daughter, Andrea, fill her head with nonsense. But you," she focused on Papa again, "you took the only person who ever meant anything to me."

"I never killed your brother, Elenora. I would never do that."

"I want you to feel the pain I've felt all those years, Piero, but if I kill you, you'd get off easy, so…" She suddenly pointed the gun at me, and I knew by her eyes she was going to fire. Then Sienna flung herself in front of me. It all happened so fast. We were both fighting to get in front of the other, a race to be the victim. A race to save the one we loved. When the gun went off, all went silent as we stared at one another, our eyes wide, frozen in the moment, unsure which of us was hit.

La Fine

Acknowledgments

My mother, for everything you do and your unconditional love and support of my career. I'm so lucky to have you.

Maggie Savarese, for your epic beta and proofing notes on this entire series. You're amazing, and I'm so glad you're a part of my team.

My betas, Veronica Nelson, Kasey Griffin, Christina DeTorio, Rachel Womack, Jennifer Santarpia, Jamie Johnson, and Elizabeth Clark, for taking the time over the busy holidays to read and review the issues in this book.

My street team, for sticking by me when I go dark. I love you ladies.

My Blackstone Reader Group, for your humor, love, and support, but most of all for giving me a safe place to come and relax.

My career-long editor Lori, who can understand and unscramble my crazy web of a brain.

My husband Nathan, for your consistent encouragement to keep writing and for a few other things that shall remain between us for now…

My kids, Brooke and Parker, for oddly helping me with my plot ideas…I think a therapist is in my future. Ha!

My sisters, Erin and Gillian, for being my cheerleaders with every single book I write.

My friend Jill Chamness, who provides me with stories that help keep my mind dark and humorous. And to her husband, Steve, who I can toss any question at no matter how random and messed up and get an answer without so much of a blink of concern.

And finally, to all my readers who give my books a chance.

I thank you, from the very bottom of my heart.

A peek at what's to come in

Quiet
EMPIRE

Noemi Capri

The shot echoed around the property and tore through the trees, sending the birds into a frenzy above me. Their wings flapped in panic, and their screams filled the air, and it was the only thing that told me life was still happening around me. I held on to a tree trunk and waited to see who was hit. My stomach did a painful flipflop when Elenora slumped to her knees and Sienna gasped in Elio's arms.

Why couldn't she have been the one shot? Fuck!

I shut my eyes and cursed. Why was I always left to deal with the aftermath?

When I opened my eyes again, I saw Sienna kick the gun away from her mother's reach and slowly kneel next to her. She placed her ear next to Elenora's lips as though listening.

I swore to God, if Elenora told her something, I'd drive a bullet right into Sienna's skull in front of the lot of them. Who was I kidding? I was going to do it anyway, but it just had to happen then instead of later.

Everyone just watched as the two whispered together. I supposed they were giving them a moment before the bitch took her last breath and died.

I whirled around and covered my mouth, hoping Theo would deal with her on the other side.

I loathed Elenora. She got what she deserved, and it was up to me to finish the rest. A tear slipped down my cheek when I saw Theo in front of me.

I let my head slip into the last time I'd seen him.

"Do I look like I'm going to stop asking?" I pulled my arm back and slapped Theo's consigliere *across the face. I knew I looked like a crazy person, but I didn't care. Theo had left in the middle of the night to go after Elenora and their spawn of a daughter without his normal cavalry, and now no one would tell me where he was.*

"Do that again," he towered over me and squeezed my upper arm hard enough to bruise, "and I'll squeeze that baby right out of you." I ripped my arm free and stepped back, feeling a painful ache deep in my stomach. I was glad I was just at the six-month mark, or I'd be concerned for my baby's safety. Stress was eating away at my ability to make wise choices. "I'm just following orders."

"Noemi," Pippo snapped at me, "it's probably best you return home." I started to protest, but he held up a hand. "Unless you have anything else to share with us about what Bosco is up to?"

I looked away, searching my mind for anything new I could share about the Capris, but at that moment, nothing came to me. I knew the only reason I was even allowed to be on the Coppola grounds with Theo was my agreement to share any news I had about the man I was dating and the father of my child. That and the fact that Theo still wanted me and not Elenora and that baby.

"There's a taxi waiting outside." He folded his short arms and waited for me to leave. His brothers, Betto and Lotto, were never far away, and it wouldn't take much for them to throw me out of the house if I protested any more.

With a huff, I gathered my belongings, but I did hear Pippo ask for an update on Theo. I dismissed them and headed out the door and to the car.

"Where to?" the taxi driver asked.

I could go to my mama's, I could go to Bosco, but I decided to head out of town and visit my aunt. At least she wouldn't ask questions and would be happy to see me. Also, she was a nurse, so if these pains got worse, I would be in good hands. I prattled off the address, and he sighed at the distance but carried on, knowing there would be a good tip at the end of it.

Once we were on our way, I settled in the seat and leaned my head back, watching the lights of the homes we passed. I was so close to my happily ever after, of money, security, and power. I just needed to get Elenora out of the way. It was when we were on the outskirts of town that I spotted it. Theo's car was parked at the end of a driveway. If I'd blinked, I would have missed it.

"Hey," I sat up and looked back, wondering what in the world he was doing all the way out here without any of his men, "I need you to turn around."

"I'm under orders to report where I drop you off. Are you sure this is where you want me to say?" the taxi driver said over his shoulder, and I should have known Pippo would have spoken to him. After all, most of the city was under their watchful eye, and those who weren't didn't last very long.

"I don't care what the hell you tell them. I'll pay you double if you turn around and go down the driveway we just passed."

"You're the boss." Without hesitation, he whirled the car around, sending me against the door, then he jerked into the driveway.

"Stop here," I ordered, not wanting him to drive right up to the house. "Pull up behind this shrub. I can't have you be seen."

I counted out some money, skipped the tip, and tossed it over his seat.

"You'll get the rest when I get back."

"So, I'm waiting for you, miss?"

"Yes." I quietly closed the door, hoping not to draw any attention to myself in case I was about to catch him here with another woman. "I'll let you know when you can go."

"I'm leaving the meter on." He pointed to the stupid

little box that counted every minute we were in the car.

I hurried down the driveway, holding my belly, and was pleased to find the side door was open. In fact, it wasn't even latched all the way. That was odd.

"You called, and I came." Theo's voice caught my attention as I stepped into the freezing cold house. I held my breath for a moment, glad they didn't hear me as my shoes squelched on the tile floor. "Now you're here, with him," he chuckled darkly, "and you think you're going to walk away from me, take my daughter, and, what, just disappear into the night?"

"I warned you that the next time you hurt me, we'd leave." Elenora's voice was cool and calm. Chilly, almost. "You've everything you want in life, so just leave us be."

"Give me my daughter, and you'll never see me again."

"Why? So she can be treated like dirt in that house? Be undermined by your mother and hated by your father? The only way you're getting her is through me."

"She's my blood, and that means something to me."

I peeked around the corner and saw Theo's back was to me, and over his shoulder was Elenora with a gun pointed at him.

No!

"I don't love you—"

"No one loves you, Elenora." Theo half laughed. "Not me, not your parents, not even your boyfriend Francesco, who let his family kill your sorry excuse of a brother. You have no one, so put the gun down and do

what you're Goddamned told!"

Oscar came into view, and he too was holding a gun that was pointed at Theo. Oh, my God, he's outnumbered! Why did he come here alone?

"You're never going to leave us, are you?"

"Not while I'm living—"

Bang!

Theo's entire body jolted as he took a step toward her then collapsed to the floor with a heavy thud. I covered my mouth in horror and fear as she lowered the gun and let out a cry of her own. I quickly threw myself into a closet and pulled the door close to my trembling body, as tears streamed down my face.

"We need to leave now," Oscar yelled. "Come on, the guys will be here to clean this up, and we can't be here." I could hear them approach and prayed they wouldn't notice the closet door wasn't shut tight. I knew she wouldn't hesitate to kill me too.

The moment they stepped out of the house, I flung myself into the room and dropped awkwardly to the floor over his body. I struggled to roll him onto his back, and he blinked up at me in confusion as he made a strange sound.

"No, no, no, no..." I sobbed as I pressed my hands against the hole in his chest. "Stay with me."

"K-k," he tried to say, and I grabbed his hand and held it tightly.

"I love you," I choked through my tears.

"Kill her," he whispered with one last effort before his body went slack, and I knew he was gone.

I sat back against the wall with numb legs and cradled my swollen belly. The only thing that ran through my mind in that moment was he wasn't thinking of me. Even with his last breath he was thinking of her.

About the Author

J.L. Drake was born and raised in Nova Scotia, Canada, later moving to southern California. Though she loves the weather in Cali, she would sell her left kidney for a good rainstorm. Jodi's love of the seasons back home in Canada definitely appear in her books.

When she's not writing, you can often find her sitting somewhere along the coast of Huntington Beach, reading, or at home curled up on a couch with her two children and husband, binge watching Marvel movies.

Authorjldrake.com

Books by J.L. Drake

Broken

Shattered

Mended

Honor

Escape

Trigger

Demons

Unleashed

Freedom

Omertà

Courage

Darkness Lurks

Darkness Follows

Darkness Falls

Behind My Words

Christmas at the Cabin

All In

Quiet Wealth

Quiet Secrets

Quiet Power

Quiet Empire

Shadows

Whiskey

Tango

Alpha

When Two Worlds Collide

When two authors become so close, their fictional stories sometimes cross over, making their worlds collide.

Wide-release author J.L. Drake crosses worlds with KU author Vivian Fiano, merging a mafia boss with an obsessive stalker.

You just met Cavaliere Bianco, the obsessive stalker who will stop at nothing to get the woman he wants. To read more about his story and those who are caught in his crossfire, check out Seductive Prey, book 1 of The Relentless Trilogy.

Seductive Prey
Graceful Abduction
Delicate Recovery